Prelude

By Arlie J. Marx

This is a work of fiction. Names, characters, places, and incidents either are the product of the author's imagination or are used fictitiously, and any resemblance to actual persons, living or dead, business establishments, events, or locales is entirely coincidental.

Table of Contents

Prologue: New Freundburg, Year of the Revolution, 19th day month of Zasit, 11 AM

The elf warrior led her ten-man squad down the main road to the docks. They were a detachment of the 1st Regiment, the King's Own. They proudly wore their uniform, chainmail with the silvery steel color of mithril covered by a white tabard. On the tabard was their unit patch, the king's coat of arms: a golden sword, tip down on a field of green. Their guidon bearer carried a pennant with the same heraldry.

The ten men were tall and burly. Marching lockstep in their matching uniforms, they seemed from the same mold – a different mold than their leader. She was slim and a head shorter. She was also the only elf.

Onlookers reacted as the squad marched by. Mixed in with the usual 'long live the king' were shouts at the elf woman. Some were jubilant, "Hail Muriel!" Some even sang a few phrases of the song that still circulated the taverns commemorating how she had thwarted an assassination attempt on the King a few months prior. Others shouted out sympathies for her brother. He had fallen at the queen's side when Prince Victor's hold was overrun by raiders the prior year. There were also those that sneered and shouted insults. They were few, but they were nasty. They taunted her about her size, about her being an elf. They taunted her men for following her.

This was not the first time Muriel and her men had come across such insults. The first had been a month previous. Each time after the protesters were angrier and bolder. The soldiers had learned to impassively march through the harassment.

The squad rounded a corner into another neighborhood and were suddenly faced with far worse. A mob crowded their passage down the street. The shouts now were insults about elves, calling her a creature of evil, mixed with chants of 'Elf Go Home!'. Many wore the tip down red triangle symbol of the One Father.

Muriel considered turning around and finding another route, but any other route could be just as easily blocked. She certainly couldn't return to the palace. She was to meet Cedric, Patriarch of the One Father, when his boat docked at noon. Her squad was to render him a welcome fitting of the head of a major religion of the kingdom and then escort him to the One Father compound.

Muriel had doubts that she was the right one to lead the welcome. Cedric's sermons were a big part of what stirred up the anti-elf sentiment. Yet she had little choice. The commander of the guard was required by protocol for anyone of Cedric's prominence, and she had her orders.

Muriel resolutely marched forward. Her men followed. A few tense minutes and they were past the crowd. Not long after that they were to the docks.

Muriel looked over the quays for Cedric's ship. There wasn't one but two ships with the point down red triangle tying up. She halted her men and tried to figure out which ship Cedric was on.

Gangplanks suddenly rolled out from both ships and men in platemail with One Father livery charged down onto the docks. In a blink of an eye the gaggle of dock hands, city guards, and customs officials gathered for the docking were overrun and cut down.

Armored men kept coming off the ships. Muriel quickly lost count of how many. Ships of that size could carry a 200-man company on a short journey, they both must have brought a full load.

Her first instinct was to charge in, but common sense immediately prevailed. There were simply too many. She would have to trust that the watchers posted in the castle towers overlooking the city would see what was happening and send reinforcements. It went against her grain, but she waited for the reinforcements.

The attack swept across the docks to the customs house and the barracks next to it. Resistance crumpled, within moments One Father troops were in both buildings. Others peeled off, leaving the docks for the nearest buildings beyond. One squad barged into a tavern on the far side, followed by screams and the sound of smashed furniture. Another squad came towards Muriel. They spotted Muriel and her men and charged.

Muriel refused to retreat. This group was small enough for her squad to handle. She motioned her men to engage.

The fight was short. The plate armor of the One Father troops gave them an advantage, but the warriors of the King's Own were the best in the kingdom. All ten of the One Father troops went down, while the king's men lost but one.

She looked back to the docks. One Father troops carried chests from the custom house back to the ships. The tavern next to the dock was in flames, bodies lay in the street where they had been cut down escaping the fire. Soldiers had moved to the next in the row of taverns.

She anxiously looked to the castle, then to the street. Where were those reinforcements?

She felt a nudge on her shoulder, one of her men getting her attention. She looked to where he pointed; smudges of smoke rose above the rooflines from the western edge of the city. While there were occasional fires in the city, she realized these were too widespread and the timing just too perfect for it to be simple coincidence. The city must be under attack from there as well. That meant there would be no reinforcements for her. She weighed what the king would do and decided he would likely move to the castle. She decided to fall back to the castle.

She ordered a quick march. They carried their fallen with them.

Several blocks over they bogged down. People filled the streets, gawking at the columns of smoke. Others ran up from the docks, screaming about the attack. Panic was born.

Muriel worriedly glanced up at the castle to gauge how far they had come and stopped in her tracks. The king's pennant was down, instead a pennant with the unit insignia of the 23rd flew.

Muriel's mind flooded with questions. What was a Wizard's regiment doing in the city, let alone in the castle? Why did their pennant fly there? That would only happen if they had taken the castle, but why would they attack? How could the castle have fallen so quickly? So much, so fast. It was hard for her to grasp.

She turned her squad from the castle towards the palace. Hopefully the king hadn't gotten caught in the castle.

They waded through the throng milling in the streets. Suddenly, people dove to either side of the street. A patrol with the patch of the 9th, another Wizard's regiment, moved towards them.

They quickly closed, swords flashing. Moments later only the troops of the 1st still stood, but now Muriel was down to seven men.

They moved on, no longer able to carry their fallen. Muriel made note of where they were left behind, but she had no confidence she'd survive to pick them up.

Chaos. Fleeing people were everywhere, heading every direction, clinging to whatever possessions they had grabbed. Some made sense, a child with a doll. Others did not, a woman with a ball gown. No one knew where the danger was, or where safety was, they simply fled. Looters, civilians as well as soldiers from invading regiments, scurried between buildings mindlessly destroying as they smashed and grabbed what caught their eye. They also preyed on those running by. The woman with the dress was suddenly grabbed and dragged screaming into a building.

Explosions! Everyone on the street cringed as fresh clouds of smoke rose from buildings several blocks over, wizards' work.

Muriel grimly moved her men forward. She had no choice but to ignore what swirled around her. It was simply beyond what her seven soldiers could make right.

They came to an intersection strewn with armored bodies.

Muriel's green eyes flashed in anger. Several of the fallen were King's Own; her brethren, men she had shared food and drink with the night before. It was no consolation that many more wore the point up triangle of the One Son.

Concern mixed with Muriel's anger. The One Son and One Father religions called each other heretics and had street fights with each other, yet there were troops from both in the attack. How, why, had opposing factions united to attack the king? And of more immediate concern, the King's Own was badly outnumbered. It was the only regiment quartered in the city. It faced at least two regiments of regulars as well as ecumenical troops. Her regiment had already taken loses. At least a quarter of them were in the castle when it fell. She wondered how many more lay dead in the streets. It dawned on her, holding the city was not an option. The best they could hope for was to rally to King Valeric, and then somehow get him out of the city.

She looked to her men. She saw from their faces they had the same thoughts. A grimness settled on them. They continued towards the palace.

The sounds of panic passed. Those who could had left the city. Those that hadn't now were scattered bodies, their once prized possessions trash littered around them. Mixed in were a few corpses in armor, where citizens had stood and fought.

Their path crossed that of other armed groups, none were of the 1st. Muriel directed her men around what she could, but skirmishes were unavoidable. They left a trail of dead, including their own.

They stopped in front of a Precinct Garrison of the City Guard. It wasn't a fort, rather a home to one of the city constable units. The constables had defended it valiantly, the fallen a testament to the battle, but they had lost. The building was in flames.

Muriel was bone tired and battered. Somewhere along the way she'd lost her helmet. Her short light brown hair was plastered to her head with sweat. Her men, now only two, were no better. They needed to rest.

Incongruously, a small park in front of the garrison lay untouched in the midst of the destruction. Two benches under a tree beckoned to her.

A few steps, and she sat with sigh. Her men joined her. They spoke a few moments of the fallen that they knew, a few more about duty. They avoided discussing how unlikely it was that they'd make it to the palace, or what would happen if they did.

Their rest was short. Through the haze another squad headed their way. The three bolted behind the garrison building before they were noticed.

Muriel peeked around the building's corner, relying on the smoke to mask her. She watched the squad come down the road. It was another squad from the 9th. Towards their rear was a man in robes directing the soldiers. Only a wizard would so calmly walk through all this not in armor.

Muriel's eye's narrowed, he was one of those blowing up the city. Eliminating him would be a boon to anyone still fighting. She took only a brief moment to consider, they weren't likely to survive the fight, but it needed done. She turned to her men, they quickly agreed, the wizard needed to die.

The chaos worked to Muriel's favor. The troopers were nearly up to them when a couple looters bolted from a house down the street and fled. The entire squad turned to face the movement, a few broke ranks to follow. The wizard screamed at his men to return to the formation.

The solders stopped half a block down, more out of breath than in response to the wizard. They were near the building the looters had fled. Its ornate front drew them with promises of rich furnishings inside. They took steps towards the house.

Muriel knew this was their chance. Muriel closed her eyes and took a deep breath. It only took a couple heartbeats for her to summon and focus her remaining strength through a battle spell. Her eyes opened and locked on to the wizard. Another deep breath and calm spread through her body, she was ready. She charged. She was aware of the men on either side as they moved forward with her, but for the moment the wizard was her world.

The wizard's back was to her, focused on his men. The men didn't heed his orders and continued to the house. He conjured a fire ball and cast it at the house to stop them. She was nearly on top of him when he heard her running footsteps. He turned just in time for her sword to slice through him.

An armored man next to the wizard also reacted. He raised his mace, not in a swing but as part of a spell.

Muriel quickly refocused on him; he must be their cleric. She instinctively threw herself at him. The cleric desperately brought his shield between them.

Her body slammed into the shield. He staggered back, his spell broken.

She landed on her feet and immediately rebounded, sword slicing the air.

He raised his shield to protect against her onslaught. She adjusted her swing low. Her mithril blade cut through his steel chain armor where it protected his knee.

He attempted to swing his mace at her as his ruined leg gave out underneath him. The swing lost its strength and went wide, as he tried to shift his weight to his good leg.

Her sword came around, slapping the mace upward. He had no time, no ability, to counter as she slammed her offhand dagger into his exposed armpit. Her mithril blade overcame steel chain. She twisted the dagger as she pulled it out.

The cleric went down, blood gushing down his side.

Muriel turned to see how her men fared.

One man was down with bodies strewn around him, the other still fought but was sorely pressed by three soldiers.

Muriel's attention was diverted by the two soldiers returning from down the street. They came at her from either side. She parried a blow. She shifted allowing another blow to glance off her armor. The mithril chainmail saved her from serious harm though she had a new bruise added to those collected through the day. She counter attacked. A flurry of blows and she killed both. She turned back to her man.

He still fought, desperately parrying attacks from the last two soldiers as they battered him. Blood flowed from a wound at his collar. He stumbled and fell.

Quick steps to them and her blade sliced the first soldier. A twirl and her blade plunged into the other. She was the only one left standing.

She bent over to pull her man up, but he had passed. Fighting back tears, she gently patted his shoulder. "Well fought. Rest in peace my friend."

She straightened up. It was a struggle. Her spell and the adrenaline of the fight faded, replaced by weakness. Her chest heaved from her exertions.

She was surprised she was still alive, but she needed to get out of the middle of the street if she wanted to stay that way. She took stock of the buildings around her. Which one would be a good place to hold up and figure out a plan?

She suddenly realized where she was. The row of mansions was only a block over from the palace plaza. She doubted she'd make it going up and down the streets, but maybe she could reach the palace if she cut through one of the buildings.

She ducked through the kicked in door of the nearest mansion. She moved down the entry hall, stepping over a small broken table. A few steps down, her foot skidded on spilled oil from a shattered lamp. She fell against the wall but kept on her feet. She moved on, passing stairs to the second floor, and instead turned into a side room.

Furniture was smashed. Clothes laid torn. There was a smear of blood on the wall.

She crossed the room to an archway on the right. There was a hall to the back of the house. It gave her a line of retreat if anyone showed up. This was as safe as she could be under the circumstances.

She contemplated sitting on the floor, then decided against it. She was so tired; it would be easy for sitting to turn into stretching out and falling asleep. She settled for leaning back against the wall and sliding down to a squat. It was good enough for her to catch her breath, and she could launch herself to standing.

The minutes crawled, oddly it remained quiet.

Her breathing calmed; her strength returned. She stood up and moved to the kitchen at the back of the house. It also had been ransacked, but the water pump still worked. She worked the handle as she put her face under the water to rinse it off, then drank deeply. It refreshed her as much as the squatting had.

The kitchen window looked out back to a tall stone wall and a large stone building behind it. She recognized the building, had been given a tour of it. It was a restored ruin from an older era, turned into a museum when King Valeric rebuilt the city. The front of it faced the plaza, only a building down from the palace. All she had to do was get over the wall, through that building, and she'd be within a short sprint to the palace.

She crossed the back yard to the wall, where she was stymied. She could barely touch the top with her fingertips. She jumped to grab the top but couldn't get a hold on the smooth stone. After several failed attempts, she stepped back and reconsidered.

A tree next to the wall caught her eye. She tried to climb it, but her gear made it awkward. She managed to shimmy up far enough to grab a branch and use it to get an arm over the top of the wall. A heave and she swung a leg over, then she rolled her body over the wall. She hung a moment by her fingertips then dropped to the ground.

She looked around. The yard behind the museum was landscaped. It was pretty, but more important she was alone.

She remembered a special part of her tour reserved for only the most trusted of the royal guard. She walked over to bushes in a corner. The bushes hid a grate, leading to an escape route. It had not been disturbed. If she could get the king this far, they should be able to make it out of the city.

She turned her back on the grate and entered the building. No surprise, the building had been ransacked. There hadn't been anything of real worth in the displays, but that hadn't stopped looters from smashing things. She saw a goblin banner laying torn on the floor. Valeric had been so proud of that, he'd personally defeated the goblin leader in the last fight clearing the ruins.

She worked her way to the front of the building and peered out. Fighting had been fierce, but it was done. Bodies near her were a mix of 1st and 9th regiments. Buildings, including the one she hid in, were heavily damaged by magic. Some were in flames.

She could see the palace. Smoke hung over the complex, the front gate was bashed in. In front of the gate stood a man in robes and another in heavy armor. She recognized them both. The one in robes was the leader of the Wizard's council, Malenkai. The other was Rhyfelwyr, the senior colonel of the Wizard's regiments and commander of the 23rd. Between her and the two figures, a company formed up in ranks. She could see additional squads coming into the plaza. It was over. The palace had fallen.

Muriel gave into her grief and anger. Malenkai! This was all his fault. Yes, Ecumenical Council troops were also in the city, but rumor had it that Malenkai often manipulated Cedric. She yearned for vengeance, but she'd never make it past all the soldiers to get to him. If only she had a bow. For the first time she wished she had trained as an archer instead of a blade master. She struggled to neither weep nor scream in frustration. She forced herself to think. What to do now?

The scene playing out in front of her broke through her frustration. The wizard and the general gestured, heated words were exchanged. She couldn't make out what they were saying over the orders sergeants barked at the forming lines of troops. She wondered what could vex them so. They already had their victory.

Hope sprung within her. Valeric was not there in chains, his corpse did not lie at their feet. Had Valeric escaped? The escape route had looked undisturbed, unused, but what else would steal the satisfaction of victory from them?

She needed to find him. She retreated through the building, to the grate.

She knelt and reached through the grate. She found a loose stone an arm length's down and pushed it to the side. She squirmed to reach further. Her fingers found the exposed latch. She pulled the latch, and the end of grate was released. She raised the grate and put her feet to the rungs on the wall of the shaft and climbed halfway down. She turned back to where she had been kneeling. With a small spell, grass straightened erasing her tracks. She pulled the grate down until the latch clicked. She pushed the stone back into place over the latch then dropped down to a passage dimly lit by shielded glow stones.

She trotted down the passage. It wandered but was easy to travel. There were several openings to side passages, each with a latched grate. She ignored them. They were not part of the escape route. She had no knowledge of where they led and she had no desire to become lost under the city.

She traveled for over a mile, before she came to another ladder up.

She climbed to the top and listened. It was quiet. She sniffed the air. There was a strong scent of disturbed herbs mixed with a faint smell of smoke. She uncovered the latch and opened the grate, lifting it a few inches to peek out. She couldn't see past trampled plants. She lifted the grate further to look over the plants. She was in a garden between a tree and a corner in a wall. She climbed out, crouching as she quietly closed and secured the grate. She peeked around the tree.

She knew this place. It was the Sun Temple she had visited just the previous ten day. She was in the temple garden. The wall behind her was the priest's residence, the worship house to her right.

She stood up and walked around the tree, passing the door into the worship house. The door was ajar. She glanced in. Bodies were strewn inside. Parishioners seeking sanctuary had found the sword instead.

She heard creaking and looked up to its source. A body swung from a rope. She stepped back to see more than just the soles of boots. She recognized the priest. Tears ran down her cheeks. She had talked to him just the other day. He was a kind, gentle man, so reassuring. He made it seem finding her a midwife in a city of humans but a small chore. He had promised to help her find one. It had been a joyous moment. Now he was dead.

Through the tears she also realized this meant Valeric must not have come this route. He would never have let one of his clerics swing from a tree. Her hope for Valeric faltered, was he caught somewhere in the city? Or worse, dead?

In that moment she also thought beyond her duty. From the moment the battle had started, her reflexive reaction was her duty to lead her men and fight her way to Valeric. Her training and decades of experience had taken over and driven away any thoughts of her pregnancy. She had done her best, but her men were dead. There was really nothing she could do for Valeric. Perhaps another day, but not today. It was time to be more than just a warrior and think of her baby.

She needed to flee the city.

She was near the western edge, only a few blocks to the outskirts. The city wasn't walled, she could just walk out. However, beyond would be refugees and perhaps formations of the invading soldiers. She needed to not attract attention. After that? Where to go? She didn't know. She'd leave that for later.

She went into the worship house. She took several minutes working through the bodies to find a cloak and a carry bag that didn't have much blood on them. She took off her tabard, carefully folded it, and put it into the bag. She wrapped the cloak around her, hoping it would hide her armor. She tried to mess up her hair to cover her ears, but it wasn't long enough. She settled on pulling the hood over her head.

She took another look at the priest in the tree. There was one last act of defiance she could do against the usurpers, for Valeric, for her. She swung her sword and cut the rope. The body dropped to the ground.

She left the temple moving directly to the city's edge. She cut across yards, past burning buildings, and finally into the woods outside of the city.

There were no troops, but there were scattered camps of refugees. The once proud citizens of the capitol were shattered. They numbly clung to each other and wept. Her heart ached for them, but she couldn't help them. They didn't look up as she crept by.

Finally, she was past it all. She took a moment to look back. Dusk descended, yet the sky was lit. Large swaths of the city were in flame. Valeric's city was dead. She shook her head. Humans! How could they do this to themselves?

She turned her back on the city and continued on, she had much to do if she and her baby were to survive.

Part 1: Finding the Warrior's Path

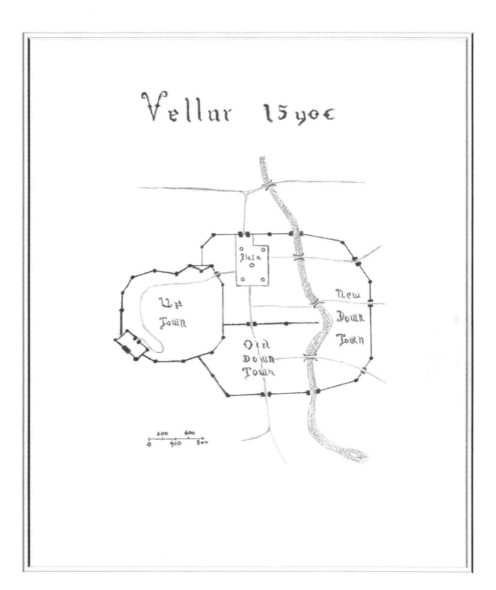

City Map, Vellar City Archives

Chapter 1: City of Vellar, 15th Year of the Council (YOC), 39th Day of Fall, Noon

A young lad with brown hair, in the simple linen shirt and britches of a common street person, sat precariously on a stool he was too big for. He bent intently over a table too short for him as he worked on something inside a small wooden box.

His green eyes narrowed in frustration as the piece he was inserting broke. He pulled out the broken pieces of a metal coil and set them aside. He searched through the small metal parts strewn on the table. He then looked up to the bins on a shelf along the back of the table and searched through them. He pulled out a fresh metal coil. This time he was successful in installing it within the box. He took a 'L' shaped piece and a tiny pin from the parts on the table. He huddled over the box, tools in both hands, connecting the pieces.

He straightened up and set his tools on the workbench. He closed the box lid. He inserted a key in the side and turned it several times. He crossed his fingers, then he lifted the box lid. He was rewarded with notes of music. He opened and closed the box several times to start and stop the music. Satisfied, he cleaned up his mess, carefully putting the tools and the parts into the bins where they belonged.

He sat back and looked over to the two gnomes who shared the room with him.

The gnome brothers were nearly mirror images with the typical white beard and a tall red cap of a gnome elder. They sat at their tables focused on their projects. One worked on the articulations of a puppet, making sure the joints moved smoothly. The other carved on small wooden pieces that he would turn into one of the intricate puzzles he was famous for.

The boy watched the gnomes, but quickly became bored. He squirmed on his stool. He sighed. He drummed his fingers on the worktable top.

Eventually one of the gnomes looked up at the boy. "Sturm! Stop that."

"Stop what?"

"THAT!" The gnome pointed at the boy's tapping fingers.

"Oh. Well, I'm bored. There's nothing to do here. Can I go out?"

Gnumph shook his head disapprovingly, thinking human children could be so capricious! "You were the one who decided to finish that music box. It's done? Good. So yes, get yourself out of here before you drive us crazy. Maybe you could even go talk to your mother and find out why she didn't want you around your home these past few days. Muriel always had a mysterious side to her, but this is odd even for her."

Sturm turned to run out the door but the other gnome, Gwiz, interrupted him. "Hey! Just a minute. Are you really going out like that?" He gestured at Sturm's clothes.

Sturm dutifully brushed off his shirt and then tugged at the bottom of it to straighten it. He awkwardly tucked it into his pants. He ran his fingers through his hair. He still looked wrinkled, and he had done nothing to the oil smear on his chest.

Gwiz shook his head. "I'd never hear the end of it from your mom if I let you out like that. Stand still a moment."

Sturm rolled his eyes. Sometimes it seemed like Gwiz out mothered his mother. Before Gwiz could take exception, Sturm took a deep breath and stood very still.

Gwiz muttered a few words and snapped his fingers. The stain on the shirt fell out, as did the creases, leaving the shirt looking freshly cleaned.

Gwiz nodded. "Much better. Now then, how about instead of wasting the rest of the day you do something useful like take run your new music box over to Wally's shop. Maybe he'll buy it. Just be back when the clock strikes the afternoon four, so you don't miss dinner."

Sturm pulled a satchel out from under the table and carefully put his box into it.

Gwiz continued, "While I'm thinking on dinner. Since you'll end up at the market plaza anyway, why don't you drop by Fallon's stall and pick up some turnips? Do it on the way back. It should still be early enough that he has some left, yet late enough he'll be easy on the haggle so to not have to take them home with him. Here, take this skilling with you for the purchase. And I want my change back."

Sturm slung the satchel over his shoulder then took the medium sized copper coin from Gwiz. "I'll be back with the turnips and your change, I promise!" Then Sturm was out the door before Gwiz could have any more 'good' ideas for him.

Outside, Sturm paused to close his eyes and breath in deep. In some areas of the city this could be an unpleasant experience, but the gnomes lived in a well-kept section of the city and only two doors down from the best bakery in the city. Sturm savored the smell of bread baking.

He opened his eyes. Like so often, his glance went upward to Uptown.

Vellar was an ancient city, with many expansions; Uptown was the original city on top the hill. The wealthy lived there next to the citadel and the garrison. It had the thickest walls and highest towers.

Sturm had wandered most the city but had never been able to get into Uptown, city guards at the gate turned away downtowners like him. He had managed to steal glances through the gate, but that had only further piqued his curiosity. There were huge houses of stone, not fieldstone but quarried stone worked by masons with arches, pillars, carvings, and inlays. House guards stood at the doors protecting whatever was inside. Sturm could only imagine, if the exteriors were so grand, what was inside? How did the wealthy live?

He shook himself from his reverie, maybe someday he'd own a house up there, but not today.

He looked up and down the street of two-story buildings typical of his section of Downtown. The lower floors were of gathered field stone, with shops. The upper stories of wood were the living quarters.

He stepped out towards Wally's shop. Along the way he waved to the shop keeps, who waved in return and smiled. He took a cross street, cut across an alley, and after another turn was at Wally's.

Sturm entered the shop to find Wally busy with a customer. Sturm went to the window display where the gnomes' wares were displayed. He imagined his music box displayed there, picking out the perfect spot to show it off.

Sturm's attention was drawn back to the front counter by the customer's loud remarks.

The man arrogantly stood as if he were a lord. In spite of his posturing, he bore a patch bearing the device of one of the uptown houses marking him as a servant. He showed Wally no respect. He demanded, then questioned Wally's ability to understand the demands.

In response, Wally was polite and patient.

The conversation finally ended with the customer directing Wally, "Remember, five days hence, no later!"

Wally, half bowed. "I understand. Trust me, I would never disappoint your lord." Wally was going to say more, but the man was already out the door.

Sturm walked over to Wally. "Wow, who was that?"

"Just another uptown dupa! Of course it will be ready, it will be ready tomorrow but he's in such a hurry he's gone before I can tell him. So, anyway... How are you Sturm? What are you up to today?"

With a flourish, Sturm pulled out the music box and set it on the counter. He proudly announced, "Good day sir! I bring to you our latest creation. Perhaps you know of someone who would like to acquire it?"

Wally chuckled at Sturm's theatrics as he picked up the box. He inspected it carefully, turning it one way then the other. He opened the lid and listened to its merry tune. "This is a fine music box. I'll be happy to take it. I know an artisan who has a commission from an Uptown gentle wanting to impress his lady. A music box would be just the thing to add to it. How much does your mother want for it?"

Sturm shook his head, working hard to cover a grin. "Mom didn't make it."

"Alright then, how much do the gnomes want?"

The grin broke through. "They didn't make it either."

"What? Did you make it?"

"Yes, I did!"

"Ha! Good for you. So, how much do you want for it?"

Sturm hesitated. He wanted to ask for a silver skilling. Any amount of silver was a lot of money to Sturm. A skilling was a full ounce. Would he be too greedy if he asked for it? The only way to know was to ask. "The gnome's normal price is a silver skilling. Do you think it would be worth that?"

Wally turned it over in his hands as he considered. The workmanship was on par with the gnomes. It was worth every bit of what Sturm asked, plus a nice commission for Wally to pocket. "I think we can get that price for you though I don't know how many skillings are still out there. Ever since the revolution they're changing all the coins. They're even melting down the old to make the new, like they want to pretend the King's coins never existed. Instead of Skilling, Gulden, and Thaler they now mint Eagles, Lions, and Griffons. The Eagle is the same weight as the Skilling. We'll see if we can get you one or the other for it, after my commission of course. Good enough?"

Sturm thought about it for a moment. The commission part worried Sturm, but he knew Wally had to make a living off what he sold. Sturm decided to accept the offer. They shook hands on the deal.

Sturm returned to the streets, free to head towards the plaza. He hadn't gone far before he came across his friend Ken. The two looked much the same in both coloring and dress, but Ken was three inches taller than Sturm.

Sturm enviously looked up at his friend. It hadn't been long ago that they were the same height. All of Sturm's friends had hit a growth spurt leaving Sturm the runt of the group. Sturm feared he'd stay short, like his elven mother. It was a constant worry Sturm had shared with his mom but got little consolation. She had a rote response for him to be patient, that his human heritage from his father would soon assert itself and he'd grow big and strong. She then deflected questions about his father so Sturm had no idea how big or how strong that might be.

Sturm was glad he had come across Ken first. Ken, unlike the other boys in their group, seldom picked on him for any of his many faults. When Ken did, it was about Sturm's eyes. Sturm's eyes shifted color drastically with his mood from drab olive to a bright forest green. Who else had eyes like that? Only his mom. He consoled himself with the thought that at least he hadn't inherited her pointy ears. It was bad enough seeing the humans of Velar react to her 'disfigured' ears. He could just imagine the grief he'd take on the street if he had them!

Sturm was quickly distracted from introspection by Ken's jokes. They kidded back and forth as they headed down the street to the river. At the canal they took the short cut along the precarious path between the river and the old city wall. Clambering over the fallen stone blocks was more fun and quicker than the longer route of crossing the bridge into new Downtown then crossing back on the other bridge into the plaza district.

A hundred feet down they were back to road, at the southernmost buildings of the plaza district. These buildings were temples. The boys hardly glanced at the buildings. They didn't feel a need to have their souls saved and they didn't need any healing. They hurried past the buildings to the fountain at the southwestern corner of the plaza. They paused to consider their path to their usual hang out, the theater near the northeast corner. The plaza was huge, part park and part marketplace packed with merchant stalls. The boys knew by experience cutting across the plaza was slow going. The quicker path was along the edges, where a 10-foot swath was kept clear as a road, but should they head east or north?

East drew them. It led to the tavern district. The previous year they had discovered how interesting the tavern serving wenches and dancing girls were. However, while the tavern keeps didn't care how old the boys were, they did care the boys had no coin and had run them off. The boys decided to give the taverns a wide berth until they had the coin Sturm would get from selling his box.

They headed north. They passed the warehouse district on their left. The imagined riches within the warehouses tempted the boy's imaginations, the stories about what happened to people who broke into those warehouses kept them from investigating.

They reached the fountain in the northwest corner and turned the corner, putting them on the road that passed the Uptown gate on the way to leaving the city through the main gate. The stalls changed over from goods made in the city to the farmers' market. Sturm spotted Fallon's stall and made note of its location for latter. They passed the Uptown gate and the buildings outside the plaza changed over to municipal buildings including the constable barracks, jail, custom house, and city clock. The boys had to watch their step to stay out of the way of richly dressed people with entourages.

The boys reached the northeast fountain and a cluster of stalls dedicated to food and drink. They weaved their way through the people waiting in line. They were momentarily blocked by gawkers surrounding a jumble of musicians and wandering entertainers, then the boys burst through to the open area in front of the stage.

They knew better than to hang out close to the stage. The area was for paying customers only. The boys skirted around to their spot on the far side of the stage, beyond where the actors passed a donation hat yet close enough to watch the show.

A couple of their friends were already there. They exchanged greetings and settled in. As time passed, others in their group showed up. They joked and messed with each other but were mindful to keep it low key whenever constables wandered by.

Three girls joined the boys. Sturm recognized two, sisters to one of the boys. The third Sturm had never met before.

The boys showed off for the girls by picking on Sturm. The two sisters quickly joined in on jokes about Sturm's height and his eyes. Sturm hated the negative attention. He had few comebacks, and those he had felt lame as he said them. He got up to leave when the new girl told them to shut up, she liked his eyes.

After a few moments of awkward silence, the group resumed their chatter, but it was no longer about Sturm.

Sturm sat back down, amazed. No one had stuck up for him before. She was cute too. He tried to talk to her through the chatter.

Ken interrupted Sturm by elbowing him then pointing toward the customs house where tents were going up. It wasn't every day that booths went up there, it meant a caravan was outside the gate.

Sturm watched as racks were quickly assembled within the tents and stocked with exotic merchandise. A man took position in front of the tents and shouted for the crowd's attention. He bellowed out with a heavily accented voice, hawking the wares. Many of the words and the phrasings were odd, he was using trade-speak.

The merchant bragged that the clothes were of the finest quality and were the latest fashion from the court of the Sultan. He claimed his spices were the tastiest and most aromatic in all the kingdoms and that the efficacy of his herbs was unmatched in fixing anything that might possibly ail you. He held out a hide, stroking it while extolling how tough it was yet soft and luxurious. He claimed it came from a fierce strange beast with three horns on an armored head.

A woman's voice suddenly cut across the merchant's words, hailing the crowd. The woman stood front-center on the stage calling for people to draw close. She was witty and outspoken, drawing laughter as she heckled those that didn't heed her. Once she had enough people gathered around her, she regaled them with a few jokes, then got down to how wonderful the play was going to be. She enticed people to sit and enjoy the show.

The play was one of several the troop did. The kids had seen it many times. Reprised, it wasn't all that funny, but the kids made great sport whooping at the punch lines. Then the play was done. The boys returned to their shenanigans. The girls seemed amused but not impressed and giggled amongst themselves.

Sturm assumed he was again the butt of their amusement. He gave up on trying to talk to the new girl. His attention wandered from them back to the plaza. He became lost in the bustle and noise. Each merchant attempted to hawk their wares over the other. The rough rural accents of the farmers intertwined with more refined city accents, which clashed with the lilting accents over by the caravan stalls.

Sturm jumped in surprise as a puppet on a string was shoved in his face. A wandering performer made the puppet dance. Sturm was uncomfortable in being singled out, but he couldn't help but join his mates in laughing. The performer then rejoined his wandering troop; a tumbler doing back flips, two jugglers, a woman on stilts and a clown trying to get under her skirt.

Sturm's attention was diverted to the crowd parting for a group of guards in chainmail on horseback. The guards carefully walked their horses past the people as they traveled from the outer gate to the Uptown gate. Sturm had learned to look at the chest of their tabards to tell who they were. City guards wore Vellar's stack of gold coins on green. House guards wore the badge of their house. This group had a unit symbol of five horizontal silver bars above a slash and three vertical bars below on a green field for the 53rd frontier guard's regiment.

Sturm made another attempt to talk to the girl. He pointed the troops out, trying to impress her with his knowledge. She seemed interested, but then all to soon the riders were past. Sturm was left uncertain how to keep the conversation going. The chatter from the rest of the group rolled over them and cut off anything further he could contrive to say.

Strum returned to watching the ebb and flow of the people across the plaza. He kept an ear to the chimes of the city clock. The town clock dutifully rang out the time every quarter hour with its chimes, each quarter playing more of a tune while figures walked through more and more of a story. On the hour completed the tune and the tale followed by the striking of the hour.

Sturm heard the fourth hour struck. How could it be four already, he had just gotten there! With a sigh, he bid goodbye to the group. He regretfully waved bye to the girl; he hadn't gotten up the courage to ask her name.

Sturm wandered over to Fallon's stall.

Fallon saw Sturm and was all smiles. "Good afternoon Sturm. You just missed your mother."

"Really? Which way did she go?"

Fallon pointed down the street, toward the warehouses.

"What is she doing over there? Well, thanks, I'll catch up to her in a moment. I need to buy some things for the gnomes. What do you still have?"

The haggle was short.

Sturm ended up with the turnips and he still had two copper pence for change. Sturm wistfully admired the pile of apples in the stall. His stomach growled.

Fallon caught Sturm's focus on the apples. "They're three for one of those copper pennies."

Sturm sadly shook his head. "Those are Gwiz's. I have no money of my own."

Fallon grinned. He took the largest apple, looked it over, polished it a moment on his shirt, and handed it to Sturm. "Here lad, you can pay me the next I see you."

Sturm's face lit up. "Thanks!" He mentally promised to pay Fallon back once his box sold.

Sturm walked off happily munching on the apple, heading down the street Fallon had pointed out. The purchase had taken only a few minutes, so Sturm expected he'd quickly catch up to his mom.

Shouts erupted ahead, from an alley to the right. Sturm didn't make it all out, but it was something about a woman being attacked. Worried, Sturm dropped the apple and ran to the alley. He edged past a couple of people peering around the corner. Then he was transfixed by what he saw.

A woman sprawled on the street, panting in exhaustion. She bled from several wounds. She struggled up to her hands and knees. A hooded man stepped behind her, gathered her hair in his fist and yanked her back onto her haunches. Her back arched, exposing her neck.

Sturm clearly saw her face, her pointed ears. It was his mother!

She tried to twist but the man's hold was too tight. Her elbow slammed his crotch, but to no effect. The man put a dagger against her throat and slashed. Blood gushed from the cut.

Sturm was stunned.

The executioner tossed her aside. She writhed on the ground, a pool of blood formed around her. The man noticed the spectators and turned to confront them.

Sturm fixated on the man. His black goatee and dark chilling eyes locked into Sturm's brain.

The man sneered at the gathered people, as if daring any to respond.

Something inside of Sturm snapped. He found himself charging down the alley screaming. Lucky for him, the others followed.

The man's eyes widened with surprise, he looked over to his accomplice standing a few feet away who had a hand over a bleeding wound. He glanced to three others on the ground. Two were dead, one not far behind them. He looked back to the accomplice and motioned with his head to leave.

Instead of attempting to take the wounded man, the accomplice finished him off with one sudden stroke. The two men turned and fled down the alley, quickly disappearing around a building.

The mob chased them around the corner.

Sturm went only so far as his mother's body. He dropped to his knees next to her. Tears rolled down his face. He gently turned her over, praying she was somehow still alive. Her front was drenched in blood. Blood oozed from her throat wound.

He shook her. He implored her. No response. Her unblinking eyes stared past him.

Sturm was bewildered. Who were these men? Why had they attacked his mom?

He looked to the men she had killed for an answer. The closest man had a rough look to him, as if a street thug or ex-soldier. He had wielded a sword. The sword was well honed, the handle worn. Sturm patted the man down finding only a coin purse. Sturm looked inside the purse and was shocked by the gold coins within. There were seven freshly minted griffons, each coin worth a fortune. He took the coins as wergild. After a moment of reflection returned one of them into the purse. The crowd would return soon. Empty purses would cause the crowd to look to him.

Sturm quickly searched through the other two bodies with similar results.

Sturm returned to his mom's body. He quickly looked through her things. All she had was a few copper coins, and a few vegetables. Her belt knife, covered in blood, lay next to her. She had nothing that the men could have wanted.

Sturm heard the crowd returning from their pursuit. They were clearly out of breath, yet still able to loudly cuss over how they hadn't caught the murderers. Sturm's time was up. He still had no answers. He stepped back from the bodies.

The first one back questioned Sturm, "Find anything?"

Sturm hid his emotions with a shrug. "She's dead. Nothing I can do for her."

The man looked across the bodies. "Yep, they're all dead. What happened anyway?"

Others joined them, surrounding the scene, fixating on the bodies. One pointed to Sturm's mom. "Hey, it's the woman with the deformed ears. Who would have wanted her dead?"

Another replied, "I don't know. She's just a street vendor of herbs and trinkets. Maybe she walked in on something, wrong place wrong time?"

"Yeah. She couldn't have taken down these three. They look like they were real fighters, look at their swords. I bet they were fighting each other, and she got in the middle of it."

A man snatched up a sword. "Heck if I care, but I fancy this sword." He held it in front of him as if daring anyone to take it from him.

No one argued with him, they were too busy following his lead. In a blink, people swarmed the bodies, searching through pocket and pouch. They even pawed at Sturm's mom's body.

Sturm's face clouded up with anger. He started to admonish them, but he was interrupted as a woman stood up whooping with joy. She held up one of the gold griffons Sturm had left behind. "Praise the gods, look what I found!"

A man next to her grabbed at the coin. Another man blocked the first, starting a scuffle. Others piled in. Fights broke out at the other bodies as coins were discovered there as well. Swords were picked up and brandished. Things turned ugly.

Sturm realized it was time to go. He slipped away, doing his best to not let the 18 heavy coins he had taken clink together. He made it to the corner and turned onto the street, away from the crowd. He walked trying to look 'normal' while fighting back his tears, and his fears. A couple of blocks down, he saw a small recess and slid into it. He let loose. Tears flowed as his sense of loss overwhelmed him. The vison of his mother's execution replayed in his head. He rejected the idea she was just in the wrong place at the wrong time, which left his with why her? Who would pay that kind of coin to kill a street person?

Sturm's mind seized on that last question. His mom had always avoided talking about her past. Was she killed over something she had done? His mind jumped to his father. She had never told him of his father. Was it something his father had done? A more sinister thought crept in, had she fled his father and he had tracked her down and killed her for it?

As he cried himself out, it came to him that his mom must have known trouble was coming and she had sent him away to protect him. He could be in danger as well. The men in the alley didn't know him by sight, but that didn't mean they wouldn't track him down. Images welled up in Sturm's imagination of being stalked by the hooded man and his accomplice.

He felt the urge to run. He fought it. Running would only draw attention. He fought his panic. His mother's lessons popped into his head. He leaned back against the wall and focused on breathing, nothing else but breathing. The panic ebbed.

He noticed a wetness to the knee of his pants, he looked down and saw blood smeared his clothes. It was something that could get him noticed and cause trouble, but he had a solution for that. Gwiz didn't know it, but Sturm had figured out his clean up cantrip. It had saved Sturm on several occasions from having to explain what he had been up to: no evidence, no questions.

Sturm spoke through the words summoning the cantrip. It was a little rushed, a little ragged. He snapped his fingers to release the magic. Nothing happened. A second time, frustration seeped into his words, and again no result. He paused. He needed to pull himself together. He methodically focused on each syllable, distinctly mouthing it. He felt magic well up and release. The blood dried and fell off his clothes. He sighed in relief.

Sturm's took note of his surroundings. He was in an enclosed space. It hid him from the street, but if they found him he would be trapped.

He slipped out of the recess and into the flow of traffic. He unconsciously drifted to behind an older couple and followed them. They took him to the gate to old Downtown, his home turf.

Sturm was relieved the gate wasn't guarded, even after the small riot back in the alleyway. Then he realized; it wasn't the city guards he had to worry about, it was the people who killed his mom. They could be anyone, anywhere. They could be watching the gates. They could be watching him. He reflexively looked around.

There was no sign of anyone lurking. No one paid him any mind.

The older couple continued walking towards the gate.

He prodded himself into motion. He kept close to the couple, as if he were with them.

Past the gate, he split off into an alleyway. He turned towards home, keeping to the gaps between buildings. The vision of the hooded man dogged Sturm's steps. Was he following Sturm? Was he ahead of Sturm, waiting at Sturm's home?

Sturm stopped. He realized it wouldn't be prudent to just walk up to his front door. He worked his way down an alley behind a row of homes. He stopped at the one that was across the street from his house and shinnied up the side of the building to the roof. He glanced wistfully across to the roof top of his home. He had spent many hours there enjoying the view across the roof tops. He had also watched the people down on the street. They never looked up at him, but there was always a first time. He positioned himself to see the upper floor of his home while not exposing himself to the street.

The window shutters were closed, which was normal for no one being home.

He leaned further forward to see the street level. An errant thought crossed his mind, what if one of the killers had the same idea and watched him from a roof? He suddenly felt exposed. He glanced from rooftop to rooftop.

There was no one.

Reassured, he peaked over the edge to the street. There were only a few people, it was dinner time. Those that passed by were just his neighbors who belonged there. Nothing seemed amiss.

He turned his attention to his home. He scrutinized it for several minutes, looking for even the smallest detail. Even so he nearly missed it. The front door was ajar. The door didn't always solidly latch, his mom had scolded him many times about it not latching behind him. She had always made a point of making sure it clicked home when she left. Someone must have been in the house. Were they still there? Sturm decided he couldn't chance it. The tears returned as he climbed down the back of the house. He headed to his only refuge.

Chapter 2: City of Vellar, 15th Year of the Council (YOC), 39th Day of Fall, 6 PM

Sturm trudged into the gnomes' home drained, eyes red. He plopped down on one of their short chairs.

Gnumph looked up with a frown.

Gwiz started to chastise him for being so late but realized something was amiss. "What happened?"

Sturm had several false starts trying to relate the story through tears that repeatedly overwhelmed him. Finally, he succeeded.

The gnomes were shocked. It took several moments before Gnumph broke the silence. "I'm sorry Sturm. I don't know what to say. It could be as simple as they wanted to take advantage of her because she was a woman."

Gwiz countered, "I think there is more here than that. Someone had been to the house. Were they looking for something and when they didn't find it they hunted her down to search her?"

Gnumph replied, "Yet Sturm found she carried nothing. Hmm, perhaps they missed something there. I think I need to take a have a look-see there. I'll be back in a bit."

Sturm pushed himself up from the chair to follow, but Gwiz pulled him back down. "You did well, showed a surprising amount of sense. Gnumph will see to the house. He will come back hungry. Did you think to get the turnips as I asked?"

Confused, Sturm nodded.

"Well, pull them out and you can help me make dinner while we wait."

Before Sturm knew what had happened, he had a peeler in his hand and turnips and other root vegetables in front of him.

Dinner was ready when Gnumph returned. He came in and sat down, lost in thought. After a few moments he noticed Sturm and Gwiz stared at him expectantly. "The house was half in shambles. Looks like they were searching for something, and then left when they found it." He turned to Sturm. "Do you know anything about a hidey hole under the floorboards in the back room?"

Sturm nodded. "Mom had her sword and chainmail in it."

The surprised Gnomes blurted in unison, "Sword and chainmail?!"

Gnumph was first to recover. "After all these years, she never mentioned... Well, that explains how she was able to take down a couple of them. And it explains why there were five of them. She was a warrior, and they knew it."

Gwiz cut in, "This has the smell of a targeted killing. The house likely was searched before their attack. The armor and weapon showed they had the right target. They made sure they had everything of worth before something might go wrong. As it nearly did!"

Sturm piped up, "Well, almost everything."

"Almost? What was left behind? What do you have?"

Sturm pulled up his left pant cuff and pulled a long combat dagger from his boot. The dagger's blade was not quite the right color for steel. "This. It's also hers."

The Gnomes eyes grew wide. Gnumph waggled his finger at Sturm. "And when were you going to tell us about this?"

Gwiz hushed Gnump. He gestured to the dagger. "Let me see that."

Sturm held it out but didn't hand it over.

Gwiz gently tilted Sturm's hand up so the light glinted off the blade. He leaned close to look at the blade, then ran his finger along it. He sat back nodding to himself. "Hmm, not magical yet mithril. Unique design. Elements to catch and break a blade, a spike tip to punch through chain links, an edge to slice and yet strength to the spine to parry. It took a master bladesmith to combine all those elements together and then to work the mithril." His focus returned to Sturm. "I'm glad you didn't think to pull it on those men. They may have stopped just to take it from you. For that matter, I wouldn't show it in the streets, someone would kill you for it."

Sturm returned the dagger to his boot. "You never saw it. No one else will. It will be fine."

Gnumph pulled out a small book and held it out to Sturm. "This was sitting on the counter. It's a book of herbal remedies, and more. I can't read magic, but there appears to be minor spells. Has she shown this to you?"

Sturm took the book. "Thanks. Yes, she showed me the trick of reading the runes and had me practice a few of the shortest spells."

"Did she train you with that dagger, and maybe the sword too?"

"Yes. She started with the dagger a long time ago. The sword was only last year, once I got big enough to swing it right."

Gwiz laughed. "Ha! You have a few surprises too."

"What does this have to do with my mom being murdered?"

Gwiz mulled it over a moment before he responded, "I think that those years ago when your mom came to Vellar it was to hide from them."

"Who's them?"

"Sorry, no clue. Your mom never talked about her life before Vellar. Made a point of it. We honored her privacy."

"Are they going to come for me?"

"I don't think they know you exist. When we first met, she was hardly showing her pregnancy. However, if they find out she had a child, that could change. I think we need to get you away from here. But what to do, and where to go? Your mom set your feet on the warrior's path, but you still have a way to grow into it. Is that the path you'd like to take?"

Sturm stared off for a moment. Emotions played over his face. Fear turned into the anger. "It's either that or be a tinker of music boxes while I wait for them to come kill me like they did her. No! Someday I'll come for them!"

The ferocity of Sturm's tone startled the gnomes and left them staring at him.

He glared from one to the other, challenging them to argue with him. Tears formed and rolled down his cheek unacknowledged.

Gwiz nodded solemnly. "And someday we'd like to help you do it, that we would. Your mom was Gnome Friend. You are Gnome Friend. We stand by our friends. But how can we help you now?"

Gnumph raised a finger in the air. "I have an idea. The best thing is to send you to a sword academy. It gets you away from here while you can grow your weapon skills. Isn't there one a few days' travel north of Barzan, in Socul? Yes?" With a sudden realization, he frowned. "But how do we get you into the academy with no questions up front?"

Gwiz responded, "Don't give up so quickly. That is a good idea. Hm... How about he claims to be the umpteenth child of some knight. Some of them are always getting sent off to places like that to get them out of the way. They normally have some training before they show up, like Sturm does."

Gnumph replied, "Yes, but if the supposed daddy knight finds out, he may not have a sense of humor about it. Also, we don't know enough about their patents of nobility to fake one."

"Aren't there some open nobility patents around Vellar? There was an estate or two that had fallen into default that they let the farmers buy the land. Maybe we could do that and buy the title as well. Oh, wait, that would take not just silver but gold to do. Where are we going to get that?"

Sturm felt the weight of the gold Griffons in his pocket. "How much gold?"

"I don't know, maybe several ounces."

Sturm pulled out the coins and spilled them on the table. "Like this many ounces?"

Gwiz sat back in amazement, stroking his beard as he stared at the coins. "Yes, that should more than do. Where did you get that much gold?"

"The assassins had been well paid."

Chapter 3: Socul Sword Academy arena, 20th YOC, 40th day of Planting Time, 3 PM.

Sturm walked Paint back and forth along the side of the course, cooling the horse down from their ride, while watching his last couple classmates finish the course.

Sturm was a mix of tired and nervous. The tournament was his graduation. It was also an opportunity for prospective employers to come watch and evaluate. The obstacle course was the last event. He mulled over his performance in the events.

The first event had been the individual melee. He had hadn't run into trouble until the last round where he was paired with the biggest and strongest kid in the class. Sturm had always had problems facing him. The fighting style at the academy was human style bashing that favored size and strength. Sturm started the match by trading blows, which got him nowhere. Sturm had realized that continuing the fight like that would only have worn Sturm down until he lost. Sturm had thrown caution to the winds and used one of his mother's moves. He had only practiced it in private, yet he pulled it off. The speed and precision of elven sword fighting had caught his opponent flat footed and won the event.

The next event was archery. Sturm had never mastered archery. He knew it was his own fault, an attitude thing. He had never warmed up to the trainer that had taken over during Sturm's second year. The new guy switched everyone from drawn to cross bow and spent most of the sessions bragging while belittling the students. So, this was Sturm's weakest event, but he felt he had minimized the damage to his overall score. He had managed to get all three bolts into the first-round target and even two in the second round after the butts were pulled back. It was a passable showing. Hopefully, it was the last time he had to touch a bow.

Sturm turned back to the riding course, scoring his points there. They had done well on the early jumps, but they had lost points when Paint stumbled going over the last obstacle. It wasn't Paint's fault; it was a rough course and Paint was getting old. Sturm considered how to take the jump differently next time... Sturm's train of thought stopped. There would be no next time.

Sturm pulled Paint's head close and give him a hug. Sturm had met Paint the first year, when assigned to muck out the stables. They had quickly bonded. It was

Paint that the first-year boy, missing his mom, had come to hug and cry on. Now their time together was nearly done.

Sturm's attention was brought back to the course by the crowd's cheers of encouragement turning to shouts of alarm. The horse had refused the last jump, rearing. The rider was thrown. Luckily the boy kept his wits and rolled away before the horse came back down. A collective sigh of relief swept through the crowd as the boy bounced back up waving.

The riding scores were quickly announced and then the final scores. Sturm had held on to 3rd place! Ecstatic, he hugged Paint again, telling him how good he was.

The stands emptied. The other graduates led their horses past Sturm back to the barns. Sturm dawdled, rubbing Paint's forehead.

One of the younger students ran up. "You're still out here? Go ahead, I've got him."

Sturm hesitated. The lad would take over Sturm's duties in the stables, and was gentle with Paint, but Sturm was loath to let the horse go.

The boy continued, "No, really, I have him. I'll take good care of him, just like you showed me. I'll brush him and make sure he gets the grain you set aside for him. You need to get to the feast, and good luck with that!"

The feast was where Sturm would have a chance to meet the guests, talk to them about jobs, yet Sturm still hesitated holding Paint's cheek strap. He jumped at a voice behind him.

"Aye, why don't you turn him over?"

Sturm turned around; it was one of the visitors looking to hire. The man was dark haired, a couple inches below six feet tall. He had strong arms, and a wide girth.

Sturm bowed politely. "Sir. It's just... well... I normally groom him myself."

The man flashed a smile at Sturm. "A good habit, but the other boy has him. That's not the whole reason."

Embarrassed, Sturm looked down at his feet. "No Sir." After a deep breath, Sturm finished, "It's the last time I'll see him."

"And you need your goodbye's?"

Sturm nodded.

"I'm sorry that you can't take the school horse with you."

"Thank you, sir. I know I can't. Even if I could, he's really too old to be going long distances on the trail, it wouldn't be fair to him. I'll still miss him though."

"I don't know if it's much consolation right now, but with a silver griffon a month pay plus end of trip bonuses, you could afford a horse of your own in a year or two."

Sturm sighed, "If only I got such an offer." That was twice the pay he hoped to get.

The man laughed. "You just did."

Sturm was startled. "What?"

"Aye, that was an offer. My name is Fazio. I saw you on the field. Impressive showing against that big guy. You're Kian Terter, yes?"

Sturm nodded. That was the name he now went by. The patent of nobility they had bought was the Terter estate. Kian had been chosen as a first name, after a Highlander troubadour popular when Sturm had left Vellar.

"Good, I have it right then. I run caravans from Vellar to Venub and all points between. I occasionally even make runs to the southern and western lands, wherever the profit is. I treat men based on what they do. You do equal work; you get equal pay. You'll be a guard, and you'll help out with the animals. A lot of the new swords think they are too good to be taking care of the horses. I won't have that problem with you, will I?"

Sturm shook his head.

"Good. So, will you come work for me?" The man spat on his palm then held it out, offering his bargain.

Sturm quickly spat in his and took the hand, sealing the agreement. "Aye sir!"

"Then you don't need to go to the feast. Take your time with your friend. I head back to the caravan route in the morning. I expect you to be with me." The man winked and turned towards the main hall. No matter his advice to Sturm, Fazio was not one to miss a feast.

Part 2: The Delivery

Vellar to Bridgeport Route Overview, Tionol Archives

Chapter 4: Caravan Route between Barzan & Sulvi, 25th YOC, 9th Day of New Spring, 6 PM.

The Cathar Cartel caravan stopped for the evening at a leveled off campground just off the road. Sturm rode the final sweep around one side of the encampment, one of his men did the other.

Sturm generally took the chore. Sturm's chainmail coat was just as heavy as anyone else's, but the ride gave him a few moments of escape from the responsibilities and headaches of running a caravan.

His warhorse Val, short for Valiant, loved it as well. The freedom to run, no longer bound to the plodding walk of the draft animals, provided a moment of exhilaration.

Sturm reined Val in at the top of the last rise of his side of the pattern. His gaze swept across the rolling sea of grass as his other rider approached. A moment of banter and Sturm sent the rider back to camp.

Sturm didn't follow, unwilling to give up his freedom quite yet. Instead, he stretched then leaned back in his saddle and relaxed. He pulled his helmet off and ruffled his sweaty short hair. Rubbing his scalp felt good. He didn't want to think about how hot it would be if he grew his hair out, even braided in the current style. It wasn't the original reason he had cut it short, that decision came after watching how his mom had died, but it was a good reason on its own.

He looked down at his helmet, a metal cap with a nose guard. It was covered with dust from the day. He pulled up the corner of his tabard and slowly wiped the dust off. Then he changed tabard corners and wiped out the inside for good measure. Reluctantly, he put it back on.

He took a last look about. The grass rippled in the wind, undisturbed by man or beast.

Sturm turned Val towards the camp and let him amble, still in no hurry. Back at camp, his evening would be occupied with preparing for the next day. There were ten wagons to inspect to see if they needed any repairs. There were forty draft horses to look over and see if any had thrown a shoe or were chafing from their harness. There were ten drivers he had to ensure were in good spirits. There was also his five outriders and their horses to check on.

Val stopped to nibble at a grass stalk.

Sturm shook his head; of the thousands of blades of grass around them, what made that one so delectable? Sturm gave Val a minute, running his hand through Val's mane reminiscing. It was nearly the first anniversary of when he had bought Val. Saving the money had been a major accomplishment, war horses were expensive. Sturm didn't regret a single copper of it. Warhorses were a breed above. They were bigger than draft horses and had their endurance. They were faster than a common rider. They were also smart and trained for combat. It had taken Sturm a month to master the various signals from his hands, knees, and feet to communicate to Val and then to practice them until they were second nature. Along the way he and Val had bonded.

The clash of metal on metal, sounds of battle, brought Sturm out of his memories. He urged Val to top the rise. The camp was just below him. The drivers and his men fought bandits in leather armor. He drew his sword and spurred Val into a gallop.

The first bandit didn't see them coming. Sturm didn't slow down and simply rode him over.

The second bandit had the chance to react and swung at Val. Sturm kneed Val a command. Val pivoted leaving the blade to slice empty air. The swing exposed the bandit's side to one of Sturm's men. The man slashed the bandit, the bandit went down.

Another bandit came at them. Val reared and lashed out a hoof catching the man in the chest. Warhorses didn't always need commands.

Sturm was the only one mounted. He had a vantage to look over the fight. He saw his people being forced apart where they could be individually surrounded and cut down. Out of the corner of his eye he noticed two bandits split off to one of the wagons. He ignored them and rode through the battle, chopping his sword downward to either side.

The bandits didn't know how to fight against a mounted warrior and the tide of battle quickly turned. The last bandits turned to run, but only made it a few steps as Sturm's men cut them down.

Sturm turned Val in a circle, sizing up the situation. Val hadn't been wounded, but it seemed all of his men had been to one extent or another. They needed the medical supplies in the wagons. He remembered the two bandits who might still be among the wagons. He shouted out a caution then rode through the wagons looking for the bandits.

The bandits were gone. Sturm saw a couple of boards on the ground under a wagon. He jumped down from Val and examined under the wagon. The boards had been pulled from the wagon bottom exposing a small compartment. He had never heard of such compartments.

Sturm swung back up on Val in time for two of his men ride up to him. He queried them, "Either of you see the two that split off over here? See where they went?"

They had been too busy fighting to notice any of that.

"I didn't either. Did you see where the attack came from?"

Cade shook his head. "I was helping unhitch a wagon, sorry."

Ned was more helpful. "I did. Follow me." He spurred his horse and they rode at a full gallop.

As they crested the fourth rise, Sturm had a brief glimpse of several tethered mounts and a bandit shoving something into a saddlebag, then Sturm's attention was focused on a mounted bandit directly in front of him. Sturm had no chance to maneuver.

The bandit saw Sturm, his eyes widened in shock. The bandit drew his sword while desperately spurring his horse to get out of Sturm's path. Their swords met as the horses collided and tumbled.

Sturm instinctively shoved away from his saddle making sure to clear his horse. He landed, rolled, and ended up on his feet. Somewhere in all that he lost his sword, so he pulled his dagger. He orientated on the horses flailing to get up, then pivoted, looking for his opponent. His view crossed his men fighting the other bandit, as Ned's sword chopped into the bandit's knee. Sturm pivoted further and spotted his bandit several feet away, struggling to his feet. The man hadn't fared well. He was gasping to get his wind back while frantically searching the ground for his sword.

Sturm closed and then lunged with his dagger. It wasn't an eloquent move, but it connected before the man realized Sturm was there. The bandit collapsed.

Sturm went to Val. Val tossed his head and snorted in irritation but wasn't hurt. Miraculously, the bandit's horse wasn't either, though it was badly shaken.

Sturm looked over to his men. The other bandit was down, but so was Cade. Sturm ran to Cade and pulled him up to sitting. "Where did he get you? I'm not seeing the bleeding."

"He didn't. Not this fight. Back at the caravan I got a cut on my leg. It was hardly a scratch but now my leg is burning. It won't hold my weight. I feel weak."

Cussing, Sturm looked at Cade's eyes. They weren't focused. For that matter Cade had turned grey. Maybe it was shock, or maybe it was something else, but Cade needed care quickly. Sturm directed Ned, "Take him back to the caravan and get him patched up. I'll grab these mounts and I'll be right behind you."

Ned nodded in reply, but he moved slowly as they got Cade on his horse.

Sturm helped Ned onto his horse. "Are you alright?"

"I'll be fine boss. Don't worry, I'll get Cade back to camp." He grabbed Cabe's reins and spurred his horse.

Sturm quickly gathered the reins of the bandit's horses and strung them through a tether line. He mounted Val, and rode led the other horses back to camp where he was met with a grim sight. A gravely wounded driver had died. The rest were as bad off as Cade. They had already gotten into the healer kits and used everything in them, but with little effect.

Sturm went over to one of the bandit bodies and examined their sword. The blade had a discoloration, as if it had been coated. Sturm knew better than to touch it.

Sturm went to the captured bandit mounts and desperately emptied the saddle bags of the nearest one, searching through the contents.

Ned came up, pale and unsteady. "Boss, what are you doing?"

Sturm answered without stopping his search, "I think the blades were poisoned. I'm looking to see if they carried any antidote with them."

"Poisoned? Crap! Here, let me help."

"Check the bandit bodies to see if they're carrying any."

Sturm went from horse to horse but no sign of an antidote. Sturm turned to ask Ned if he had found anything, but Ned was face down three bandit bodies over. Looking around, Sturm could see it was too late for all of his men.

He numbly stared at the bodies. It was all so quick!

Once Sturm's brain started functioning again, he went to the horse that the one bandit had shoved something into the saddle bag. He looked through the items he had tossed during searching for an antidote. In the midst of normal travel kit items was a small sealed wooden box. It was small enough to fit in the compartment under the wagon.

He wondered if there was anything else hidden in the wagons. He went wagon to wagon and searched under each. Most of the wagons had secret compartments, all empty.

Sturm wondered how many times, in all his trips as caravan guard, something had secretly ridden along. He also wondered how it was that the bandits went directly to the only one with something in the compartment.

Sturm considered the box. Why was it worth men's lives? He wanted to look inside it but decided to not break the seal. Opening sealed containers in a shipment was a violation of the contract and he would forfeit his men's wergild to their families. His remaining option was to deliver the box. The next city on the caravan route, Sulvi, was also the headquarters of the cartel. Perhaps he could parlay delivery of the box into some answers.

Sturm's attention returned to his men. His first thought was to bury them before he left but he realized there were too many. It would take him all night and well into the day. He couldn't chance getting caught in a follow up attack.

His next thought turned to the horses. There were too many to lead to Sulvi. He couldn't just leave them here vulnerable to predators. He unhobbled those already tethered for the night and dropped saddles from the mounts. He hoped that setting them free would allow them to defend themselves, or at least allow them to run from danger.

Storm mounted Val, then took a last look around the ambush site. He felt like he was abandoning his men, but there was nothing else he could do. He shook his head sadly, then turned his horse east and rode.

Chapter 5: Sulvi, 25th YOC, 10th Day of New Spring, half past 7 AM

Sturm was waiting when the city gate opened. He hadn't bothered to clean the blood splatter from his armor. His clean up cantrip didn't work while he wore his armor, and he hadn't taken the time to take the armor off to clean it. The Sulvi gate guards stared at his state, but they recognized him and waved him through.

He rode from the city gate toward one of the city's landmarks; the tall, silver dome atop the main building of the Cathar compound. Rumor was the silver wasn't just paint, but real silver. Sturm's past dealings with the trade cartels made him believe the rumor.

The Cathar estate covered two acres. It was surrounded by twenty-foot walls, opulent with statues and friezes that hid strong defenses. The style of the towers and gate was of the southern kingdoms with minarets decorating their tops. The stout doors of the gate were open, with a guard to either side.

Sturm had Val top shy of the guards.

The guards nervously eyed the tall warhorse and the blood splattered rider. They exchanged glances. Neither wanted to be the one to demand his business.

Sturm's patience was quickly exhausted. He squeezed his knees and Val trotted past them into the courtyard. The gate guards shouted at his back. He ignored them and rode to the large fountain in the center of the courtyard. He dismounted and let Val drink from the fountain's pool.

Men responded to the shouting, streaming from the stables and barracks on the right and the smithy on the left, grabbing whatever came to hand as they readied for a fight. One of them recognized Sturm and shouted, "Sir Terter! You gave us a start riding in like that. What are you about?"

Sturm forced a smile as he replied, "My apologies, but I have ridden long and hard to report to Lady Cathar."

"Really? Well, out with it then. We'll pass the news to her, if it's important enough."

"Is one of her caravans being ambushed important?"

The guard's eyes popped in surprise. He ordered the other guards, "Keep an eye out here. I'll take the news in." He hastened to the main building, disappearing inside.

The guard quickly returned and escorted Sturm inside to an upper floor antechamber. The guard directed Sturm to wait and then left.

Sturm pulled the wooden box out of his satchel. He stood quietly and waited. As the moments passed, he looked around the room. It was richly done with rugs, tapestries, and silver lamp sconces. Across the back wall was a satin curtain in the Cathar house colors, a silver domed building on a light blue background. There wasn't much furniture, only an ornate settee and a side table. On the table was a silver tray holding a decanter with a dark red liquid and two stemmed glasses. The decanter and glasses were of matching cut crystal. The room had a single window. Even that was a sign of wealth. It wasn't a typical opening in the wall with a shutter for weather. No, this was a combination of clear glass to afford a view across the city with a leaded colored glass border for decoration. Windows like that were found in cathedrals.

The satin curtain fluttered, then parted. A woman stepped through, then she paused letting the curtain drop back behind her. She was perfectly posed to capture Sturm's attention. She wore a bright red silk sari, which set off her dark coloring. Cinched at the waist, it highlighted her figure. The matching ruby earrings, necklace, and rings spoke not just of money, but of wealth. She was beautiful with the almond shaped dark eyes of the kingdoms to the south. Sturm recognized Hermanji, the head of the cartel.

She assessed Sturm. She wrinkled her nose as she saw the dried blood. Her gaze continued across him lingering on his green eyes. After a moment, she nodded towards the box without taking her eyes from his. "So, what have we here?"

Sturm bowed and offered the box to her. "Lady Cathar, I think you already know since I was ushered in on such short notice."

She took the box, gently caressed the lid with a fingertip, then looked back into his eyes. "Yes, but I wonder if you know."

"No, the box is still sealed. I only know I lost five men, so it must be important to someone."

"And the rest of the caravan?"

"You lost all of your drivers. I had to leave the rest of your goods and let your horses run free."

Sadness crossed her face. "The entire caravan, gone?"

"Yes. I'm sure the goods would all be salvaged by now, except for that." Sturm gestured towards the box.

"How interesting, that you are the only one to survive."

Sturm was immediately angered. Was she insinuating he hadn't done his part in the fight? He blurted, "I wasn't the only one to survive the fighting, but I was the only one lucky enough to not be wounded by their poison blades. I had two men at my side when the last of the raiders fell. They died within a few minutes after the fight."

She nodded, apparently pleased by his reaction. "Lucky? Hmm, perhaps the only one good enough not to be wounded? So, how did you come by the box?"

Sturm stared at her; emotions roiled. Had she had provoked him on purpose? He was angry with her, yet not certain if he really should be. It had been her caravan; it was her right to question his abilities and motivations. He was also mad at himself for firing up so easily. He swore it wouldn't happen again. He took a deep breath and forced himself past his anger before he answered. "Two of the raiders split off from the fight to loot the wagons. The fight at the wagons didn't last long, and I was able to catch up to them as they reached their horses."

"And that was all they took?"

"Yes."

"They were lucky to find the box so quickly."

"There was no luck to it. They went to one wagon, right to a secret compartment under the wagon. I never knew the wagons had secret compartments. How did they know? Did you know about them?"

She smiled at him, a dazzling smile. Instead of answering him, she turned and set the box on the table. She stood a moment tapping its lid lost in thought. Coming to a decision she broke the seal and opened the lid, revealing a turquoise glow from a stone within.

She appraised the contents for several moments. She closed the box and returned her attention to Sturm. "You wear the blood of your foes." She clapped her hands and called out, "Tej!"

The door opened and a young woman bearing a strong resemblance to Hermanji stepped in. She bowed. "Your wishes, m'lady?"

"Take his armor and clean the blood from it. His britches are ruined, find him a new pair."

"Yes, m'lady."

The women stared expectantly at Sturm. Sturm hesitated.

Hermanji chided Sturm, "Surely you don't feel you're in danger from two unarmed women. Off with the armor. Give it to Tej. It will be cleaned as we talk. You can keep your pants, for now."

Sturm undid his chain coat then handed it to Tej. Tej accepted it and bowed her way out of the chamber.

Hermanji took up the decanter and pulled the stopper. As she poured a generous amount of the dark red liquid into a glass, she asked, "Would you like to join me in a glass of port? We have some business to discuss." With a teasing laugh, she continued, "Do not worry, it will be a most congenial discussion. Really."

Sturm didn't particularly like port, however he wanted to hear her out. He took the offered glass.

She poured a second glass for herself, then lightly clicked it against his in a token toast.

Sturm waited for her to sip from her glass before he followed suit.

She was amused by his hesitation. "Please enjoy your drink. If I wanted you harmed, it would have happened without you ever seeing me. I have no interest in that. I know better than to blame you for what happened to the caravan. So, can we talk business now?"

She curled up cat like on the settee, settling herself in. She idly sipped at her drink, her eyes never leaving him, waiting.

Sturm responded, "Go ahead."

"You have done well for us in the past. I have heard that the other merchant houses are pleased with you as well. You've drawn your blade only when you needed to, and you've always used it well. Today, you've also shown you're more than just a useful blade."

She paused to sip her port, then smiled at him again. It was a disarmingly sweet, innocent smile. "So, you have caught my attention. From time to time, I have special jobs that I need done. I need special people for those special jobs, people I can depend on."

Sturm looked at her suspiciously. She was playing with him. He weighed her words, looking for what lay hidden behind them. What kind of jobs were they? Dirty jobs, the type people didn't come back from? He decided he wasn't interested, but he needed to keep her talking so he could turn her back to the box and the ambush. "Really? What makes you think I'd be who you need? I just got all my men killed. And then, maybe I already have something else planned right now."

"Yes, really. They died, but you survived. You brought the box back to me without getting greedy and attempting to get a... Let's just call it a bonus. And you didn't get into Cathar business, you didn't open the box. These three qualities make you a valuable commodity for House Cathar." She paused for his reaction but saw none. "Let me guess your thoughts. You want to know what happened, and why. You want to know who needs to pay for this. Yes?"

Warily, Sturm nodded.

She continued, "You came here as much for answers as to fulfill your contract. I appreciate that. I also would want answers. Further you want to punish who did this. I have as much right, as much responsibility, to not let this go unpunished. House Cathar's reputation is at stake. If this goes without ramifications, I will look weak. Bandits will no longer fear us and will attack my caravans. Other houses will be tempted to test us, to steal our contracts. Our routes would disappear."

For a moment they exchanged stares, then she continued. Her tone changed as she pitched her deal, "Whatever you do about this, people will think you do it in my name. This also means any consequences that may rise from your actions would also extend to House Cathar. Because of this I ask, even insist, that you work with me on this. If you do, there would be benefits to you. House Cathar has many resources. I can send people with you. Also, House Cathar rewards those who uphold our interests."

The last thing Sturm needed was people he didn't know and couldn't trust. He blurted out, "I'll do this alone."

Taking that as agreement to the partnership, Lady Cathar stood up and stepped over to Sturm. "As you please. Let us toast to our new relationship." She touched her glass to his. After a sip of her port, she continued, "Now, let me tell you a few things. First, few know of the secret compartments on the wagons. We often transport items of high worth; secrecy helps to protect them. This is one such contract. Please do not spread this knowledge."

"Whose contract?"

She looked at him for a moment. With a slight shake of her head she replied, "I'm sorry, I'm not at liberty to say. Part of the contract was confidentiality for the client. I will ask them if I may share that with you. Will that do?"

Sturm had lived with similar contracts the last several years. You fulfill the terms, or you don't work again. She could be lying to him, but if that was in the contract she wouldn't budge. Sturm shrugged. "I guess I can't blame you. On the other hand, you can't blame me if I find out on my own."

"Kian, please! Give me a few days to get permission. In the meantime, just focus on finding out how the ambush came about."

Sturm had half a mind to just plow ahead on his own. He bet the owner of the box would know who wanted it bad enough to kill for it. Then again, how would he find who that was if Hemanji didn't tell him? That would leave his next best route the person who had placed the box in the wagon, the Cathar trademaster in Barzan. That brought Sturm back to Hemanji. Putting the question to the trademaster would have fewer consequences with Lady Cathar's blessing than without it. Sturm gave her the tiniest of nods.

She continued, "You are right. The bandits were not 'lucky' in finding the box. They knew which caravan, which wagon, and the existence of the secret compartment. They would only have gotten such knowledge from our trademaster in Barzan. He was the one who placed the box."

She leaned close, looking up into his eyes. She put her hand on his chest, speaking softly, "He is key to this, but I doubt this was his idea. He isn't that smart. There is someone else behind it. We need to know who he told, and who is behind this. Unless the bandits told you something you haven't mentioned?"

"No."

"Unfortunate. So, you need to get from him who he talked to."

"Then what?"

"After, only after, you find out who; you can do whatever you feel is appropriate. If this is from him being stupid, I don't care what you do. If he betrayed us, caused our men to die, stick his head on a pole in both our names. After that, return to me and we can discuss what happens next."

"And you said House Cathar rewards well?"

With a laugh she replied, "Of course."

"What?"

She pressed her body against his, her lips to his ear. She whispered seductively, "What do you want?"

Sturm was tongue-tied.

She leaned back to look at him, amused at his confusion. She caressed his cheek. "Oh, you are a pretty one. Someday we will play. Yet, you are more than just a pretty face. Return to me with word of who caused the attack." She tilted her head up while turning his head to her, her lips brushed his. She turned and walked out through the curtain she had come in.

Sturm was left staring at the swaying curtain. He glanced down to the box left on the table, apparently forgotten. He stared at the stone within the box a moment, then shook his head. He walked out the door he had been ushered in.

Hemanji re-entered. She returned to the box, caressed the lid thoughtfully with one finger. "Yes, my pretty boy. I can trust you. How unique in this world. How very unique."

Chapter 6: West of Sulvi 25th YOC, 10th Day of New Spring, Noon

Sturm left Sulvi in much better condition than when he had arrived. He had cleaned up, eaten, and even had a nap. He felt revitalized.

Lady Hemanji had done her part. She had her people feed, water, and groom Val. She had saddle bags packed with trail food, grain for Val, and a healer kit. It wasn't a typical healer kit; she had added antidotes for several common poisons.

Sturm traveled west from the gate following the same caravan route he had been on the previous night. It was the fastest route. The roadbed was kept up for the wagons, and the grades provided easy travel.

Sturm considered his confrontation in Barzan. Jurik, the Cathar trademaster, didn't have it in him to so obviously cross Hermanji. So, who did? How could Sturm get Jurik to tell him? The idea of subduing Jurik and then beating the answer out of him was tempting but Sturm rejected it. An alternative plan formed in his mind, but it required him to ride to his estate and enlist the help of his godfathers and then ride back. It also required that word of the ambush didn't make it back before he confronted Jurik. Could he make it to his estate and back in time?

Sturm looked over his route map. Distances were marked in terms of days of travel for a caravan wagon. Sulvi to Barzan was normally eight days with seven prepared campsites in-between. His caravan had been ambushed at the third campsite out from Barzan. Caravans moved slowly. A rider would cover the distance much quicker, especially a motivated rider on a warhorse. He figured he could over the distance in a single, long, day. The distance from Barzan to his estate and back to Barzan would be another day.

Sturm tried to place caravans on the route with respect to the ambush site. He didn't have to worry about the next caravan coming out of Barzan, it wasn't scheduled to leave until the 12th. That left the caravans camps he had passed on his ride to Sulvi. He had no way of knowing which way they were traveling. The closest had been camped two days away from the ambush site. If they traveled toward Barzan, he would pass their new campsite near dusk. They would be only one day away from the ambush. If they discovered the ambush at the end of that day, they would send a rider to Barzan to report it who would make Barzan's gate opening at dawn. That scenario didn't give Sturm the time to visit the gnomes. His plan hinged on what that caravan was doing.

He pushed Val but he also paced his progress. The fastest way to travel was keeping his horse fresh. That meant alternating riding with leading Val. It also meant taking breaks and occasional water.

He passed a caravan that had left Sulvi that morning. Dukar colors flew from their pennant: a rearing draft horse on white. He had ridden for Dukar on occasion, some of them knew him and waved as he rode past.

Another hour passed; he came up on a caravan coming from the west. They looked to be foreigners and sported a horse tail banner instead of colors. He'd seen that once before. They had been from a kingdom west of Vellar, beyond the wastelands. He gave them a wide berth and rode past them with his right hand up, open, and visible to show he meant no harm. One of their guards followed him around, watchful, but also with an open right hand visible.

He came across two more Cathar caravans, both headed towards Sulvi. He rode past them acknowledging their greetings.

An hour before dusk he passed the campsite located a day of wagon travel from the ambush site. There was no caravan. An hour later he caught up with it, they had just settled in for the night. They had made good time, which was good for them but bad for his plan. Irritably he turned Val to skirt around the encampment, then caught sight of their banner in waning light; a winged pig flying over a handful of coins. His dejection turned to elation. It was his old mentor Fabio. Leave it to Fabio to push for a 6-day run.

He slowed Val to a walk and turned towards the camp. He greeted the guard who stepped forward. "Hail Rath, how have you been?"

Rath's face split into a grin. "Ah, Kian! Pleasure to see you again. I've been good. Having work is always good, eh? How about you? What brings you down the road alone?"

"Bad news I'm afraid. I was ambushed up ahead of you. Oh, don't worry, we got all the bandits. I just had a ride to Sulvi to report the loss to House Cathar, and now I'm riding back to Barzan so they know on that end as well. It's a royal mess."

"Sorry to hear that. That is a lot of long riding. You must be tired. You can hitch up here if you'd like."

"Thanks. It'll be good to see the old crew. Let me unsaddle and feed this guy."

Rath stepped up to help. He'd had been with Sturm when he bought Val. He ruffled Val's forelock affectionately, then whispered into the horse's ear – loud enough for Sturm to hear, "So you're still letting this big oaf ride you!"

Sturm poured grain into Val's feed bag while Rath grabbed one of the watering buckets and filled it from the barrel on the nearest wagon.

A wide girthed guard sauntered over. "Who do we have here? Oh, its Kian!"

"Evening Fazio. Good to see you again."

Fazio beamed as he wrapped Sturm in a bear hug. "It's been what, most of a year? I hear you have your own troop now."

"Yeah, we were doing pretty good, at least until the other night."

"What happened?"

The three of them walked over to the campfire and sat down while Sturm caught them up on the ambush omitting only the box.

Fazio shook his head in sympathy. "Poison blades? That's a bad business. And this far out? There are a couple of small bands that wander through here, but they are backward and poorly equipped. I doubt they'd know what to do with poison if they had it, so not them. Who could it be?"

Sturm shrugged. "I don't know. When I talked with House Cathar in Sulvi they had no idea. Maybe their trademaster in Barzan will know."

"Yeah, maybe. You'd think news of any new bandit bands would reach a trademaster's ears quickly, but that one is such an idiot. Have you had to work with him? Oh, what am I saying, of course you have! So, you know what I mean."

Sturm grinned and nodded.

One of the drivers walked over awkwardly juggling three bowls of food. He grinned at the group around the fire. "Geesh, these are hot, but you gotta love that new cook stove. Here's last night's stew, already steamy. Hey, we have a visitor.... Oh, Kian, it's you! Here, take this bowl and I'll get another." The driver handed each of them a bowl.

Now it was Sturm's turn to juggle, shifting the hot bowl from hand to hand. He belatedly hollered to the receding back of the driver, "Thanks Karl!"

Sturm set the bowl down and stirred it to cool it down. He watched the steam and enjoyed the accompanying aroma. He decided Fazio must have gotten a new cook with that new stove. The cook he remembered never made a stew this good.

Several guards and drivers joined them, each with their bowls. Most knew him and greeted him. A loaf of bread appeared and was passed around. Sturm tore off a chunk for dipping into the broth.

Sturm savored each spoonful; it tasted as good as it smelled. Everyone else seemed to agree as they dug in, with occasional grunts of appreciation.

Fazio finished first. "Oh, that hit the spot! And a long hard day of traveling can make a pretty big spot to fill!" He patted his belly and let out a loud appreciative belch. "Ah, there we go. Ha! No one tell Getti how good her food is, she'll want me to pay her more."

One of the men snorted with laughter. "Ha, you married her so you wouldn't have to pay her." He started to say more but was interrupted by the cook walking up to the fire with a jug in her hand.

She was pretty, with her long dark hair tied back. If the saying 'never trust a skinny cook' was true you'd have her cook your every meal, there was nothing petite about her. She gestured at the man. "Will you think it as funny when you're cleaning the dishes? Ha, why don't you go and find out!"

The man good naturedly grumbled as he got up and gathered the bowls.

She added as he walked off, "And the longer you take, the longer it be till you get to the jug." Then she turned to the rest. "Anyone for music and drink?"

Drovers and guards seldom passed up either. A couple of the men scrambled to get their instruments. Fazio liberated the jug from her, took a swig then handed it to Sturm.

As her gaze followed the jug, she realized there was an unfamiliar face. "Ach, a visitor! No one told me. Good evening sir."

As Sturm swallowed a mouthful of harsh liquor, Fazio jumped into answer, "My beloved, this is Kian. Kian this is my little Getti."

"The name is Bridgette. How he gets Getti out of that I don't know. I think he does it just to piss me off." She glared at Fazio, who made puppy eyes back at her. After a moment she chuckled. "But how can I stay mad at him? Are you the same Kian he talks about so much? Are you coming back to work for him? He'd love that!"

"Hush, me darlin'. He's a caravan captain now. He's beyond a gold a month from me anymore." Fazio turned to Sturm, "Though, if you ever need to, you're welcome here."

Sturm cuffed him on the shoulder. The offer meant a lot to Sturm, but he couldn't find the words to say it so settled for a simple "Thanks". He hid his awkwardness by turning to Bridgette. He politely did a small bow. "Pleased to meet you."

Further talk was drowned out as one of the men returned with a concertina and started up a lively toon. Another brought a small drum and joined in with a background rhythm. A third pulled out a couple of spoons, clapping them together, adding to the beat. The toon was a popular ditty about a wandering rover. Several knew the words well enough to bellow them out, their enthusiasm making up for lack of hitting the notes.

Sturm's arm was nudged, reminding him to pass the jug. Bridgette motioned for him to join in the singing as she settled in next to Fazio in front of the fire. He watched them a few moments. They were having fun joining the bellowing, trying to outdo the other. All sense of their words was lost through their laughter.

Sturm was happy for Fazio. He was also envious. The man didn't have just a wife, but a partner to share his life.

Sturm thought about the women he'd met. There weren't many, he'd been focused on getting his guard company going as well as his estate. For a moment, Hemanji crossed his mind. She was certainly attractive. Then he laughed at himself, remembering the details of their meeting. She seemed interested, but it was in what he could do for her. He was only a commodity for her. That's not the relationship he saw in front of him with Fazio and Bridgette.

The jug came back around to Sturm. He took a deep swig and passed it on. His thoughts turned to the families of his men, waiting for husbands who would never return. How would he tell those families what had happened? He hadn't set foot inside Vellar's walls since his mother was murdered. He just couldn't bring himself to do it. Now he had to go, but facing the families...

The jug came around a third time. Sturm took the jug, but then shook his head and passed it. He really wasn't part of this party. Another round or two and he'd be befuddled, but he still had a long ride ahead of him.

Sturm stepped over to Fazio and bent down to speak into Fazio's ear. "Thanks for the hospitality, but I need to push on. If I sit here any longer, I'll fall asleep for the night. The sooner I get to Barzan the better."

Fazio looked up at Sturm, "You sure?"

With a small shrug followed by a nod, "Sorry to say it, but I am. I'll see you next time Fazio."

"Next time Kian. You always have a place at my fire."

Bridgette reached over and squeezed Sturm's hand. "Good to finally meet you. Fare thee well."

He bowed to Bridgette, patted Fazio on the shoulder, then waved goodbye to any who looked up as he walked to the horses.

Chapter 7: West of Sulvi 25th YOC, 10th Day of New Spring, 11 PM

As he approached the ambush site, Sturm decided it was a good place to give Val a rest break. He dismounted and led Val towards the wagons as a cool down walk. His scrutinized the wagons, wary of predators.

Looters had found the caravan. Wagon doors were broken open. Goods were strewn around the wagons where they had been tossed out the doors. Sturm dropped Val's reins, loosened his sword, and made sure of his dagger as he circled around the wagons to where he'd laid out his men. What he found was a grisly sight.

Scavenger animals had been at work, the bandit bodies were already picked clean of meat though they had ignored the poisoned corpses of Sturm's men. However human scavengers had so such qualms and had liberally taken equipment from all the corpses.

Quiet noises from the wagons caught Sturm's attention. He doubted the wagon horses had stayed close. Was it people? Was it merely a raccoon digging around in the foodstuffs?

There was a horrific scream and a figure in rags jumped at Sturm from the top of the nearest wagon. Sturm pulled his dagger as he sidestepped. He grabbed the man's shirtfront and rotated while directing the body past him. Somewhere in the midst of the move Sturm's dagger found the man's gut. The man landed behind Sturm writhing from his wound.

In his peripheral vision, Sturm saw Val rear and a hoof lashed out at a man lunging for his reins. There was a sickening crunch of bone as the looter's body slammed backwards into a wagon. That one didn't look as if he'd be getting up again. Several more looters came from around the wagons.

Sturm drew his sword and twirled it menacingly, causing them to hesitate, as he assessed what he faced. They were a sorry lot. Five wore ill fitted chainmail, looted from his men. Some had been lucky enough to loot boots that fit, but the others had their feet bound in cloth. The only worthwhile weapons they had were taken from his men or the bandits. They all looked desperate for a meal. On second thought, desperate seemed to sum it up for them.

Before they could regroup, Sturm addressed them. "Do I have to kill all of you?"

One in looted armor took a half step forward. "Ye do if ye to stop us from taking what's here. I fancy yer kit too. And that horse could hook up to a wagon 'n let us take a lot more in a trip."

"You saw how well my horse would cooperate with that."

The man shrugged in response.

An idea came to Sturm. It would mean a delay but the stop at Fazio's camp meant no rider would be sent to Barzan and bought Sturm more than enough time for his plan. "Tell you what, I'll leave you to your loot, but you'll have to do me a favor in return."

The man looked Sturm over, sized him up. He glanced at the two fallen men, then back to Sturm. Warily he replied, "'That would be what?"

Sturm indicated his fallen drivers and men, "You've already taken anything of worth from these bodies. Now give them a proper burial. You can use the shovels that are with each wagon. It doesn't have to be fancy, just a trench long enough to lay them side by side. A marker stone at each corner of the trench so I can come back and find it later."

"What be they to you? E'en wolves won't touch 'em!"

"They were my men, and this was my caravan." Sturm decided to help them make up their minds. He suddenly mounted Val. Strum knew that a warrior on a warhorse was intimidating. He hoped it would keep them from doing something stupid.

The looters stepped back and brandished their weapons. In response, Sturm swung his sword back and forth. Val snorted and stomped. The looters kept their distance.

After several heartbeats, the leader broke the standoff. He turned to his fellows. A muffled discussion followed. There were mixed responses. A few shrugged, one shook his head and raised his weapon defiantly.

The leader abruptly decided for them. He went to the nearest wagon and returned with a shovel. They all watched as he went to one end of where the bodies lay and then took a couple steps down from the feet. He shoved the shovel tip into the ground, looked up at Sturm, "Here?"

Sturm nodded. Others, muttering, slowly followed the man's lead and pulled shovels from the wagons. The defiant one took a few moments of glaring, but eventually joined the rest.

The wounded man still writhed on the ground, and occasionally pleaded for help, but was ignored by the diggers.

Sturm was appalled, he couldn't imagine them just leaving the man. Sturm rummaged through his healer kit. He pulled out some strips of cloth and a jar of salve. He got the attention of the smallest of the men, a boy really. He motioned to the wounded man. "You guys don't care about him?"

The boy glared up at Sturm. "'Course we do, but ye gutted him. What can we do? Gut wounds be death wounds."

Sturm held the jar up so the boy could see it. "You know what wound salve is?

The boy shook his head. "Ne'r heard of it."

Strum looked at him a moment and decided the boy also had never heard of a bath. Sturm realized he would have to explain not only wound tending, but hygiene as well. "You want him to recover?"

The boy sullenly nodded.

"Then do as I tell you. Go to a water barrel, get a bowl of water and wash your hands off. Dump the water on the ground. Then bring fresh water to him. Rinse out his wound and wash off around it. I wish we had something to really clean it, but water will have to do."

The boy looked at Sturm like he thought Sturm was addled.

Sturm pressed the boy, "There are certain steps you must do for the magic to work. I'm not kidding. Now do it and I'll tell you what's next."

The boy sullenly complied. When he was finished cleaning the wound, Sturm walked him through applying salve and covering it with bandages.

A few minutes after the wound was wrapped, the man stopped moaning and seemed less distressed. The men stole glances from their digging, switching from the wounded man to Sturm then back to the man. They muttered between themselves, but they were more energetic with their digging.

In an hour the trench was dug. Another quarter hour the bodies were arranged in the bottom.

Sturm said what prayers he could remember as the bodies were covered.

The diggers gathered around the wounded man. He had sat up and looked much better but was still too weak to get up. Their leader stepped towards Sturm. "We good?"

It was more than Sturm could have done on his own. He hoped his men would rest in peace. He replied, "Yes. Thank you." On impulse, Sturm reached into his bags and pulled out his food wallet. He tossed it to the man. "Share it around." Sturm wheeled Val and rode west.

Chapter 8: Terter Estate, 25th YOC, 11th Day of New Spring, Noon

Val's hooves clumping on the wooden bridge marked their entry to the Vellar province. It was also the edge of the Terter estate. Another mile down a lane turned off from the caravan road. A stone marker incised with a bull's head indicated the lane led to the Terter manor house.

Sturm turned Val down the lane. A few minutes latter they came to the hamlet, overlooked by the manor house. The first cottages they passed were in ruins from neglect, a reminder of how the estate had disintegrated over the years there had been no lord Terter.   Closer to the manor house was a cluster of tidy cottages with new sod roofs, a testament to how the estate was turning around.

A pregnant woman, near to full term, stepped out of a cottage carrying a laundry basket. She spotted Sturm. She set her basket down and waved energetically as she walked towards him.

Sturm was weary, in no mood to talk to anyone, but he signaled Val to stop. He summoned a smile and waved back.

"Lord Kian. Welcome home!" She awkwardly started to bow.

Sturm interrupted her. "Audrie. No. Stop that." Not only was Sturm concerned that she might hurt herself, but he was also embarrassed by people treating him like nobility. At school, he had been just another student, lost amongst scores of noble brats. On the caravan trail, he was just another sword, nothing special.

"Yes, milord. I hope your trip turned out well."

"Not so well." Sturm didn't burden her with details of the five men he had lost, since none of them lived in the hamlet. He instead kept to a generality. "I still have a few things to take care of. I'll be leaving again in the morning. How are things with you?"

"Couldn't be better! I cannot thank you enough for all the help you and the gnomes have given us. Not a drop through the roof with the storm last tenday. We also have the best news. My brother Boiko would like to join us here. I was waiting on your return to ask your permission. The next place over is still empty. We wouldn't have to impose on the gnomes, he and my husband could fix it up. Would it be alright?"

"Of course it's alright. The unoccupied houses are available to any who care to rebuild them. New build houses are also welcome. I just ask that they're not built in the way of fields I'm planning."

She bobbed her head. "Thank you milord. Thank you! I can't wait to tell my husband! If I may?" After a nod from Sturm, she hurried back into the house.

Audrie's cheerfulness and enthusiasm brightened Sturm's mood. Yes, he had lost five men and he still was getting over that, but his hamlet drawing in new tenants was good news.

Sturm urged Val forward, to the horse barn. Its grey weathered timbers had been painted green since he'd left a few days ago. It was a bit of the gnome 'magic' that was spreading across the estate. Elsewhere, the gnomes had returned a swath of wild forest back to an orchard and a vine choked meadow had become a vineyard. A gnome steading had sprung up with each.

Sturm dismounted and led Val to his stall. Sturm was dead tired, and starving, but he groomed Val and left him with grain and water before heading up to the manor house.

Sturm walked down the main hall and dumped his saddle bags on the center table. He undid his sword belt and laid it on top the bags. Finally, with a sigh, he dropped onto the bench. He leaned forward, elbows on the table and buried his face in his hands. He took a moment rub his face, around his eyes, then stared at the far wall.

There were a couple of 'yip yaps' from the kitchen followed by a white ball of fur charging out. The puppy ran to Sturm's bench and jumped up on it to lick Sturm's face, nearly toppling Sturm. The puppy was only six months old but was already bigger than most dogs. The 'Big Shaggy' mountain dogs were a giant breed which had recently come into vogue around Vellar as guard dogs.

A grin spread across Sturm's face. "Mira! You silly thing. Did you miss me?" Sturm gave the pup a big hug then rubbed under the pup's floppy ears.

The pup moaned with happiness and leaned into the attention, nearly falling off the bench – turning Sturm's smile into a laugh.

"I do believe he did!" Gnumph sat down across from Sturm and continued, "Miss you I mean. You look tired, and worse. Deep thoughts? Is everything alright? Where are the lads? Can I get you some food?"

Sturm's smile disappeared, replaced with a grim set to his jaw. "They're gone. We were ambushed, and they're gone." Sturm recounted the ambush.

During the narrative Gwiz joined them, quietly sitting down next to Gnumph. The gnomes listened, interrupting only to encourage him on through the most difficult parts. Sturm's words trailed off, ending with his report to Hermanji.

Gnumph got up. "After that I need a drink." He headed towards the kitchen.

Gwiz called after him. "Good idea. I think we all can use a pint." Gwiz turned back to Sturm. "Alright. You had a bad day. You've also had a couple days on the road to figure things out. So, now what?"

"I'm going to find who caused this and kill them."

"It seems I've heard that from you before. How many trails of vengeance can you follow at one time?"

Sturm glared at Gwiz. "As many as I need to. There is more to this than just childish hot headedness. I haven't forgotten about avenging my mother, but I need men to do it. So, I have to start over with recruiting them. Yet how can I do that if I don't avenge the men I lost? Who will follow me?"

Seeing the anguish in Sturm's eyes, Gwiz reached across the table and patted Sturm on the arm. "Alright son, alright. Yes, you have to start over, but you'll get there. What's your plan?"

"I'm going back to Barzan to talk with the Cathar trademaster there. He hid the box in the wagon. The bandits knew which wagon to go to. He has to be involved."

"Is that talk going to get you in trouble with House Cathar?"

"No, in fact Lady Cathar is sending me. She also has a reputation to uphold."

"Fair enough. What comes after that?"

"That depends on what trademaster Jurik says. I doubt he arranged the ambush; I just can't give him that much credit. So, who did? Most any scenario I can think of, I'll need a fancy little box with a glowing rock in it to flush out who did this. Think you could help with that?"

"I can do the stone. Gnumph would be better with the box. What color is the stone?"

"Turquoise."

"A turquoise glow stone is a bit tricky, but I've made colored lights for parties before."

Gnumph returned with three tankards. He set one in front of Sturm and handed another to Gwiz, then sat down at the table. "A box you say?"

"Yes. Do you have some paper?"

Gnumph reached into a pocket and produced a small roll of parchment. From another pocket he pulled out a stylus and an ink pot. He passed them over to Sturm.

Sturm sketched the box as he described it. He handed Gnumph the sketch and asked, "Can you make one like it?"

"Sure."

Sturm switched to his next concern. "Another thing then. I need some back up. I have no idea who or how many I'll be facing. Could the two of you come with me?"

Gnumph shook his head. "Not unless you can wait a few days. While you were gone things happened here as well. A ram strayed from the north steading. They followed its tracks to the scene of a scuffle. Then they followed drag marks until they came to where it lay webbed and paralyzed. They managed to recover it, and I think it will be alright, but a spider big enough to do that is a threat to the gnomes and needs to be dealt with." Gnumph ended by looking expectantly at Sturm.

Sturm took his hint. "Meaning, by me."

"Yep! It's your responsibility as lord of the manor. Also, you're the big bad warrior here. We can help you and I'm sure some of the gnomes of the steading would come as well."

"I can't wait that long."

"In that case, one of use will have to stay behind to protect the gnome steading and make sure they don't go after it, maybe getting some good gnomes killed. I think Gwiz would be best to go with you. Either of us can sneak around, but he has a few parlor tricks that may come in handy."

Gwiz snorted then glared at Gnumph. "Parlor tricks indeed!"

Gnumph grinned back.

The grin became infectious leaving Gwiz grinning as well. "All right, all right. I agree. Only one of us should go, and me it should be. In truth, my tricks can be handy. So when and where?"

Gnump interjected, "I can have the box done maybe by noon."

Sturm replied, "I need to leave before that. I'm planning on a grabbing a few hours sleep and then traveling tonight."

"I can't rush the drying time on the glue and then the lacquer."

Sturm thought a moment. "I don't need to have the bow with me to set things in motion. Gwiz, would you be able to bring the box and meet me by tomorrow evening?"

Gwiz responded, "I'd be using my parlor tricks, but I think I can. Where do we meet?"

Sturm sighed with relief. "Great! We'll meet outside of Barzan's east gate. There is a hill just north of there with a big old oak tree. You know the place?"

"It's been a few years since I've been there, but I remember father oak."

Gnumph added, "And when you get back, we'll take care of the spider."

Sturm nodded impatiently. "Yes. But I won't be back immediately. I'll need to go to Sulvi, meet with Lady Cathar and tie up loose ends."

Gnumph winked. "I bet."

Sturm blushed and protested, "No, not like that. I meant..." He stopped, realizing Gnump was messing with him.

Gwiz decided to spare Sturm further embarrassment. "Enough! Time's wasting. Get started on that box. I'll take care of the stone and make my travel preparations. Sturm; eat, drink, sleep. Also, that puppy of yours needs some attention from you. He sleeps on your bed, even with you gone."

Chapter 9: Barzan, 25th YOC, 12th Day of New Spring, 7 AM

Bili put his shoulder to the gate to close it after the last wagon of the morning caravan. As it swung closed, Sturm popped through the gap startling Bili. "By the gods, Sir Kian! I almost slammed the gate on you. Are ye alright?"

"I'm fine Bili." Sturm was relieved by the genuine concern in Bili's voice. It told Sturm that Bili wasn't involved with the ambush. "Is your boss around."

"Yes sir. He's in his office like always."

"He let you do all the work again?"

"Not a problem. The horses don't like him much. I do the animals; he oversees the loading. I'm fine with that." It crossed Bili's mind that Sir Kian should still be on the road with his caravan. "I don't mean to be in your business, but shouldn't you still be on the road to Sulvi? Did you forget something? Is there something I need to round up for you?"

Sturm cuffed Bili on the shoulder. "No Bili, I'm good. The caravan ran into trouble, and I need to tell Jurik. You go ahead with your duties. I don't envy you cleaning up the courtyard after all those horses. I'll see you later."

Sturm carefully picked his path across the yard, avoiding steamy horse pies. He stopped to peer through the open door to the main office. Jurik sat at his desk facing away from the door, engrossed in a ledger. Sturm rapped on the door frame.

"Bili, don't disturb me..." Jurik looked around and saw Sturm. Jurik's face cycled through several expressions before he settled on a forced smile. "Sir Kian. How nice to see you. Uhm... Here for work? I didn't know you were back in town. The caravan just left, and we already have guards for it, and..."

Sturm shook his head, like a parent to an errant child. "Jurik. Come on, we both know better than that."

Jurik's composure broke. Jurik was taller than Sturm and bulkier, but it was bulk from ale and he was no fighter. Fear showed in his face, in his voice. "No, please no. I didn't know what he was going to do. I didn't even realize I had told him until after the words were out of my mouth."

"Him, who?"

"Just Rafe, that's all."

"The Dukar trademaster?"

"Aye, we were just talking shop over a few pints. We do that all the time. There's never any harm to it."

"How much did he pay you?"

"It wasn't like that. Yes, he gave me 20 ounces of gold. I was going to refuse, but what was the point? The words were already out of my mouth and that's several years pay! How do you refuse that? And... And... I thought it was harmless; he simply wanted to know when the caravan would be at Sulvi. I swear, I never thought he'd ambush you."

Sturm locked eyes with Jurik. "I didn't say we were ambushed. Word hasn't made it back to Barzan, so how did you know that?"

Jurik stared down at the floor. He broke out in a sweat. Finally, he managed to stammer out, "Rafe told me. I... I just found out last night, long after the deed. Please don't kill me."

Strum was pleased with how easily Jurik had caved but he wasn't pleased with the news. Things could be very messy if the other major Sulvi trade house was involved. "I will spare you if you to do me an errand."

Jurik nodded. "Anything!"

"Deliver a message to Rafe. Tell him it would have been so much easier if he had just talked to me in the first place. I'm sure we could have come to an arrangement. Now... Some of my men got hurt, and I'm not happy. So, it just got expensive. He can have the box for 10 times of what he gave you. I prefer it in platinum, it's easier to carry. You know the orchard a couple miles east of town and north of the caravan route?"

"The old Lancour place? Yeah, we use to ship his apples."

"Tell Rafe, that's where we'll meet at noon. If I see a lot of people, I'll figure it's a trap and I'll let you know where I'm switching the meet to and how much more it's going to cost. Or maybe I'll just take the box somewhere else." Sturm abruptly left the office and walked out of the compound into the city.

Chapter 10: Barzan East Gate, 25th YOC, 12th Day of New Spring, 5 PM

Sturm rode Val out the Barzan east gate at a walk. He nodded to the guards and exchanged a few pleasantries. He continued down the road until he was beyond their sight. He had always been genial with the guards, but that wouldn't keep them from reporting on him for coin.

He watched a few moments to see if anyone followed then he turned north towards his rendezvous. After a short ride he pulled up at the top of a hill, next to a large oak tree.

Gwiz appeared in front of him. "About time you showed up."

"You said evening; its barely evening. In any case, what do you have to complain about? It's been a beautiful day, and you got to spend it relaxing in the trees."

"Oh, sure I did. I just ran my little legs off to get here."

"You have the box?"

"No, let me go back and get it." Gwiz laughed at Sturm's glare. "Joking!" He pulled a small box from his pouch and handed it to Sturm.

Sturm examined it. He could swear it was the original. "Good job. What did you use for the stone?"

"Just a round rock from outside the door. I polished it up some. So, now what?"

"I told them to meet me tomorrow at noon and bring 200 ounces worth of gold in platinum. What's the going exchange rate these days?"

"I think about five gold to one platinum, but are you crazy? Asking for that much may make them decide to just kill you."

"I expect them to try it no matter what, but I have to make this credible. I'm not just a thug, I'm a caravan captain. I'd have a high buy out price."

"So, they show up with a small army, looking to kill you. Then what are you going to do?"

Sturm laughed and patted Gwiz on the shoulder. "My little Godfather, that is why I'm bringing you along."

"Oh... alright. So, have you any idea who'll be showing up?"

"Yes. The Dukar trademaster. And yes, I made sure. I followed Jurik to a tavern, saw them meet. After a pint and some intense conversation, they went their ways. I'm really hoping there is a third party here and the Dukar Cartel isn't behind it."

Gwiz dryly noted, "Watch what you wish for. If not Dukar, then you can bet its somebody even worse. So, where is the meet?"

"It's at an apple orchard about two miles east of here. It hasn't been well tended in years, so it'll provide plenty of cover for us to hide in. Then it's either plan A or plan B."

"What's plan A?"

"Talk to them, find out if there is anyone else part of this, then kill them."

"And plan B?"

"Quietly run away."

Chapter 11: Apple Orchard NE of Barzan: 25th YOC, 13th Day of New Spring, 10 AM

Sturm and Gwiz arrived two hours prior to the meeting time and walked the ground finalizing details.

Sturm found a bush big enough to hide him until he decided to reveal himself. He made sure he had a couple lines of retreat with plenty of trees and bushes to duck behind and to block horsemen from riding him down. If faced with too many men, plan 'B' was still an option even if they didn't come from the road.

Gwiz had traded in his orange elder's cap and blue shirt for dark green and brown instead. He wandered back and forth to either side of Sturm's bush, considering the line of sight from the road. He needed to see what he cast spells at. He found a bump of ground that only a gnome could hide behind, an unlikely spot to attract human attention. He returned to Sturm at the bush.

They settled in and waited listening to the birds and watching the antics a squirrel. A half hour prior to the meeting time, the orchard suddenly quieted.

Gwiz heard the jingle of a horse harness first. He nudged Sturm and whispered, "They're a bit early."

Sturm nodded and replied just as softly, "I told you so. And you complained about being here so early."

"I still wish I had that second cup of tea."

"Next time, now hush!"

Two men rode into the orchard and reined in their mounts. Each wore a black bordered white tabard over their platemail armor, the uniform of their regiment. Shields hung from their saddle horns. The black heraldry on their white shields matched the shield shaped patch on the right chest of their tabards; two horizontal slashes supported by three narrow vertical slashes, with a diagonal separating them.

Sturm leaned close and murmured into Gwiz's ear. "Regulars. Look at the patch, the 23rd. I've heard of them somewhere... Oh yeah, they're one of the wizard's units, 'Heroes of the Revolution'. They aren't stationed at Barzan, where did they come from?"

Gwiz murmured back. "No idea. I wonder how many are showing up?"

One of the troopers turned his horse halfway around and waved to someone behind him. He turned his horse back alongside the other.

A woman joined the troopers. She wore a travel robe patterned in red, orange, and yellow. Her long braided hair was dyed in streaks to match her robe. She sat very straight in the saddle, with a confidence marking her authority. Rafe, in his normal working man's smock, followed. After him came two more troopers. The six dismounted. The troopers left their shields on their mounts. One of the troopers took charge of the horses.

Sturm softly cussed.

"What is it?"

"It's a woman."

"Yes, but more importantly, she has the look of a Firewizard. She looks like a campfire. Now look past the woman, do you see any other problems there?"

"I hate killing women."

"What about the guys in plate armor?"

"Well, yeah, they could be a problem if I have to tackle them all together. Wish I had a mace, just bash them a few times on the head and they'd be knocked out. With my sword, I'll have to get fancy and try to slide it between the armor pieces. Anything you can do to cause them trouble?"

"Considering they're pets of a sorceress, I'd bet their armor has protections against magic. I doubt I can do much to them directly, but I have a few ideas to break up their party." Gwiz pointed to the workman. "What about him?"

"That's Rafe. I heard he was once a caravan guard, but that was a while ago. I wouldn't expect any fancy sword play from him."

"You think we can do this?"

Sturm nodded. "You got the troopers?"

"Yeah, at least for a 30 count."

"That will do. I got the sorceress and Rafe then. I'll give you a minute to get to your spot."

"Keep your wits about you." Gwiz patted Sturm on the shoulder, turned, and faded into the brush.

Sturm counted off 60 seconds as the sorceress stepped into the orchard.

She motioned for Rafe to join her, and for the three troopers to fan out. Rafe deferentially moved to half a pace behind her. He nervously scanned the orchard. He started to say something to the sorceress, but she silenced him with an imperious wave of her hand. It wasn't magic, rather the force of authority and the power behind her guild that caused him to squelch whatever he had started to say.

Sturm reached his 60 count. He stepped forward into view and nodded politely to the sorceress. "I believe you're looking for me?"

The sorceress was startled. She irritably tossed a braid over her shoulder then replied, "You are, if you have what we came for."

Sturm wanted to be in reach of the sorceress should she cast a spell at him. He made a show of taking off the backpack and then gestured with it, as he stepped forward. He placed it on the ground in front of him. "I have a fancy box. Do you have my coin?"

She nodded in reply then waved Rafe forward.

Rafe warily stepped forward to toss a bag next to the backpack, it clinked with coin as it landed. He darted to pick up the backpack then quickly retreated to the sorceress. His eyes never left Sturm until he was safely back next to her.

Rafe opened the backpack, pulled out the box. He looked at it as he turned it side to side. He nodded, satisfied, and handed it to the sorceress.

She noted the seal was intact. She held the box up in one hand and waved her other hand over it with a short incantation. Her divination spell revealed nothing inimical, though she sensed magic within the box. She broke the seal and opened the lid halfway to peak in. The stone inside glowed.

As she inspected the stone, Sturm asked, "Who do I have the pleasure of doing business with?"

Absorbed with her find, she offhandedly responded, "Let it be enough that you are dealing with the Fireguild." There was a haughtiness her words.

Sturm continued, "Just out of curiosity, what is so important about that box anyway? Why is it worth so much?"

"You don't know, do you?" She closed the box, handed it back to Rafe, then turned back towards Sturm. "Still, you ask too many questions."

Sturm, like anyone who has worked magic, could feel when magic power was gathered. He felt it now, more power than his mom or Gwiz had ever summoned. He lunged across the few steps between them and slammed his fist into her throat.

The punch was so sudden she had no chance to react. She was thrown from her feet and landed unceremoniously on her ass. Her voice box ruined; the words of the incantation turned to a gurgle.

Rafe reacted, juggling the precious box to his offhand while pulling his sword. His swing was rushed, awkward, but on target for Sturm.

Sturm stepped inside Rafe's swing, pulling out his dagger. He stabbed Rafe just below the ribcage. Sturm twisted the dagger as he withdrew it, then he shoved off Rafe to bounce back two steps.

Rafe crumpled to the ground.

Sturm unsheathed his sword to confront the troopers.

The nearest two had fallen over each other and were on the ground. They cursed as they untangled themselves and tried to stand up. The weight of their armor and the motion limits of the joints hampered their efforts. The third trooper pulled off his helm and slapped at his face, beset by insects. Behind them, the one holding the horses was being dragged back and forth as the horses reared in a frenzy.

Sturm returned his attention to the nearest two. He walked up to the nearest and kicked him, knocking him back down. The other trooper desperately managed to struggle to his feet. His sword slid out of its sheath and arched towards Sturm, but the trooper was off balance and the swing had little force behind it.

Sturm slap blocked the trooper's blade. The trooper attempted to recover, swinging wildly in Sturm's direction. Sturm stepped into the swing and met sword on sword, blocking the trooper's arm upward and across the man's face. Sturm brought his dagger up and slammed it into the exposed armpit of the trooper. Chainmail protected the exposed armpit, but it was only steel and the mithril of the dagger was stronger. Chain links burst apart at their crimp seam and the dagger slid in, grating against bone. Sturm rotated the dagger, slicing artery and nerves, then shoved the trooper.

The trooper staggered back, his sword dropping from his useless hand. Blood streamed down his side. He staggered, then collapsed to the ground.

Sturm shifted to the second trooper. The trooper had grabbed a branch and was pulling himself to his feet. Sturm's sword sliced low across the unprotected back of the trooper's knee. The trooper's leg went out from under him. He fell to the ground, blood gushing from the deep cut, his leg nearly severed. Sturm left him struggling as Sturm moved to the trooper with the horses.

The trooper faced away from Sturm, digging in his heals as he tried to keep the horses from bolting. Sturm again went for the back of the knee. The trooper fell bleeding, dropping the horses' reins, shock on his face. The horses bolted and were gone.

Sturm stepped over to the fourth trooper. The trooper was completely preoccupied slapping at the insects and only noticed Sturm as Sturm's sword swung down on his neck, a killing blow.

Sturm pivoted, surveying the bodies. The first three troopers weren't dead yet, but mortally wounded and soon to pass. The trademaster was dead. The sorceress had gotten to her knees, one hand at her throat and the other motioning towards him desperately trying to cast at him. Her magic formed around her and then dissipated as she gasped and gaged, and spit up blood. Sturm grimly walked over to her and finished her.

Gwiz appeared next to Sturm. "Good job!"

Sturm growled in response.

"What's the matter? Plan 'A' worked out after all."

Sturm wiped his sword off on the sorceress' robe. "As I said, I hate killing women. What did you do to those guys?"

"Just some parlor tricks. I sent some angry wasps towards the horses. Some of the wasps must have gone astray along the way and got inside the helm of that trooper. As for the other two, I managed to cause a rock to slide out from underfoot of one. He fell in the way of the other."

Chuckling, Sturm replied, "Very useful parlor tricks. My thanks."

"No problem. Need some help cleaning up?"

Sturm looked down at the blood splattered across his armor. He had a flash of irritation at his armor. He'd never been able to cast a spell while in armor, including the cleanup spell. He considered taking the armor off to cast it, then realized he was just being pig-headed. They had better things to do. "Yeah, I do. Just like when I was a kid, you're always making sure I'm presentable."

Gwiz rolled his eyes then cast the cantrip. The blood splatter fell off Sturm's armor.

"Thanks. Now let's look over what we have here."

Sturm knelt next to the sorceress as Gwiz went to the trademaster.

Sturm started at the top and worked his way down. Earrings, a pendant suspended from a delicate gold chain, and two rings went into a pile. The last item was her belt. The belt buckle was copper and had flecks of red, yellow, and orange gemstones. A pouch hung from the belt. He opened the pouch and turned it upside down to dump out the contents, but nothing came out. He looked inside but only saw darkness. He tentatively reached in. His hand encountered a handle. He pulled it out, to see he was holding a hairbrush. He reached in again and this time came out with a small mirror. They were added to the pile. Sturm reached in again, this time grasping a large book. The scaled hide cover of the book momentarily caught on the lip of the bag. Sturm carefully worked it free. The scales caught the sunlight and shimmered like fire. He hooked his thumb around the cover to open the book but was interrupted by Gwiz.

"Oy, I wouldn't do that."

Sturm looked up, surprised. He had forgotten Gwiz. The gnome sat in front of him with the payoff bag, a wallet of papers, and a helm. Sturm queried, "Why not?"

"It might have a protection spell on it. You open it without the right password or counter spell and bad things could happen."

"You know what it has to be, don't you? It's got to be her spell book."

"I'm thinking the same, all the more reason for her to have it protected. Probably best to just take it back to the house and take our time with it."

Sturm hesitated. The book held a promise of magic lore far beyond the few battle magic spells he had learned from his mother's book. He decided to chance it, though he'd take care in the doing. "Can you detect such protections?"

"In all honesty, the ink and the pages themselves could be magicked to protect them from aging and weathering. Any detection I do on the book would alert off those as much as anything more inimical."

Sturm stood up with the book then walked over to the nearest trooper.

"Sturm, what are you doing?"

"It comes down to sooner or later we just open it." Sturm grabbed the trooper's tabard and worked it free from the corpse. He folded the tabard over several times then wrapped it over the book's cover. He carefully faced the book to open away from him and Gwiz. He braced himself and suddenly pulled it open. He stood there several moments cringing in expectation of an explosion that didn't happen.

Sturm heard a choking sound coming from Gwiz. Concerned, he turned to see Gwiz trying to suppress laughing.

Tears ran down from the corners of Gwiz's eyes. "Sorry Sturm." Chuckling between phrases he continued, "Do you know how ridiculous you look?" Gwiz finally gave in to full out laughter.

Sturm sighed. He turned the book around and peaked inside. His face lit up. Magic runes, the script of spells, proved it was her spell book.

He settled down flipping through the book. It was in four sections. The first section was short, basic spells centered on summoning a flame. He could probably cast them after a bit of practice.

Gwiz tried to peak over the top of the book to see the text. "Well? Are we right? Is it a spell book?"

"Aye, it is. Now just hold on." Sturm flipped to the second section. These spells were more complicated. He was less certain of casting them. He flipped through the last two sections. He wasn't able to follow them at all. He leaned back with a dejected sigh.

"What is it?"

"I can't make most of these out. They're useless to me."

"Here, let me look." Gwiz took the book. He flipped through the pages. "I see what you mean. While I might be able to puzzle out one in section three in a year or so, I simply have no clue where to start on the spells at the back. She must have been a master and it will take a master to teach you."

Gwiz handed the book back to Sturm. "I know it's a disappointment but look on the positive side, there are some useful spells in those first two sections. And look at all the rest we have here. How about this helmet? I think it will fit you." Gwiz picked a helm up from a small pile next to him.

Sturm looked at the well-crafted helm. He shook his head. "It's a full helm. I hate the things. They're heavy, you can't breathe, and you can't see. For that matter the armor is distinctive, a uniform. I can't take any of it. It'll be recognized and then maybe tied back to here."

Gwiz pointed to the pile of jewelry. "What about your treasure pile? I suggest we just bag it and take it home. I can sort out what's magic and what's not. Any non-magic items we can sell."

"Yes, but again we have to be careful. A distinctive piece could get us in trouble."

Gwiz grabbed the payoff bag and looked in. "They actually brought the platinum. It has a nice hefty feel like it's the full coin count we expected."

"That'll keep the estate going for a long time." Sturm pointed to a wallet of papers in Gwiz's pile. "What are those?"

"They were on the trademaster. Looks like records of some sort, but I can't read them." Gwiz handed the wallet to Sturm. "They make any sense to you?"

Sturm glanced through the pages. "Yeah, they're trade records showing the coming and going of goods. We won't make sense of them though. Many of the goods and the people involved are just identified with a symbol. Only House Dukar knows what the symbols mean."

"So, toss them. We'll bag up the jewelry, the coin, and your book."

"No. I'll return them to Dukar."

"You nuts? You just killed his trademaster, won't Dukar just kill you in return? And for all you know, Dukar is involved."

"That was my first worry when I found out Rafe was involved, but... It just doesn't feel right."

"Oh?"

"I've worked for Dukar, even met him personally. He was a driver once and worked his way up, seems pretty straight forward. Maybe I'm naive, but I can't see him ordering an ambush."

"Powerful people do things like that all the time."

"Yes they do, but this was the sorceress' show, not Dukar's. Her power. Her money. Rafe was her tool."

Gwiz gave Sturm a long look.

Sturm pressed his case, "What do you think will happen if someone doesn't explain it to Dukar? We'll have a trade war. And who else is there to do the explaining? You?"

"I don't like it, but I guess you're right. So, what are we doing now?"

"Take this bag, it holds more that it should. Everything will fit back in it. You go home. I have a quick bit of business in Barzan. Then I'll travel to Sulvi and do my business there, first House Dukar then House Cathar."

"Barzan? What's left to do there?"

"Take care of Jurik, one way or the other."

"You need more help?"

"No, I got it."

"What do you have in mind?"

"Not certain." Sturm shrugged then continued. "My first thought is to kill him but there's been enough killing today. I also already told him I wouldn't kill him, so I guess I'll just fire him."

They spent a few minutes packing the bag. Gwiz weighed its heft in his hand. It was a fraction of the weight he expected. He tied it to his belt. "I'm off then. Don't be too long or we'll worry!"

Sturm started to reply with a 'yes mother', but the gnome was already gone.

Chapter 12:   Sulvi West Gate, 25th YOC, 14th Day of New Spring, 11 AM

Sturm's first stop, the Dukar estate, was quick to get to from the west gate. He turned left at the first intersection, then traveled past five buildings to the fortified villa at the end of the road.

The villa's walls were unadorned, solid and functional, melding into the architecture of the nearby city's walls. The gate opened to a large plaza surrounded by stables, warehouses, barracks, and the main house.

Sturm rode in, dismounted, and tied his horse up at the hitching rail. He made sure the reins were loose enough for Val to reach the water trough.

Two guards sauntered over from the main office. "Good day. State your business."

Sturm nodded in greeting. "Good day to you as well. I am Sir Kian Terter, caravan guard captain. I have information for Lord Dukar that I believe he would prefer to hear in person. Please be so kind as to send word to him."

The guards were taken aback. Their job was to keep visitors from bothering their boss, not to go summon him. The senior guard responded, "I've heard of you. You escorted one of our caravans last month." He shouted over towards the warehouse. "Trademaster Jacko, get out here!"

After a few moments, the trademaster came out.

The guard pointed to Sturm. "Do you recognize this man?"

Jacko looked Sturm over.

Sturm removed his helm.

Jacko smiled and nodded. "Now I recognize you!" Bowing, he continued, "Sir Kian, a pleasure to see you again."

Sturm returned the bow. "And I remember you. Thank you for bringing my payment so promptly last month. It's always a pleasure doing business with you."

Jacko addressed the guards, "You need anything else?"

The senior guard responded, "No. Thank you trademaster. I just needed to know he was who he claimed to be." He then addressed the other guard. "Go inside to Lord Dukar and advise him of his visitor. Return with word of what his lordship requires us to do."

The young guard bobbed his head and sprinted inside.

The senior guard turned back to Sturm chuckling. "Kids, ha! But he'll be quick on his chore."

Sturm nodded and found a place to sit on a nearby half wall. He and the guard stared at each other until the main door opened. The 'kid' held it open for two men. The first was Lord Dukar, a tall, slim man in fine robes. His arms were disproportionly beefy from years of driving wagons. The second man was a heavily armored guardsman in dwarven made half plate armor.

Sturm stood up and bowed.

Lord Dukar stopped several feet Infront of Sturm. "It's a pleasure to see you again. What is your information?"

"Milord, I am here to advise you, warn you, and perhaps even apologize to you."

"Really? An interesting combination, please, tell me more."

Sturm pulled out the wallet of Rafe's trade records. He offered them to Lord Dukar. "Let me start with these."

The senior guard stepped up and took the papers from Sturm then walked them over to Lord Dukar. He bowed as he handed them to Lord Dukar.

"What have we here?" Dukar flipped through the papers. After a moment, he looked up at Sturm. "Where did you get these?"

Sturm replied, "That would get into what I'm sure you'd rather hear in private."

Lord Dukar glanced down at the trade records, then back up at Sturm. "Very well, follow me." Lord Dukar abruptly turned and walked back inside.

Sturm followed. He could hear the clanking of plate armor behind him.

Lord Dukar led them down the entry hallway to a study. He continued across the room to behind a desk. He motioned Sturm to a chair.

Sturm's gaze slid across the room past dark wood furnishings and a lush rug on the marble floor, to fixate on a large wall map showing the Dukar trade routes. The routes extended beyond what Sturm had guessed: a spider web going from lands far to the south and west beyond Vellar, north to several major cities of the country, and east across the Danu River all the way to the dwarven hold on the coast.

Lord Dukar tossed the papers on the desk and cleared his throat, getting Sturm's attention. "So tell me, where did you get these?"

"From your trademaster Rafe in Barzan, Milord."

"Does he know you have them?"

"He's dead, Milord."

Lord Dukar was caught by surprise. He started to say something then stopped. He looked down at the papers, his index finger tapped them as he was lost in thought. Coming to a decision, he turned to his guard. "Ario, would you bring me Diago?"

Ario was clearly not happy to leave his liege and didn't budge. "Diago? Milord are you sure..."

Lord Dukar cut him off, amused, "Yes, Ario. Please get Diago. If Sir Kian does anything to me while you're gone, you have my permission to track him down, but for now I need Diago."

Ario left the room using a side door concealed by wooden bookcases.

Lord Dukar looked back to Sturm. "Ario has been with me a long time. He has only my best wishes and those of my house in mind. His job is to not trust people, please take no offence. While we are waiting, perhaps you can tell me what happened to Rafe."

"Milord, my story starts with the ambush of a caravan I escorted."

"Ambush? I didn't know one of my caravans had been ambushed. What route were you on?"

"It wasn't one of yours. I was contracted with House Cathar."

"Oh?"

Sturm continued, "It was an ugly fight, they used poison blades."

"Poison weapons? Those are bad business! How many did you lose? Did any of the drivers die?"

"I lost my five men and all ten drivers. The drivers fought valiantly next to my men."

"I am sorry for your loss." Lord Dukar's tone and expression reinforced that the words were heart felt.

The side door opened and a wizened old man shuffled in. He bowed and waited.

Ario followed closely behind him. His gaze immediately went to Lord Dukar, satisfied his lord was unharmed, he moved to hover behind Lord Dukar.

Lord Dukar waved Diago over and handed him the wallet. "Diago, please look at this and tell me what you make of it."

Diago took the wallet of papers. He turned it over in his hands, examining it, then he opened it and flipped through the pages within.

"Does it look like Rage's ledger?"

"Well, it does and it doesn't. Some entries seem out of place. They're in addition to what he's reported. Or perhaps my old memory is playing tricks and I'm forgetting."

"You forgot nothing. I also noted a few... oddities." Lord Dukar motioned to Sturm. "Please, continue."

"I recovered an item the ambushers had taken from a wagon during the fight, and I turned it over to House Cathar. Then I returned to Barzan where the caravan originated."

Lord Dukar interjected, "That was Rafe's station."

Sturm nodded. "Yes, sir. I talked first with the Cathar trademaster and determined his involvement. Then I indicated I still had the item, and it was for sale. I gave him a time, a place, and a price."

"Smart, many would have simply killed him. You still haven't gotten to how Rafe fits into this."

"The Cathar trademaster went straight to Rafe. Rafe showed up at the meet, along with a sorceress of the Fireguild."

Lord Dukar sat back, gobsmacked. "I don't believe it!"

Diago interrupted, "I do."

Lord Dukar turned to Diago. "What makes you say that?"

"The ledger Milord. Not only are some of the sums off but look at the cargo listings here." Turning the page, he pointed to another line. "And here as well."

Looking, Lord Dukar nodded in acknowledgement. "Glyphs from the Fireguild contract we had. Why is that significant?"

"Milord, look at the dates. These are months after we discontinued the contract."

Lord Dukar took the ledger from Diago and flipped back and forth between the pages. "You're right. There are many such entries continuing to the present."

Diago replied, "Exactly. So, these glyphs we chose to represent these..." Looking over at Sturm, he carefully picked his words. "...special trade items. The only ones outside of this room who know what we assigned to them are our trademasters."

"And we have trademasters at both ends of a caravan route. Diago, we need to put together a list of where the goods Rafe smuggled came from and where he sent them. Then we need to see if the other trademasters have private ledgers."

Diago bowed low. "I will do so immediately Milord." He tucked the ledger under his arm and shuffled out the concealed door.

Lord Dukar sat back in his chair and stared a long moment at the map, lost in thought. Sturm waited patiently. Eventually Lord Dukar's focus came back to Sturm. "Back to what happened to Rafe."

Sturm replied, his tone apologetic. "I was forced to kill him during the fight, milord."

Lord Dukar stared at Sturm. Several emotions crossed his face before he replied. "I see, a fight. With him, a sorceress, and perhaps others?"

Sturm nodded.

Lord Dukar's gaze remained fixated on Sturm. "That must have been some fight."

Sturm resisted the urge to squirm. He returned Lord Dukar's stare.

Lord Dukar decided to not press for further explanation. "It appears it is I who owes you an apology."

Sturm inwardly sighed with relief.

Lord Dukar continued, "Rafe did not act upon my orders, and I do not condone what he did. Please convey to Lady Cathar my condolences for the loss of her drivers, wagons, stock, and any financial loss she incurred. Tell her I have no desire for a trade war, especially when it seems we have a common adversary. Please ensure she understands this. Have her communicate to me what compensation she feels due, and I will make it right."

Lord Dukar pushed back his chair and stood up.

Sturm followed suit, thinking he was dismissed.

Lord Dukar stepped over to a cabinet and opened it. He pulled out a decanter with an amber liquid in it. "I need a drink after that news. Do you have the time to join me? It's a liqueur from Venub."

"I'm sorry Milord. It's been a long, rough, couple of days and a drink would knock me over. With your permission, I'll leave and give Lady Cathar your message."

"Of course, Sir Kian. Perhaps the next time you are in town you would do me the honor of joining me for that drink? In the meantime, leave in peace, and fare thee well."

Sturm bowed and left.

Lord Dukar poured two drinks, then walked over to Ario. He handed Ario a glass. "So, what do you think?"

"About which?"

Lord Dukar sipped on his drink. "All of it."

"If true, we have a real mess on our hands."

"If true?"

"Maybe he faked the ledger."

"Trust me my friend, few could fake the ledger even if they knew what we had assigned to the glyphs. We'll be able to confirm soon enough with the trademasters at the other end of the transactions. No, I believe him."

With a grin Ario responded, "Actually so do I, but I still had to say it."

Returning the grin, Lord Dukar gently chastised, "Always suspicious."

"That's how we survived the last trade war."

"I know. So, what about Sir Kian?"

"He didn't go into a lot of details. He does things, he doesn't brag about it. I don't know who or what he had at his back when he faced the sorceress, but he had to be good to live through it. And it took guts. It also took guts to come here."

"I know. It's easy to like him, isn't it?"

"Yeah, that's another thing I don't trust."

Part 3: To Bridgeport

Chapter 13: Cathar Estate Sulvi, 25th YOC, 14th Day of New Spring, 3 PM

Sturm rode into the courtyard of the Cathar estate.

The gate guards stood to attention as he rode through. The groomsman ran up to him to take Val, assuring him the horse would be well taken care of.

Moments later, Tej hurried out to Sturm and bowed. "Milord. Would you be so kind as to follow me?"

Sturm had only moments to contemplate how differently he was being treated as he was ushered to the room where he had met Lady Cathar a few days before.

Hemanji awaited him, seductively posed on the settee. She was dressed similar to last time, but her color theme today was earth tones. Her silk sari was in a rich brown. The jewelry she sported was amber.

"Ah, my hero returns. I have been thinking of you." She flowed to her feet. A step, then another, her arms slid over his shoulders as she pressed herself against him in a full body embrace ending with a soft kiss on the lips. She stepped back, her hand lingered on his neck before it slowly slid down his chest before she pulled it away to motion towards a decanter and glasses on the table. "May I offer you something to drink?"

Sturm was dazed from the feel of her body, from her perfume. It took a long moment for him to nod.

She poured amber wine from the decanter. She handed him a glass, clicked hers with his in a toast, and took a sip from hers. Then she continued, "What word do you bring me?"

Sturm was still heady from her perfume. He wondered if it was laced with some magical potion. He struggled to gather his wits, then responded, "I spoke with your trademaster."

She was amused by Sturm's reaction. She seductively looked at Sturm, toying with her drink. "Did you have to be... unpleasant?"

Sturm found the contradiction between her actions and words chilling. He used it to stay focused. "Yes, but not like you mean. I didn't harm him."

She tilted her head, her hair slid down over her shoulder. "I hope you are not too soft hearted. What did you find out?"

Sturm ignored the urge to lean forward and kiss her. "He had loose lips, probably for a long while. I'd guess it started with little things and grew to bigger things. This time there was pay involved."

"Yet you didn't kill him?"

"I thought about it, but no, I sent him on his way. I left Bili in charge." Sturm saw that the name didn't register, so he explained, "Bili is the handler there. He's always been good with the horses and seems honest enough. He wasn't involved in this. You should consider leaving him in charge."

Her hand was back on Sturm's chest, undoing the top tie of his chainmail coat. "As you think best. I'll at least give him the opportunity. So, who paid off Jurik?"

"The local Dukar trademaster."

Her eyes widened; her seduction act came to an abrupt halt. "Dukar? Oh, no!"

"Don't worry. I've already talked with Dukar. He was not pleased with his trademaster making side deals with someone else. He sends his apologizes to you in return. He wants no war with Cathar and is willing to confer with you to ensure one doesn't start."

"You have done well. We may yet profit from this disaster. So, if t was not Dukar, then who..."

They were interrupted by a knock at the door.

Hemanji's smile reappeared. "That must be my special visitor. I promised you I'd try to get permission to tell you who owns the box. He not only agreed but insisted on telling you in person. It is perfect timing; he is also interested in the 'who' of this matter. Additionally, he mentioned he has a request of you. I hope you'll agree." She raised her voice. "Enter!"

A tall, slim, man dressed in light gray scholar's robes was admitted. His dark hair and beard were neatly trimmed and had only a few strands of grey to them. He beamed a smile to Lady Cathar and bowed. "Hemanji, a pleasure as always."

"George, thank you for your patience." She gestured towards Sturm. "May I introduce Sir Kian Terter, the caravan leader who saved your box and brought it to Sulvi. He was just about to tell me who he found was behind the ambush."

George acknowledged Sturm with a short bow from the waist. "Thank you for all your efforts. The Earthguild owes you a debt. I am most curious to hear what you have found out."

Sturm's mind raced, a second wizard guild! Was he in the middle of a conflict between the two guilds? What would this wizard think of Sturm having killed a wizard? "Milord, I'm afraid you won't like what I have to say."

George chuckled and replied, "Please, no need for such formality. Especially since you're the only titled one here. I should be calling you 'milord'. Now then, continue."

Sturm went straight to the meat of the matter. "I believe a member of the Fireguild was behind the theft."

Hemanji's glass hit the floor and shattered, wine splattered across the floor. She leaned back against the table in shock, mouth gaping, her eyes fixated on Sturm.

A momentary glance to Hemanji and George was back to Sturm. "Fireguild you say? And how did you come to this conclusion?" George didn't sound surprised.

Sturm nodded toward Lady Cathar. "We figured the Cathar trademaster in Barzan had to be involved. The thieves went straight to where he had hidden the box. So I went to the trademaster, told him I had the box, and they would now have to deal with me. We set up a meeting. A sorceress and her guards showed up. I don't know who she was. She gave no name, and only identified herself as Fireguild. She was interested in the box. Then there was a bit of scuffle, and here I am."

Incredulous, Lady Cathar exclaimed, "Scuffle? And you are here unharmed? How did you manage that?"

Sturm hesitated to answer. Saying he had stepped up and punched the sorceress in the throat might be too graphic for Hemanji. He wasn't sure if George would believe it had been that simple.

George saw Sturm's hesitation and rescued him from a reply. "Indeed. Perhaps someday you will tell me. For now, be at ease, I believe you. Your news is more disappointment than surprise."

Lady Cathar, calmer, asked, "George, are they the reason for such secrecy in the shipment?"

George nodded. "It seemed a wise precaution even if only to guard against mere greed from the common bandit. But yes, we also worried over the Fireguild."

Sturm blurted out, "That's a relief."

"Why is that Sir Kian?"

"When you, a wizard, walked in I was afraid that not only would you not believe me but that you might also... I don't know, punish me maybe?"

George chuckled. "Wizards are people too. Some are good, some are not, and we each have our agendas. The nature of the Earthguild is to build and preserve. We often find ourselves at odds with fire, which is a destructive force. Based on that alone, I feared they would try to take the box just to deprive us of it. I don't think they even know what it is. If they did, they would have made a more concerted effort to take it."

"More concerted effort? They killed all my men and the drivers as well."

"Yes Sir Kian, more concerted. Imagine the sorceress and her bodyguards added to the bandits in the caravan ambush. For that matter, several wizards could have been there."

A chill ran down Sturm's spine as he contemplated fighting all that at once. "But what is worth that many lives lost?"

"I am not willing to answer that until we reach its final destination." George saw Sturm's disappointment, so he quickly added., "I plan on carrying it myself, and riding with all haste. Please be my escort, and I'll tell you once we're there."

Sturm hesitated in his reply.

Hermanji caught Sturm's eye and nodded, signaling for him to agree.

Sturm still hesitated. This must be the request she had mentioned, but he wasn't about to take it on just because she had nodded.

George continued, "I see your hesitation, and I don't blame you. If we do tangle with the Fireguild along the way, it could get quite unpleasant. I won't belittle that. It is because of that, and because you've already shown your honor, that I would have you with me. But no matter your answer, you are already friend to the Earthguild, and we are indebted to you."

George abruptly turned to Hemanji, his tone much lighter, "Here, let me see what I can do about that glass while Sir Kian has a chance to think." George knelt over the glass shards and summoned magic.

Sturm watched in fascination as the pieces gathered together, rearranged themselves into the shape of her glass, then melded together.

George stood up and handed the restored glass to Hemanji.

Sturm tuned out the small talk between the two that followed and weighed his options. Fire vs earth wasn't a good place to be, and George seemed to be on the weaker side. It was always wizards of fire or air who won the battles in the stories. Earthwizards weren't even in the fights. It would be smart to just walk away, yet could he? Sturm realized it was already too late, he was already in the middle of it. If, when, the Fireguild discovered he'd killed one of their casters, they'd come for him. Would the Earthguild protect him from them? George was likeable, but would he be there when it mattered?

Sturm's gaze wandered to Hemanji's glass. George's magic show had been impressive, but it was on par with Gwiz's parlor tricks. What more did the man know? What if Sturm could learn from him? If Sturm could learn to command magic, perhaps he could master the spells in the sorceress' book, then he wouldn't need George to protect him. Sturm made up his mind. "I will go with you, but there's a price."

"Of course, I did not expect otherwise. What is it that you require? Gold? Gems?"

"I will be stepping between the magic of fire and earth. A blade is not much worth in such a fight. I would learn magic."

"Oh!" After a moment, George recovered from his surprise. "I see your point. However, you don't know what you're getting into, and how unlikely you'll benefit. Normally a candidate is brought forward as a youth, considered, and if found capable allowed to apprentice under a master at the guild house. They have their entire life for what can be a lengthy journey from candidate to adept. Few are successful making it to mastery."

George thought a few moments then made his decision. "As I have said, we owe you a debt. If this is what you want, so be it. I will take you as my apprentice and teach you earth magic, but there is no guarantee of your success. Do not be disappointed if it turns out you do not have the talent. So, I will stipulate this; if after a year you show no progress, please let us offer you some other reward? Agreed?"

Sturm nodded.

George abruptly turned to Lady Cathar, "Hemanji, would you have one more who can ride as escort? One who can leave today?" With a grin he added, "And not one who wants knowledge of magic as payment."

Hemanji nodded. "I do, my guard leader Tarek. He is my best blade." She picked up and rang a bell.

Moments later her chambermaid entered. She bowed to Hemanji.

"Tej, go find Tarek and have him come here. Oh, and send in something for the four of us to eat. Some slices of meat, bread, and fruit. Also, there is wine spilled on the floor, have it cleaned up."

Tej bowed and left. A moment later, a servant quickly entered the room and wiped up the spill. A few minutes later, food and more drink were brought in and set on the table.

The three exchanged small talk and trivialities over the refreshments for nearly an hour before there was a discrete knock at the door.

Hemanji snapped out, "Finally!" She took a breath, forcing herself to release her impatience. In a normal tone she continued, "Yes Tarek, enter."

Instead, Tej bowed her way in again.

"Tej, what is it? Why has it taken so long?"

"Mistress, I am sorry. I only just found him. He had stepped out to a tavern. He is taking a few moments to make himself presentable and then will be right here."

"That is alright Tej. You did well."

Tej, bowed her way out.

Hemanji bit back angry words. They were meant for Tarek and not her guests.

Sturm saw Hemanji's discomfiture. He returned to their conversation before Geore also noticed. "What was I saying? Oh, yes, my years growing up at the Academy were not so different from those your apprentices go through when you think on it. Yes, they learn spells and I instead learned to swing a sword, but we still have to fetch the water for the masters. Yes?"

George chuckled. "True. In both environments the apprentice has to show an interest and a discipline to excel at their lessons. You have already gone through all that and even advanced to being a guard captain, a master of your craft. Hemanji has told me you've done well at it."

"I've run several trips up and down the route to Vellar. Last year I also had a contract where I delivered to Venub."

"Oh, did you get to see the ships?"

"No sir. Once we were at the city gates, the wagons were taken over for escort to the docks. They have laws against armed men from outside the city. I don't know what a large city has to worry about from a hand of caravan guards and two hands of drivers, but you don't argue with the men at the gate."

"My understanding is that it's not due to paranoia, rather it is because of labor agreements. Even the frontier guard had to make special arrangements as part of those agreements. Well, I hope you'll find our little journey beyond the cities of the Triangle to be a bit more interesting. In particular, the Great River..." George's attention was diverted by the door opening. "Ah, this must finally be Tarek?"

Sturm turned and froze. The man had a face he knew, a face that had visited him countless times in his nightmares. The features had a few added lines to them, but the cold dark eyes were unchanged. The eyes of his mother's executioner. Even this close, the eyes were so dark Sturm could not tell if there was any brown to them or if they were black. Sturm was torn between running and pulling his sword. He was saved from anyone noticing his reaction by Hemanji's admonishment of Tarek.

"You didn't even knock."

Tarek responded, "I was told to come immediately."

"You know better than that. Do not forget your place again."

As Tarek opened his mouth to reply, Hemanji cut him off sharply, "Tarek!" The next words softened as she motioned to George. "We have a guest who would employ a rider as escort. I am sending you."

Sturm recovered from his shock. The urge to run disappeared, the urge to draw steel didn't. He countered it with common sense. This was not the time or place for that fight. There were too many things in play, too many people involved, too many questions unanswered. He had found the executioner, but who had sent him? Tarek was with House Cathar now, but was he back then?

Tarek looked between Sturm and George. He decided to address George. "How long a journey, and to where? How many in the entourage?"

George nodded politely. "Well met Tarek. There will be three of us. Be prepared for a long ride, though I would guess we only need to take three day's rations with us for man and horse. As we cross the river, there is a place we can restock."

"Which river?"

"The Danu."

"Where after that?"

"I'd rather not tell you that yet."

Sturm barely paid attention to the interchange, instead he measured up Tarek. The man was as tall as Sturm, muscular. Tarek had prospered the last decade hiring out his sword. He would be dangerous in a fight. Sturm needed time to not only answer his questions, but he also needed to learn about his enemy before he fought him.

Tarek addressed Sturm, "Are you part of this?"

The direct query caught Sturm unprepared.

George answered for Sturm. "This is Sir Kian, my bodyguard."

Tarek shook his head. "I use my own people."

"He is coming. I require only one more guard."

"I'll send one of my men."

Hemanji curtly contradicted him., "No. You are going."

"Really? With only this kid to cover my back. And we haven't even discussed price yet."

Hemanji glared at him. "You will go, and he will pay the normal rate of one silver ounce per day. Paid to the Cartel."

Tarek glared back at her. "I am worth more than that!"

"Not this trip! Go, prepare."

Chapter 14: House Cathar Courtyard, Sulvi, 25th YOC, 15th Day of New Spring, 7 AM

The three met in the courtyard. Sturm was in his chainmail coat, the wizard in grey riding garb. Tarek was in heavy armor with breastplate, pauldrons, and schynbalds strapped over his chainmail.

George was irritated. Tarek had convinced him to not leave until the morning. Now they were met with further delay. The courtyard was a scene of confusion as a caravan prepared to leave. Men ran in and out of the stables leading horses to the wagons. Others carried goods from the warehouse and supplies from the kitchen. Two more were busy topping off barrels with water from the well. These preparations blocked George and his party from their horses and supplies.

George turned to Tarek, harsh words formed, but before he could say anything Tarek excused himself and walked over to the caravan guard captain.

Tarek exchanged words with the captain, then returned. "Sorry for the delay. They're almost done. Once they're out of our way we can bring our horses out, fill our canteens, and saddle up."

George worriedly eyed the caravan. "Are they going to be in our way on the streets?"

"No, they're going west towards Barzan. You said you wanted to go to the Danu, right?"

George nodded.

"That's east, the other gate. So, Bridgeport, right?"

George hesitated, then laughed. "So much for me being circumspect."

"It's where your guildhouse is, and it's the closest city on the river. So, may I make a suggestion?"

George nodded.

"There are two routes we can take. The easiest is the caravan route. We'd eat up the miles faster, but there are a lot more miles. It swings south to Venu and then back up to Bridgeport. There is also a courier route that splits off from the caravan route where it turns to Venub and goes straight to Bridgeport. It is not as well maintained as the caravan route and goes up and down hills instead of around them."

"The courier route would be quicker, since it's more direct?"

Tarek nodded. "Assuming we're on horses and not on a wagon. I know you have a fine rider, must have some warhorse in him, but what about your hired help?" He shifted his attention to Sturm. "Hey, kid, you know how to ride?"

Sturm nodded.

"Good. Once they're done with the caravan, have a stable hand hook you up with one of our riding mounts. I'm sure he can find you a gentle one. Think you can handle getting three days grain ration for all three horses while I go to the kitchen and get our food?"

Sturm bit back a retort, and again only nodded.   It served Sturm's purpose for Tarek to hold him in contempt. It would cause Tarek to underestimate him, making it easier to kill Tarek later.

Chapter 15: House Cathar Stable, 25th YOC, 15th Day of New Spring, 8 AM

Tarek stomped into the stable. He tossed a sack of food at Sturm and handed another to the wizard. "Took longer than I expected. Stupid cooks forgot about us. They were none too pleased having to carve up the last ham and giving us the last loaves of bread. They were holding that back to have for themselves. Oh well. They have all day to bake up more bread and to go to market."

Tarek looked at his horse, then glared at Sturm. "What? You didn't saddle my horse?"

"Sorry, I wasn't sure you allowed anyone to touch your mount."

Tarek grabbed a saddle and blanket. "Probably best you didn't. You might not have gotten the saddle cinch tight enough. What have you got there? A warhorse? How did you get one of those?"

Sturm watched as Tarek stepped into a stall. Tarek's horse was a quality rider, the same kind of southern breed and warhorse mix as the wizard rode. It was an expensive mount, but it wasn't a warhorse.

Tarek interrupted Sturm's appraisal of the horse, "What? Can't catch your tongue? I asked you a question."

Sturm shrugged. "What do you think I did? I saved all the money I earned and spent it on him."

Tarek led his horse out. "Hey, don't get snippy with me. Why aren't you mounted up and ready to go?"

Sturm hesitated. He had Tarek's attention. Once they were riding, they'd be traveling hard and fast – not conducive for conversations. How could Sturm turn the conversation to his questions?

Tarek was losing patience, "What are you staring at?"

Sturm decided to go the most direct route. "At you. Sorry. It's just... I've seen you before. But not in armor like that."

"Really?"

"Yeah. Pretty certain. You ever done any work in Vellar?"

Sturm's question caught Tarek as he was mounting. Tarek hesitated, then finished swinging his leg over. "Yeah, a long time ago."

"Maybe a decade ago?"

"Maybe that long."

Sturm kept his tone as casual as he could, "I thought so. Back when I was a boy, I was in Vellar and there was a big commotion. I ran to see what it was about. There were five of you and a woman. Three of your men were down. I got there in time to see you finish off the woman. That was you, right?"

Tarek hesitated, then nodded. "Yeah. We had a bad day with an elf woman. What's it to you? Hey, that was the day some crazy kid charged us. That wasn't you, was it?"

Sturm coolly replied, "I remember the kid. Yeah, he was pretty insane. Lucky for him a bunch of people followed. Lucky for all of them they didn't catch you, right? That was part of why I remembered it. Another part is it was the first time I saw someone die. It made a big impression on me. I've always wondered what it was all about."

Tarek shrugged. "It was about nothing. We had a commission from the Tionol, and we executed it all legal like. That's all."

The answer gave Sturm pause. The Tionol was the council that ran the country. Her murder went far beyond Tareek's blade. Sturm pressed for the connection. "How did the Tionol know she was in Vellar? Why were they involved?"

"I don't know. She was an elf, they are banned from human lands. I was told where she was and what to do. That's good enough for me."

"How did you hook up with the Tionol? Those commissions fairly common?"

"Kid, you ask a lot of questions. We've been doing commissions for a lot of years. The pay is good, and it keeps us in the good graces of the councils."

Sturm saw Tarek losing patience. He took a verbal jab to see what came out. "So, did the commission say to kill her or did you do that for fun? You sure it was a real commission? Law or not, she was just some street woman."

Tarek glared back at Sturm and replied testily. "Some people are not what they seem. She obviously wasn't. She took down three of my men. Yeah, it was a real commission, properly signed. So, are we done now?" Tarek spurred his horse out the stable, across the courtyard to the gate.

Sturm mounted Val, then felt a hand on his knee. He looked down to George.

"Young man, while you managed to get a reaction from him, are you sure that is what you really want? We have a long journey."

Prodding Tarek had felt good, but Sturm realized the truth to George's words. "I'm sorry. You're right, I shouldn't make trouble. It's just hard for me to respect a man who murdered a street woman. And did you hear? Do you see nothing wrong with execution orders?"

With a soft laugh George replied., "My naive friend, there is much that goes on in the City of Councils that I find distasteful."

"What do you mean?"

"The Tionol is actually a combination of three councils: the Convocation of Wizards, the Ecumenical Synod, and the Assembly of Nobles. The Convocation is run by one man, the Synod by another, and they often work together. The things I have seen done as they feed their greed, their hunger for power, or that of their cronies..." George trailed off, then shook his head.

"But doesn't the Earthguild have something to say in the Convocation?"

George snorted. "We're supposed to. However, the Guilds of Fire, Air, and Necromancy are aligned together. Water is left in confusion, leaving Earth to stand alone in opposition. Time and again we are ignored, or overruled."

"What about that last group, the Assembly of Nobles?"

"They are supposed to be a power, but they are in disarray. Many voices, but none to lead, so only noise results. When one does step up and manages to sort them out, something happens. Some have suddenly become a puppet of the Fireguild, or they have a hunting accident and end up dead."

George mounted his horse, then continued. "In the midst of all this, questionable arrangements are made and become motions that are voted on. Once something is passed, it becomes law. Even death warrants for an innocent are legal and supposedly proper."

"Something should be done!"

"You're right. So why don't you do something?"

Sturm was taken aback. "What do you mean?"

"You are a noble. Where are you from?"

"Vellar."

"That makes it easy. Their seat at the Tionol is empty. Get yourself into it and make changes."

"And then not go hunting?"

With a bitter laugh of agreement, George nodded. "Yes! Enough of these musings, we need to ride and catch up with Tarek."

Chapter 16: House Cathar Stable, 25th YOC, 15th Day of New Spring, 9 AM

Tarek led, half a furlong ahead of the other two. He kept a fast pace. He occasionally looked back to see if the others kept up with him.

George rode along softly humming some ditty, enjoying the ride.

Sturm kept pace with George. He paid little attention to the song; his thoughts were in turmoil. After so many years, pieces to the puzzle of his mother's death had fallen in his lap. Yet how these pieces fit together was boggling. He had never imagined that it would involve someone in the Tionol. George's advice to take the Vellar seat at the Tionol went far beyond anything Sturm had envisioned doing. For a few moments he imagined himself there, strutting around making laws. He quickly dismissed the vision of grandeur. Lording it over people just wasn't him. He had no interest in controlling others, or of power for power's sake.

Sturm's thoughts moved on to Tarek. For the last decade the man was the embodiment of evil in Sturm's thoughts and dreams. He had murdered Sturm's mother, and so should die. Now, certainty turned to confusion. Tarek had fulfilled a commission from the Tionol. How many times, in how many cities, did sheriffs do the same thing when enforcing the law? Were they murderers? Was Tarek a murderer, or was he an enforcer of the law? Sturm's mind balked at the thought of Tarek being guiltless, yet would killing Tarek be justice or just another murder?

Storm sorted through Tarek's explanation. It boiled down to his mom being an elf. Sturm mulled that thought around. He and the gnomes had many discussions on that being the reason. He had been taught the revolution was as a result of the elves exerting influence over the king, turning the king against his people. A short human-elf war had followed the revolution, culminating in the humans' victory at Jukai.

The depiction of the elves didn't fit well with Sturm's childhood memories of his mom. He could not imagine his mom involved with bringing harm to the kingdom. She had been sweet, caring, and patient. She was that way not only with him, but with everyone. She had lived humbly and in peace. She had human friends.

Sturm also wondered how the Tionol had found out about an elf in Vellar. No one in Vellar knew what an elf was. To them, his mom was just a downtowner with deformed pointy ears. Perhaps it had been the pointy ears?

Sturm realized there was another equally important question. Why had Tarek brought four men with him? Yes, he had needed them, but how had he known that? That had to be in the commission, put in by someone who knew her past.

Sturm's mother had never told him of her pre-Vellar past. Sturm needed to find out who that someone was and learn what they knew. Sturm needed to follow his clues to the capitol.

Chapter 17: On the Road East of Sulvi, 25th YOC, 15th Day of New Spring, 1 PM

The caravan route had gone from a straight road heading east between farmers' fields to weaving between forested foothills. A few miles into the hills the caravan route turned south, down a valley. A narrower courier road continued east over a hill. Trees crowded the road and arched overhead giving the road a feeling of being overgrown and dark. Tarek led them east.

After a couple hours, Tarek reined in his horse at the base of a hill and waited for George and Sturm.

George pulled up near to Tarek. "Why the stop?"

"I'm worried about what's on the other side of the hill. Heavy brush closes to the edge of the road. It's a prime spot for an ambush. I'm going to ride ahead and check it out. Give me a couple of minutes, then follow." Not waiting for an answer Tarek turned his horse and spurred it over the rise.

Sturm stared at Tarek's back. "That was abrupt."

"Yes, but I suppose he's still miffed at you over the conversation in the stable. Don't let it distract you. What is of importance is that he is concerned about ambushes on this road. He hadn't mentioned it when we planned the ride last night. I would rather not ride into an ambush, even if it wasn't meant for us. Perhaps there is another path..." George trailed off as he scratched his beard in thought. He dismounted and squatted next to his horse, with his hands on the ground. Magic formed around him as he mumbled. He slowly faced around from the nearly easterly direction of the road to almost due north. With a satisfied grunt, George stood up and wiped his hands off on his pants, then climbed back on his horse. "Well, then. I think we've given Tarek more than enough time. Sir Kian, if you would, please go and bring him back here."

Sturm was curious about what he'd seen George do but held his questions. He kneed Val into a trot to the top of the rise. On the other side, he saw Tarek had been right; the underbrush crowded the road creating an opportunity for an ambush. Tarek was half a bow shot down the road, facing back toward Strum.

Tarek waved for Sturm to ride up, as he called out. "Where's George?"

Sturm pulled up next to Tarek, crowding Tarek's sword arm, their horses facing opposite directions. Sturm took a long moment to look around. He didn't see anyone, but there could be an unseen army in the brush.

Tarek prompted, "You going to answer me?"

"George wants you to come back and talk to him." Sturm turned his horse away from Tarek and went back up the road, not giving Tarek a chance to reply.

Tarek stared at Sturm's back for a moment, then he slowly wheeled his horse around in a slow three-sixty, pausing for a moment broadside to the road. He made an odd open-handed gesture on the side away from Sturm. He completed turning his horse and followed Sturm over the rise.

Tarek pulled up near George, his irritation plain, and demanded, "Why didn't you come? We could be half an hour up the road by now."

George calmly responded, "While I applaud your caution, it seems to me if even this road could harbor an ambush, then we need another route."

"Another route, really? We're in the wilderness, this is the only road."

"There seems to be another way not far from here, follow." George turned his horse north and rode off the road into the trees. He led them a few miles to a twenty-foot-wide flat swath across the forest floor. Hills in the way of the old road had been cut back, their sheer rock faces smooth and bare. The only impediment was that trees had reclaimed the road. Some of the trees were huge and centuries old.

Sturm queried George, "Where does this road of yours go?"

"I believe, due to its age and its direction, it's to the old kingdom city of Lanaick. That's on the Danu."

Sturm was a confused. "The kingdom? These trees are a lot older than the couple of decades since the revolution."

"Not that kingdom. The old kingdom, centuries before the kingdom you've heard of."

George saw he needed to explain. "The old kingdom had several major cities along the Great River. They enjoyed great prosperity from the trade along the length of the river. Not much else is known of them other than they all fell or were abandoned within a short time of each other, as that kingdom ended. Lanaick was one of these cities. There is only ruins and a small fishing village there now."

Tarek interrupted, "So now you want to go there?"

"Sure, why not? From there we can ride down the river road to Bridgeport. Come along." George spurred his horse.

They rode from there in silence, George ever ahead, leading down the roadway just north of east. Tarek was to one side. Sturm was to the other side, keeping an eye on both George and Tarek.

An hour prior to dark, George pulled up his horse and dismounted. On one side a hill rose steeply, exposing an overhang of rocks forming a shallow cave.

George walked over to the cave. "Yes, this will do nicely. A cozy spot, I can bed down here and throw a ward across the opening and be as safe as can be. However, there is only room for one. You gentlemen will be on your own. I'll be safe enough, but you'll have to figure out something for yourselves."

Sturm was relieved. Maybe it wasn't fair to Tarek, but Sturm didn't trust Tarek to watch over him as he slept. With George's directions, he didn't have to.

As the three took care of the horses and made camp, Sturm took in the area around them. One of the trees caught his eye. It overlooked George's nook yet was far enough back to be beyond their campfire light come nighttime. It looked stout enough for him to climb, even with the weight of his armor. Its heights offered a safe haven above where people could attack him, or even notice him. He glanced over at Tarek's armor. The strap on pieces added weight and restricted movement. They would stop Tarek from climbing. That decided Sturm, that tree is where he would spend the night.

Food was pulled out and turned into a meal over the campfire. Few words were exchanged.

George finished his meal, bid them a good rest, and crawled into his nook. A buildup of magic power, a few mumbled words, and a small flash resulted in a muted glow extending across the face of the hole. The warding dimmed George's profile as he pulled his sleeping bag around him. The ward slowly became opaque, looking like a wall of rock, completely hiding George as he nodded off to sleep. Unfortunately, the ward did little to block his snoring.

Tarek looked across the fire to Sturm. "So now what? Take turns on guard?"

Sturm shook his head, keeping his tone light. "I think I'm going to follow the wizard's example and find a safe spot to hole up until daylight."

Irritation crossed Tarek's face. He opened his mouth to say something, then bit it off with a shrug.

Sturm grabbed his saddlebag and bedroll. It took only a few steps for him to disappear into the dark beyond the campfire's glow.

Sturm moved slowly, carefully picking his steps, while wending a circuitous route to the tree. He couldn't be completely silent, but the sounds he made were minor, random, and he hoped lost in the background sounds of the forest. He stopped several times to listen. Each time he heard only the rustling of leaves or the scurrying of an unseen nocturnal animal. It reassured him that he wasn't followed.

Sturm made it to the tree. He set his gear down and pulled a coil of rope out from a saddle bag. The rope was of very strong fibers, so it was thin, allowing for a long coil to fit in the bag. He tied one end to the saddlebags and his bedroll, then the other end to his belt.

He took his time climbing the tree, careful to not bang his sword against the tree or to shake the branches.   He stopped where a couple of strong branches ran close together, high enough where he could see George's nook.

Sturm pulled his equipment up. Then he looped the rope back and forth between the branches. He laid his bedroll and saddle bags across the web to complete his nest. Sturm gingerly eased himself onto his bedroll taking care to not shake the branches. Sturm stretched out on his back with an internal sigh of relief, he was settled in without causing a disturbance to give himself away.

He glanced over to check on George, all was quiet. He took another look towards the horses but found he had no line of sight through the foliage. He had to trust Val to take care of himself. He also had no line of sight to the campfire, so he had no idea where Tarek was, but he was confident Tarek also had no idea where he was.

Sturm looped the last couple feet of rope over him and tied it off with a quick release knot. He didn't fancy rolling over in his sleep and falling out of the tree. One last thought, remembering the wizard's snores, Sturm tightened his chinstrap to keep his mouth closed. He settled in and closed his eyes. He quickly drifted off to sleep.

Chapter 18: Triangle Foothills, 25th YOC, 15th Day of New Spring, 11 PM

Sturm suddenly was awake. It took him a few moments to realize why. Below, in front of the wizard's grotto were two men. Their heated discussion had wakened him. Sturm didn't recognize them. They were in leather jerkins and brandished weapons. Sturm couldn't make out what they were saying but from the way one kept pointing his spear at the wizard's grotto it apparently wasn't a social visit. It was time to climb down and see what was going on.

Sturm didn't see any immediate danger to the wizard, so he took a few moments to drop his equipment and then let himself down from the tree. He carried his equipment with him to where the horses had been hobbled, only to find the horses were gone and a new trail had been forced through the brush to the south. He dropped his gear and followed the trail.

He quickly caught up with the horses. They were led by another man in leather. It was slow going for the man, Val was balking at being led, and the man was having to urge Val forward using carrots. Sturm followed, careful to not alert the man.

The man stopped.

Sturm quietly circled through the brush, closing in on the man.

The man gave a whispered call. There was a reply from ahead. The man got the horses moving again, and brought them up to a picket line with four horses and a man tending them. The two men conversed, as Sturm worked his way to where he could see the men without they seeing him. He waited. He was confident he could quickly take out one of them, but the second would result in a longer fight. Two to one odds would quickly turn into four to one if the ones from by the wizard joined in.

Sturm's patience was rewarded. The man turned over Val and the other two mounts, then left heading towards the camp. The horse tender busied himself tying the leads to bushes. Val was uncooperative, distracting the man.

Sturm pulled his dagger and slunk to behind the horse tender, then lunged. A quick overhand stab, the dagger plunged into the base of the man's neck. Sturm quietly eased the body down to the ground.

Sturm wiped off his blade on the man's shirt and took a moment to look around and listen. It was quiet except for the horses, nervous from the sudden movements and the smell of blood.

Sturm sliced the reins of the unfamiliar horses. They ambled away from the body and the blood scent.

He grabbed the reins of his group's three horses and led them to a spot deeper in the woods and out of sight. He left Val unhobbled, able to defend himself. The others he secured. He returned to where he had left the other four finding they had not wandered far. Sturm picked some small stones and threw them at the horse's rumps causing them to bolt. Sturm melted back into the forest.

Sturm followed the trail back to his gear. He carried it with him as he made his way to where he could see the camp, and the wizard's nook. There was no sign of either the men or Tarek. The wizard's ward was still intact.

Cursing broke out over where the attackers' horses had been.

Sturm stepped over to the wizard's nook and dropped his gear. He drew both sword and dagger and faced the remains of the campfire. The magic of the ward at his back dissipated. George stepped out with his staff in hand.

Before they could exchange words, a figure stepped into the campfire light from the far side. After a momentary start, they recognized Tarek.

Tarek sheathed his sword. "Good, they didn't get to you. I ran them off, no help from Sir Kian here." Tarek glared at Sturm. "I hope you have a good story."

Sturm glared back at Tarek. Tarek's words didn't ring true. If Tarek had confronted them, Sturm would have heard more than just some curses and Tarek wouldn't have rejoined them so quickly. So, what had Tarek actually done? "Better than yours. The horses had been moved. I retrieved them so we can get out of here."

The two warriors glowered at each other. George broke the standoff. "Good. We need to move out quickly before they return. Lead us to where you took the horses."

It took only a few moments to get to the horses, but then they were slow to leave as Tarek fumbled with his saddle bags.

George lost his patience. "Tarek! What ails you? We need to be off!"

"It's dark, I can't see what I'm doing. I don't even know how we're going to travel though this forest in the dark."

George reached into his robes and pulled out a small stone. With a word it dimly glowed. George held the stone, shielding it with his hand so it illuminated only Tarek's things. "Get on with it."

Tarek hesitated.

Sturm stood near, ready to go. He had Val's reins in one hand and his sword in the other. "Just drop the gear and let's go."

Tarek glared at Sturm, but then finished tying up his bags.

Sturm moved to mount Val, but George stopped him. "Tarek is right, we can't just ride full tilt through the dark forest. We'll have to lead the horses. Follow me."

George affixed the stone to his staff, grabbed the reins of his horse, and led them into the forest. He returned to his road, keeping up a fast pace, adeptly picking his way between the trees with the aid of his light stone.

Sturm and Tarek subtly jockeyed back and forth for position, each trying to keep an eye on the other. Eventually Tarek ceded position to Sturm. Tarek was night blind and had so much trouble avoiding trees that he ended up focusing on simply trying to keep up with George. Sturm had trouble only when the glare of the stone was in his line of sight, momentarily blinding him.

Chapter 19: Triangle Foothills, 25th YOC, 16th Day of New Spring, Dawn

Once the darkness hiding obstructions gave away to the light, the three mounted up. They rode for hours, little was said.

George called a stop. Their way was blocked by a ravine. There had been a bridge, but most of the span had fallen.

George urged his horse to the lip of the ravine and looked down. The sides of the ravine were steep, too steep for the horses. Large stone blocks from the bridge were strewn across the bottom.

Tarek sidled his horse to also look into the ravine. Tarek didn't seem particularly disappointed as he pronounced, "So much for this road of yours George. I don't know if it's worth riding up or down the ravine to look for a way across. There probably isn't one if they had to build a bridge here. So, now what? Turn back?"

George shook his head. "Let me try something first."

George got off his horse, handed the reins to Sturm, then stepped onto the remaining bit of bridge. George took a deep, slow breath followed by a slow exhale. He began an incantation.

Sturm watched as magic energy surrounded George, in a glow. George raised his staff and directed the energy to the blocks below.

George stared in intense concentration, beads of sweat on his forehead. A large stone block slowly floated up from below and attached itself to the bridge. The seam between stone and bridge faded, melding it to the bridge. The process had taken several minutes.

Tarek snorted. He walked off to tether his horse. He rummaged around in his saddlebag, pulled out some food, then sat down under a tree.

George saw Tarek's movement out of the corner of his eye. "Yes, Tarek, this may take a while though it may not be as bad as it first appears. I still have a trick up my sleeve. Please stay alert and make sure I am not interrupted."

Tarek shrugged as he bit into a loaf of bread.

George went to his horse and pulled the box out of his saddle bag. He opened it and gingerly removed the stone within. He returned to his spot on the bridge and repeated his casting using the stone instead of his staff.   The stone brightly glowed in response to George's magic.

A stone block rose out of the ravine and attached to the bridge. A second block quickly followed, then in rapid succession many more. The last block flew up, added itself to the bridge, making the bridge whole.

George let out a sigh of relief. He returned to his horse, put the stone away, and mounted up. With an "Are you coming?" thrown Tarek's way, George rode across the bridge.

Sturm followed. On the other side, Sturm looked back at Tarek. Tarek looked surprised, and perhaps even disappointed. Tarek scrambled to his feet, mounted his horse, then joined them.

George gestured for both Tarek and Sturm to ride further down the road. "One more thing for me to do. Gentlemen, stay clear of the bridge."

George dismounted again and stood on the edge of the bridge. He raised his staff and brought it down with a flourish to tap the bridge, releasing his magic from the stones. The stones rumbled and shifted, then tumbled into the ravine. "That should take care of any pursuit." George returned to his horse, mounted, and led them down the road.

Chapter 20: Triangle Foothills, 25th YOC, 16th Day of New Spring, 3 PM

The kept up a fast pace. Oddly, the horses remained fresh and needed no breaks, until in the mid-afternoon the horses surprised their riders by suddenly coming to a stop.

Tarek responded by sawing his reins back and forth and spurring his horse. His horse snorted, and shivered, but didn't move.

Strum leaned forward to speak softly into Val's ears. "Come on boy, why are you stopping?" Val shook his head in reply.

George urged his horse as well, but then stopped. He looked down at his horse's hooves. He whistled and waved to Sturm and Tarek. "That's enough, they aren't going anywhere."

A man stepped out from behind the trees. He blended well with the forest, dressed in brown and with a green cloak. He carried a walking staff. "You are correct, sir. I've entwined the horses' hooves. They could not move if they wanted to, however I've also ensured that they do not want to."

As he spoke several other men showed themselves. They were similarly dressed, but instead of a stick they carried loaded crossbows. The bowmen were alert, but none had their bows pointed at the riders.

George nodded to the men, then addressed their spokesman. "Good day sir, my apologies if we have trespassed on your land. Please do not take exception to us. We're merely passing through in peace."

"Oh, I take no exception. I simply heard that there were travelers on the ancient road and I'm curious. It's been generations since there has been such news. Plus, the bearers of the tidings were quite excited, their stories of two headed monsters were worrisome."

George laughed. "Two headed monsters? No, not at all. Have they not seen riders before? And if they don't know horses, how could they have gotten word to you ahead of us? Magic?"

Now it was the robed man's turn to laugh. The man touched a bird shaped charm hanging from a thong around his neck as he replied, "Magic? Aye, the magic of the forest around you. The birds on wing fly far faster than your mounts can travel, even on this road."

Suddenly it added up for George. "Oh, how dense of me. My apologies friend druid! But what are you doing so far south from the circle of power?"

"So far south? We are only hour's walk from there, and its due east."

"Really? So, we're not headed towards Lanaick?"

"No, that is a good day's travel south of here. It's probably simplest just to continue on this road to Kunalas then follow the river road south to Lanaick."

"Actually, I really meant to get to Bridgeport. I only thought this path led to Lanaick."

"Ah, Bridgeport! That makes more sense. Well, you have almost made it to the Danu where our Druid's Circle overlooks the river."

Tarek broke in, "But how did we get here so fast? I expected another day before we came to the river."

The druid responded, "You are on a road built long ago for fast travel. Unlike today where important people use magic to speed their trip, the road was imbued with magic so all may travel quickly. The road yet holds some of that magic."

The idea of a magic road piqued Sturm's imagination. "So your circle of power is at the end, but where does the road start?"

The druid shrugged. "The history of who came down this road has been lost. Where they came from likely no longer exists. Only our circle of power endures, as it will forever – Danu willing."

The druid turned back to George. "If you wish to continue to the Danu through Kunalas, you are welcome to pass. You'll have to swear the pax, the oath of peace, for your time in the sacred district."

George bowed. "Thank you for your hospitality. I would be pleased to make such a pledge. Could you send word to the Great Druid that George of the Earthguild is passing through? Perhaps he would take a few moments to greet an old friend?"

The druid returned George's bow. "I will send a messenger ahead, milord." He looked to Tarek and Sturm. "And you gentlemen, you care to journey through as well?"

Sturm quickly replied. "Yes, sir."

Tarek hesitated; he wasn't certain what the pax was or how it might get in the way of what he had to do. The druid calmly stared at him. Tarek realized the only way he'd stay with George was to also agree. Tarek finally nodded ascent.

The druid smiled. "Good! Please dismount. Each, in turn, will need to place your hand on my staff and swear the oath."

The druid stepped up to George first, he held his walking staff in the middle and raised it parallel to the ground to chest high between them. George laid his hand on it. The druid locked eyes with George, said a few words of an incantation. Then he demanded of George, "Do you swear to uphold the pax; to bring no harm to man, woman, or protected beast for as long as you remain in the sacred precinct? Or forfeit your life if you break your oath."

George responded, "I so swear!"

The druid stepped over to Tarek and then Sturm, repeating the Oath ritual with each. When he was finished the men with the crossbows relaxed.

The druid released his spell on the horses and addressed his guests. ""Welcome. My name is Oliver. Let me show you the way to the hostel. We'll find you some beds for the night. You can start your journey down river in the morning."

Oliver turned and headed down the old roadway, George fell in next to him leading his mount. George asked a few questions, and they were quickly wrapped up in a discussion about the forest, the weather, the river, the harvest.

The others fell in behind. Sturm chatted with the guards, discussing crossbows and armor. Tarek followed near the rear, quiet, a scowl on his face.

Chapter 21: Kunalas, 25th YOC, 16th Day of New Spring, 4 PM

The road emerged from the forest, and then split into three. Oliver called a halt.

The view was idyllic. To the left the road curved down into the river valley passing farmer's fields, lush and green with the beginnings of the year's crop, to a fishing village on the river. Smoke drifted up from chimneys as dinners were being cooked. A small craft piled with nets dropped its sail as it coasted to the dock. It slid in beside a barge already tied up. The crew jumped out and tied it to the wharf. Across the river, near the far bank, a large merchant craft was being towed upstream by mules.

The middle road ran straight ahead to a promontory. This road was well tended and lined on both sides with totems. A double circle of huge stones stood on the promontory, dwarfing a group of people that were walking toward the stones. The stones were perfectly aligned, straight, and topped by lintels.

The road to the right headed south, going down to the river then following the river bank. It was also well tended until it disappeared into the trees.

George called back to his guards, "Walking through the stone circle is amazing. Maybe Oliver would be so kind as to give you two a tour of it. I'll continue down to the village to pay my respects to the Great Druid and arrange our further travel."

Oliver chimed in. "I'd be pleased to take you, if you're interested."

Sturm readily nodded.

Oliver turned to Tarek, "And you sir?"

Tarek shrugged. "Sure. Why not."

"Good. Hand your horses over to my men, they'll get them bedded down for you." Oliver waited for the handover then led them down the road.

As they walked past the totems, Sturm started a question, hesitated, then with a sheepish grin started again, "Excuse me friend druid. I don't mean any disrespect. But how should I address you?"

The druid chuckled. "By my name of course, I have no title. And you gentlemen are?"

"Pleased to meet you. I am Kian Terter."

"Tarek."

"Pleased to meet both of you as well. Many visit here, and we give tours all the time." Oliver gestured to the people near the stones. "I see a tour group near the outer stones. If we hurry, we should be able to catch up to them and save you from my feeble attempts as a guide."

As Oliver picked up the pace, he continued. "You've missed the part about our Path of Honor marked by these totems. The totems represent and respect past leaders. The newest is nearly three hundred years old. The oldest? Unfortunately, they're lost to us, predating our records. On the right are the leaders of the people, the earliest were chiefs followed later by kings. On the left are the spiritual guides, the Great Druids and High Priestesses. As you can see, there are many generations. It is said most are buried within the circle."

Sturm asked, "Why so long since the last one?"

"On the king's side, the last one was put in place when the last king of the old kingdom died. We would have placed one for King Valeric, but the Tionol didn't allow it. On the spiritual side, the last pole is for the previous Great Druid. It may have been long ago by your standards, but not by ours. Two back is for the last High Priestess who died before the schism."

Sturm interrupted, "Schism? What is that?"

"The schism was a dark time. The Priestesses and the Druids both worship the Goddess, but in different ways. There was contention over these differences. Why? It makes no sense to me. They can believe what they want about the Goddess and follow their tenants, as can we. If the Goddess isn't angered, why should we be? However, back then the differences led to battle. Both sides lost. Centuries later, distrust still lingers. They stay up in their mountains, we in our river valley."

As an afterthought Oliver added, "Perhaps someday there will be an age where wisdom returns, and we'll start talking to each other again." Oliver shrugged and continued walking down the path.

They crossed the last span of road and caught up to the tour at a ditch in front of the outer ring of stones.

The tour guide waved to them without interrupting his spiel. He motioned to the stones as he extolled, "Imagine hauling them around for a day's bread, eh?! But they're small compared to the inner circle. These outer ones are twelve feet tall, but the inner ones are three times that. We're going to move along now. My apologizes to the new commers. You missed the parts of the quarrying and why they were brought here. Oliver, can you catch them up after the tour?"

Oliver nodded.

"Good. Then let's continue." The guide stepped onto a bridge of wooden planks, waving the tour to follow. "Come along. Mind your step now. Use the cross bridge, the ditch is muddy at the bottom."

On the other side, the tour guide walked up to the closest stone. He reverently touched it with his fingertips. The fingertips then went to his head, his lips, and over his heart as he mumbled a blessing. He then stepped past the stone and waved the tour to gather around him.

The tour followed over the bridge, passing the stone to stand by the guide.

Sturm's turn came. As he set foot on the other side, it was as if he'd stepped through a veil. He was immersed in energy. It was odd: it was magic, yet it wasn't. Instead of coming from within, it enveloped him. He felt the promise of great things he could do, if only he could somehow harness and shape this energy.

Behind him, Tarek nudged Sturm. "What's got you? Step forward, you're in the way."

Sturm stepped to the side and watched Tarek step through the veil.

Terek showed no reaction, oblivious to the energy. He walked over to join the rest of the group.

Sturm's gaze shifted to Oliver, who followed Tarek.

Oliver reacted. It was subtle, he stood a bit taller. He reached out to touch the nearest stone and blessed himself before he joined the rest of group.

Sturm followed Oliver, covertly running his fingertip along the stone as he passed it. He nearly jumped at the surge of power. He wondered if they were similar to the Earthwizard's stone.

The guide continued his discussion. "One of the names for this place is the Circle of Power. You may not feel it, but Danu has blessed these stones and imbued them. We also call it the Circle of Life or of Healing. Even if you can't feel Danu's power, if you have cuts or scratches you should be feeling them itch as they heal. Anyone feel it?"

A middle-aged woman waved her hand and nodded enthusiastically.

"Ah, good. So, you see. This healing power increases towards the center. Ahead of us is the inner ring, though maybe we shouldn't call it that. It's really not a circle. Rather its two sets of three connected stones, on either side of this main avenue we're on. Let's walk to the center." He led the group down the avenue.

Sturm hesitated as he passed the inner stones. His eyes followed the nearest stone upward. It seemed to reach up and touch the sky.

Inside the inner ring was a garden, maybe a hundred feet across. In the center was a stone block, an altar. The guide led them towards the alter. "This is the most powerful place of healing. It is said a king with a death wound was once brought and laid on this stone. In moments he stood up restored. He returned to his battle. Unfortunately, like so many of my people's stories, his story had an unhappy ending."

One of the tourists obliged the guide by asking the question, "How so?"

"Well, you see, the battle was already lost. When he returned to the battlefield, he saw his friends and allies fallen. In his grief, he charged in and died. Though he took many enemies with him, he was still dead. That second time there was no reprieve from death. I suppose there is a moral there about accepting one's fate, but I'm not one to subscribe to it."

Tarek broke in, "Can the stones restore youth?"

The guide chuckled. "There is always one who asks that. No, it heals. An old person with rheumatism will be able to click their heels and dance a jig, but they will still be old. Being around it daily does extend life. If you aren't ravaged by sickness, you live longer. So, if you're concerned about a long life, renounce your warrior profession and move into the village – become a druid!"

The crowd nodded and laughed along with the guide. Tarek frowned.

They stopped at the altar. They were surrounded by the garden. The plants grew as tall as a man, with small yellow blooms. A pretty lass tended them, harvesting leaves from the plants.

The guide coughed once to get her attention. "Hello Heather, how goes the gardening?"

She looked up, then smiled and waved at the group. "Oh. Hello all. Welcome to the Circle."

An older man in the tour pointed to the plants. "Young lady, what are you tending there?"

"Sir, this is the sacred herb Isatis. The leaves are used to make healing poultices. Plants growing within the circle are particularly potent. The medical corps, tending wounded warriors, praise the virtue of what we send them."

A couple of the people in the group, including Sturm, stepped up to get a closer look at the Isatis plants. Tarek held back, looking Heather over instead of the plants.

At first, she didn't notice. She was focused on explaining the growth habit of the plant, how they tended it, and then how it was processed for the poultices. Eventually she looked over and Tarek caught her eye. She nodded and then looked back to the people around her, answering a question. After a few moments she looked back. He still stared at her. She flushed, but ignored him, going back to her discussion.

Tarek continued to stare, now with a cocky grin. Tarek suddenly felt a hand on his shoulder, it was Oliver.

Oliver advised him, "Heather is only fifteen years old. I don't know how men treat girls where you are from, but here she is a child and protected."

Tarek laughed, a short but mocking sound, and responded loudly enough for Heather to hear. "Where I come from, if she looks like a woman, she gets treated like one."

Oliver's eyes narrowed. "Behave!"

Tarek responded with a dangerous note to his voice, "Or you'll do what?"

"I don't have to do anything. You'll be breaking the pax. You will be harming her." Oliver stepped back, to see how Tarek responded.

Tarek bit off a reply. He remembered there had been a ritual to the oath. Heather was a cute little thing, and Tarek was used to getting his way, but he decided she wasn't worth testing out the pax. His thoughts were interrupted by one of the women in the group.

She was definitely full grown. She walked up to Tarek with an inviting sway to her hips. She whispered into his ear. He smirked.

He looked sideways at her, then across the rest of the group lingering a moment on Heather, then back to her. He nodded. "I like the sounds of that." He put his arm around her, they turned and followed the road out of the circle.

The tour guide was distraught, things like this simply did not happen during the tours. "Well, that was... interesting. Uhm... Unless there are further questions for Heather, there is still one more stop on the tour."

He paused for a few moments, but no one had a question. "Good. Then let's head to overlook. It has the most spectacular view of the Danu at any point along the river." He led the tour east, to the tip of the promontory.

Oliver caught Sturm's attention. "What kind of man is Tarek?"

"Tarek is a hired blade George picked up in Sulvi. He was recommended based upon his skills with a blade."

"I hope you're not of his same type."

"Uncle Oli, this one here is different." She gave Sturm a smile. "You were very respectful with your questions. You have quite an interest in the plants."

Sturm nodded. "I'm interested in what they can do. I recently lost my men to poisoned blades in an ambush. With these plants, maybe it would've been different."

Oliver sensed Sturm's sincerity and relaxed.

Heather took Sturm's hand. "I'm so sorry. Plants, even Isatis, are useful only with a few minor natural poisons. The more serious poisons are created by alchemists and must be treated by alchemist means. However, Isatis is very useful for healing wounds. I will get you some of the salve. Don't leave without seeing me, you hear?" With a peck on his cheek she quickly turned, gathered up her cuttings, and ran out the circle towards the village.

Sturm was left staring at her back.

Oliver chuckled. "Well, I guess that's that then. You have your orders for the morrow. In the meantime, would you care to go see the view before the sun sets? Or would you rather just go to the hostel for some food and drink?"

The reminder of his lost men soured Sturm's mood. "All due respect to the view, I'd rather just get something to eat."

Chapter 22: Dancing Bear Hostel, Kunalas, 25th YOC, 16th Day of New Spring, 5 PM

Oliver guided Sturm to a three-story building with a sign of a dancing bear, and circled around to a stable. Sturm checked in on Val and found him groomed and comfortably bedded down in a large paddock. The paddock was clean and smelled of fresh cut grass and herbs. Sturm was tempted to grab his bedroll and join Val. Sturm then realized that his bedroll, and his saddle bags for that matter, weren't there. "Hey, where's my kit?"

Oliver responded, "In your room of course. Come, this way." The two walked around to the hostel's street entrance and into the foyer. It was unattended. There was a desk with a ledger and a bell. Oliver rang the bell sharply.

A couple minutes later, a woman rushed in drying her hands with a dish towel. She looked like a scullery maid with her brown hair tied back, a smudge of flour on her cheek, and a light dusting across her smock. Her face broke into a wide grin when she spotted Oliver.

Oliver grinned back. "Hi sis. May I introduce Kian Terter. He came in with the wizard George. Is his room ready?"

She smiled at Sturm and curtsied. "Pleased to meet you. I am Amber. And yes, we have rooms waiting for each of the three of you." She pulled a key from a pocket and handed it to him. "Yours is on the top floor and to the river side. I hope it will please you."

She turned to her brother. "Oliver, can you show him the way? I'm in the middle of making dinner." She didn't wait for an answer and rushed out the door she came in.

Sturm turned to Oliver. "She didn't mention the cost."

"If I remember right, the room is a small silver and dinner is another three small coppers. You don't have to eat here, but the other public house is more for drink, and I wouldn't recommend it even for that. They serve a green mead that will give you a headache. Come to think of it, you probably don't have to worry about the price. If George is a friend to the Great Druid, I suspect you'll be here as the guest of the Great Druid."

Oliver led Sturm up the stairs to his room. It was small, but well kept. The shutters were open; the view of the river was unobstructed by the cottages between the hostel and the river. Sturm's saddle bags lay on a dressing table, his bedroll on the bed.

Oliver kept Sturm company as he sorted out his things. Oliver was interested in Sturm's travels, and the state of the magic road. Sturm was interested in the village and its people.

Wonderful smells wafted up from the kitchen. Sturm's stomach took notice and growled.

Oliver heard it and grinned. A moment later Oliver's stomach growled as well. "It seems time for dinner."

"Just a second." Sturm unbuckled his sword belt and hung his sword belt over a bed post. He then undid his chainmail coat and dropped it on the bed. "Ah, much better. I've been wearing that for days." Sturm took a moment to stretch his arms and rotate his shoulders. "Now I'm ready."

They went down to the ground floor, to the public room, and chose an unoccupied table. A serving wench appeared, introduced as one of Oliver's cousins. She set mugs and a frosted pewter pitcher of water on the table. After a moment she returned with plates and utensils. Another woman placed steaming platters heaped with fish and greens between the settings.

The frost on the pitcher caught Sturm's eye. He wondered how they chilled the pitcher on such a warm day. Surely there wasn't a wizard hidden away casting cold spells on the pitchers. Then he was distracted by the meal on the platter. Sturm had read stories about the Druids and their odd connection to animals. Eating fish seemed contrary to the stories. Curious, Sturm turned to Oliver to ask but then stopped and waited as Oliver prayed over their food.

Oliver finished and noticed Sturm watching. "What is it?"

"I was just giving you a moment to finish. But I have a question about the dinner."

"May I guess? You wonder about the fish. We get that all the time from visitors. The easiest explanation is we don't eat what we can talk to. We can't talk to fish, so they're fair game."

"You can talk with other animals?"

Oliver nodded, "Yes, it's not such a big thing. People talk to their pets all the time. The pets understand. Have you ever taught a pet a trick?"

"Aye, I have a puppy back home. I've been teaching him things like shaking hands or to fetch a ball. But that's not talking."

"Actually, it is. He's understanding and responding to your words. When he barks, growls, whines, or whatever, he's talking to you. It has meaning, even if all you can do is guess what means. Now, imagine if you did understand."

Oliver paused a moment to let Sturm think on that, then continued. "There are birds who can learn to speak our language. I can see your disbelief, but I'm serious. One is the large mountain raven, another is a brightly colored bird from the jungles of the southern continent. It was one of the ravens who told me of your ride through the forest. As for the other animals who are not as gifted, we craft charms and cast spells to talk with them. These work with the furry critters, many of the birds, even a few reptiles. It doesn't work with fish, or insects for that matter. Good enough?"

Sturm nodded, and piled food onto his plate. Two bites in, he nearly dropped his fork as a bear wandered into the room.

Oliver saw Sturm's eyes widen and turned to see what caused it. He chuckled and waved to the bear. The bear nodded and wandered over to their table.

Oliver scratched around the bear's ear and offered her a piece of fish, which was accepted. Oliver turned to Sturm. "Sir Kian, may I introduce Ms. Fuzzybutt. Our name for her is from when she was a cub. Among bears she's known as 'Mighty Roar'. You don't want to hear my rendition of what that sounds like in bear."

The bear sat down and nodded politely to Sturm.

Oliver turned back to the bear. "Will you be performing tonight?"

She replied with a series of mews, then she leaned towards the fish and sniffed.

Oliver pulled a piece off the platter and tossed it to the bear. "That's too bad, I was looking forward to it. But I don't blame you, keeping up with cubs can be quite a chore. At least they're napping now. Would you care to join us?"

Oliver turned back to Sturm. "Oh, I'm sorry. I suppose we should leave a spot for your unpleasant companion."

"Tarek? No worries there. Though, it would be nice to save George a spot."

"I expect he'll be supping with our Great Druid. They'll have a lot of catching up to do."

Chapter 23: Great Druid's Residence, Kunalas, 25th YOC, 16th Day of New Spring, 5 PM

George waited in the dining room of the Great Druid's residence. It had been years since his last visit, but the room hadn't changed. The walls were adorned with murals of forest scenes. The wooden pillars were carved to appear as trellises with grape vines. A pair of birds chirped from the high rafters of the vaulted ceiling.

An acolyte entered the room. He fussed over George and topped off George's mug. He engaged George in small talk as he laid out two place settings, facing each other, in the middle of the long dining table. The small talk abruptly ended as the Great Druid hurried in. The acolyte bowed his way out.

The Great Druid shook hands with George in greeting, the hearty clasp of long-term friends. "Ah, George! It has been moons since I saw you last! Sorry to keep you waiting, I was healing a lad's broken leg at the far end of the village." He stepped around the table to take his seat.

"Sylas! Good to see you. If you still came to the Tionol meetings, it wouldn't have been so long,"

"Well, that didn't take long. Is that your purpose then, to have me return? George, nothing has changed since last I was there."

"I'm sorry, that's not what brought me here. However, you are needed there..."

Sylas cut George off. "I already know your argument. I've heard it many times before. Yes, we need to stand up for a good cause. And yes, when someone stands up for what's right, they'll need my council and protection. But that protection didn't help the Lord of Tulchow last year, did it. It was his son's accusing look when he assumed his father's seat that I realized I was no longer doing any good."

"You couldn't have helped it. He wasn't an accomplished blade, and I suspect he was betrayed by some of the very people he depended upon for protection."

"He was as good as any other who would stand up." Sylas picked up his mug. "Leave it be. Let's toast to better times, both past and future."

George raised his mug acknowledging the toast. Both men drank to the toast.

The acolyte returned deftly placing a plate of steaming fish and green vegetables in front of each man.   He then returned to his station next to the door.

George set his mug down and resumed the conversation. "Well, perhaps you're right about Lord Tulchow. Then again... One of the men who came with me is a noble over by Vellar."

"I was told about your guards. Is he the one with the little pointy beard?"

"No, the other."

"That's good. I heard complaints about pointy beard. So, what about the other?"

"Remember this name, Sir Kian Terter. There seems to be more to him than most nobles. First off, I think he cares about people. Certainly, he cares about the men he lost in an ambush."

"So? He managed to lose some men in a fight. As much as he cared about them, that's not exactly a glowing recommendation for what we're about."

"My second point is he's quite capable. It was a nasty ambush involving betrayal and poisoned blades. He defeated the ambush, then settled with who set up the ambush."

"So, who was that? Some local bandit leader?"

"No, the Fireguild. He killed one of their wizards."

Sylas let out a low whistle. "The Fireguild? Really? That's impressive. How did you get involved with someone at odds with them? You're normally so cautious, so wary."

"He was protecting Earthguild property."

Sylas set his ale down with a thud, some sloshed onto the table. "What?" After a moment he continued, "What was the Fireguild doing? And with you in the middle of it. George, are you trying to get yourself killed?"

George grinned. "When there is good cause..."

"What is this good cause?"

George pulled the box out of his satchel. He opened it and set it on the table in front of Sylas.

Sylas eyes widened in surprised recognition. "A power stone!"

It was George's turn to be surprised. "How do you know about power stones?"

"Seriously? What do you think the sacred circle is? In any case, I visited Eldrin back when he was restoring Bridgeport. He showed me the remaining power stone there. The stones he created were amazing, but they paled next to the older stone."

Sylas continued while he scrutinized George, hoping for a reaction. "You don't have Eldrin hidden away somewhere making more stones, do you? That would explain why there has been no word of him since the revolution."

"Take another look. This was not made by Eldrin."

Sylas picked up the box and examined the stone at length. "Oh, I see. Another of the older stones, and still with its power. Where did you get it?"

"I heard a rumor out of the desert of buildings oddly untouched by the sands, reminiscent of how Bridgeport was preserved. I went and investigated. When I found this, I was worried others would hear about it and waylay me."

Sylas interjected, "Others? As in the Fireguild?"

George nodded. "I returned by one route, and I sent the stone covertly to Bridgeport via another. I was ignored, but the caravan with the stone was ambushed and the stone momentarily taken. T was Sir Kian's caravan. He retrieved the stone and returned it to me. The ambush showed me my folly. I decided speed was more important than being circumspect. I carried the stone and traveled with Sir Kian and with pointy beard, the head guardsman of House Cathar."

"Then, somehow you ended up here on your way to Bridgeport?"

"Aye. I've only traveled to here riding the river road. I never knew there was a route from the west." He then recounted the details of the journey from Sulvi.

Sylas sat back with his mug in hand as he listened. When George finished, Sylas nodded thoughtfully. "They may yet follow you. So now what?"

"I need to get to Bridgeport."

"You have good timing. Our merchant ship will be leaving with the new day for the coast. A stop along the way at Bridgeport's eastern bridgehead was already planned. You should be safe on the ship; I doubt you would be ambushed mid-river. I'll make sure the boatmen are prepared for you and your horses. In the meantime, I'll keep a guard posted."

"I appreciate it." George finally took a bite of the fish. It had cooled during the discussion, but even so it was every bit as tasty as it smelled.

Chapter 24: Kunalis Docks 25th YOC, 17th Day of New Spring, 8 AM

Sturm stepped out of the hostel, saddlebag over his shoulder, a breakfast biscuit in hand. He looked down the street to the dock. The Druid's 'merchant ship' was really a large barge with a mast. Three men transferred goods from the dock to the deck. Val and the other two horses were in a small corral in the center of the barge.

Sturm heard rapid footsteps behind him. Sturm turned, his hand reflexively went to his sword.

It was Oliver. "Morning Kian, did I give you a start? Sorry! I'm in a rush. Did you have a good sleep?"

"Morning Oliver. I did at that, easy to do with a full belly. I loved the food. I'd take the cook home with me if I could. What did your sister put into the dishes?"

With a wink, Oliver replied. "A secret recipe I will never reveal."

Heather rounded the corner of the hostel, package in hand. She rolled her eyes. "Secret recipe? What, that fish? My goat's ass! And like he would know, never a step into the kitchen. Give me a moment and I'll write it down for you." After a brief hesitation she asked, "You do read, right?"

Laughing, Sturm replied, "I can give it a try. How do you know the secret recipe?"

"It's my mom's place. I help. Hold this. I'll be right back." She shoved the package into Sturm's hands and disappeared inside. Moments later, she reappeared. "Here."

Sturm took the piece of parchment she handed him. He looked at it, then turned it. Looked at it some more, then turned it again.

Heather shifted foot to foot, concerned. "You can't read it?"

A grin tweaked at the corner of Sturm's mouth as he turned it again, and Heather caught on. "Fool!" She punched him on his arm. "Here, give me the package back."

She pulled open one corner of the wrapping and slid out another slip of parchment. "This is a bit different. Can you read it? And no messing around this time!"

Sturm took the parchment and looked it over. He shook his head. "No, I can't. It looks like the script of alchemists. I've seen my godfather write with it. If that's what it is, he should be able to decipher it for me."

"It's the same script. So, your godfather is an alchemist?"

"He dabbles in it."

"What? Alchemy isn't safe to just dabble in. He could blow something up!"

"He dabbles in most things. He's a Gnome, it's what they do."

Heather's eyes widened, her tone turned to excitement, "A Gnome!? That is so cool!"

Sturm mouthed the word 'cool' and looked to Oliver for help. He hadn't heard that one before. He didn't have a chance to ask.

Heather plowed on. "I've always wanted to meet a gnome. What is he like? Do they really wear pointed hats? Are they as short as they say? Do they have long beards? If so, how do they not step on their beards? Do they live under trees? Does he have a Gnome wife? How big are their babies? Do they have any...?"

Oliver cut her off. "Heather! You're not giving Kian a moment to answer, and we don't have time right now. We need to get down to the ship." The two men started walking down to the docks.

Heather followed along, "But I want to know about the Gnomes. Please, Sir Kian, tell me!"

Oliver started to admonish Heather, but Sturm interrupted him. "It's alright Oliver." Sturm then addressed Heather, "I'll try to answer, just take a deep breath after each question to give me the chance. I have two Gnomish godfathers. Neither..."

Heather couldn't contain herself. "Two? Two! Oh, I so have to meet them." She turned to Oliver and continued her tirade. "Uncle Oli, you have got to let me go with you!"

"Heather! We're not taking him home. He's traveling to Bridgeport with his two companions. I don't even know where Kian lives."

Heather quickly turned back to Sturm and asked, "Well, do you live there?"

"No, I live outside Vellar."

"Vellar, the trade city? Oh, no. That's like the other side of the world! But that's where the Gnomes are?" Heather's interrogation was interrupted as the hostel door opened behind them.

Tarek stepped into the street with the woman from the day before hanging on his arm. He tried to disengage, but she pulled herself against him and gave him a full kiss on the mouth. When she was done, she gave him a light shove in the direction of the dock. As he walked down the street, she loudly bid him farewell, possessively watching his departure. As he passed Heather, the woman's satisfied smile turned into a smirk.

Before words could be exchanged, there was shouting from the docks for the passengers to hurry up. Loading was done and the barge was ready to set off.

The four hastened to the barge. Heather nagged Oliver until he allowed her to journey with them on the boat. They gingerly stepped from the wharf to the deck.

The three-man crew sprang into action. Mooring lines were tossed onto the boat, then oars were shoved against the dock. The barge drifted back, out of reach of the dock. Two of the men used their oars to pole the barge further away from the dock and turn the nose down river. The third carried his oar to the rear of the barge and set in into a oarlock. He dipped the blade of the oar into the water and used it to steer.

When the river became too deep for poling, they put their oars into oarlocks on either side of the barge and started rowing with the man closest to the land pulling twice for each pull by the other. The barge moved towards the center of the river, into the main channel. The side oars were then stowed, and a sail was raised on the mast.

They passed a couple of small sailing boats floating in place midstream. The crews waved and exchanged quips about the fishing, and then they were out of earshot.

Heather watched the bank as they passed the promontory of the Great Circle. She clapped her hands and exclaimed. "It's like I'm running, but I'm not even moving my feet!"

Tarek rolled his eyes. "You're kidding, right?"

Heather, her excitement deflated, shook her head.

One of the crew scolded Tarek. "That wasn't nice." His tone turned gentle as he addressed Heather. "Missy, this your first trip on the river then?"

Heather gave him a wounded puppy look and nodded. "It's also my first time away from Kunalas."

"I would have thought your pa had taken you out on the river before he passed, bless his soul. Well, It's alright. You just ignore this outsider. Maybe it's not exciting to him, or maybe he just wants to pretend it's nothing. But you go ahead and enjoy the trip. I'll tell you though, some of this is more fun and exciting than others. It's like the druids teach, there is balance to everything. It's easy heading down, current to our back, but coming back – now that's a whole 'nother story, it is."

"What do you mean?"

"Heading back up, we fight the current every inch of the way. It would be too much for the three of us to pole our way back up from Bridgeport."

"So, what do you do?"

"Mules, to tow the boat upstream." The crewman pointed to the far bank. "Look over there. See the tow road? It stretches the length of the river. Downstream traffic over here, upstream over there. Keep your portside to the center and you stay out of trouble."

"Where do you get the mules?"

"We either bring them, or hire'm."

"But why don't you use magic?"

The man laughed. "We have no magic. I don't know we want any. I heard a story of a Waterwizard once, from maybe a century ago. He didn't have any mules and was too good to pay the toll. He changed the flow behind him to push his boat upstream. Tried, I should say. Messed up the river good he did, fishing wasn't the same for years. Of course, ended up not doing him any good either. The river current from the front and his magic current from behind was too much for his boat, it flipped and broke apart. And that was the end of him."

"You made that up!"

The man at the steering oar broke into the conversation. "No ma'am, he spins a lot of tales. I wouldn't trust how big he says his catch is. But that one's real, though not as old as he says. I was a kid when it happened. Boats went out and rescued a couple of the crew that had managed to swim away. It happened halfway between here and Bridgeport. I can point out the spot when we pass it." He shook his head then continued. "Wizard folk got no sense. We have a system that worked since always, he should have used it."

He pointed at the horses. "That is where we normally have our mules. This trip though, we'll have to pay the tolls. Any one stretch doesn't charge much, but it's a lot of miles and a lot of payments. A copper here and a copper there adds up to a silver or two by the time we're home."

Talk of a Waterwizard had caught George's attention. Talk of the mules caused him to be thoughtful for a moment, then he reached into his belt pouch and pulled out two coins. He stepped over to the man and pressed the coins into the man's hand.

"Eh, what's this? Two silver! No sir, here, take them back. I wasn't looking for charity with my story. I was only wanting the missy to understand the whole of things."

George firmly shook his head. "No, you take them to pay for the return trip pulls. It was not my intent to put the three of you to any hardship by our hopping aboard. It's only fair I pay for your tow back up stream."

The man looked George in the eye, then nodded. "Thank you, sir. If you ever need another boat ride, just look us up. My name is Artem. The storyteller over there is Dima. The quiet one is Jakub – you'll forget he's there but he's a great hand on a boat. Time and again I'll think it's time to do something and he's already doing it."

Jakub smiled and nodded as he went over to a long bench seat on the starboard side.

Artem laughed. "And there he goes again, one step ahead of me. Yes, Jakub it's time to pull out the fishing gear. Bridgeport is always a good market for fresh caught fish, and we should be getting there before the market closes."

As Artem talked, Jakub pulled out a couple of poles, lines with hooks, and a bucket filled with loose dirt and earth worms. The boat had several brackets along the sides. After a moment of consideration Jakob went to the port side and set up the poles there.

Tarek had no interest in folk tales or in fishing poles. He looked around for a comfortable spot to settle in. He decided on a bench near the front of the barge and sat down on it only to be shooed off by Jakub. Tarek protested, "Really? I'm trying to sit, why is that a problem?"

Dima laughed and answered for Jakub. "Sorry friend, but that is our cooler we keep the fish in after we catch them. No one wants to buy stinking fish at market. You can sit over here next to this hay bale. It will make for a good back rest."

Heather interrupted, "My dad never said anything about coolers."

"The coolers are new, since he passed. We fill them with ice from that icehouse the druids built. What was it, last fall?" Getting a nod from Oliver, Dima continued. "Right handy they are. The ice keeps the fish fresh all day."

Sturm was surprised. "Icehouse?"

Oliver responded. "Aye. That's where Heather's 'cool' comment came from. Chilled drinks in summer were 'cool'. Then everything else the kids liked was cool. I have to admit I rather like ice in my tea, though not in my ale. Anyway, the icehouse was an unintended bonus when we built the hot house for a freeze tender tropical crop."

"What does a hot house have to do with an icehouse?"

"Balance. To create a hot house, we also had to create a cold house. Like the wizard of the story, there are consequences to what you do. In this case they've all been good. We have tropical fruit year around, and we have ice year around."

Tarek settled in, his back against the bale. Jakub handed him a wide brimmed straw hat. After eyeing it a moment, Tarek took it and put it on.

Heather returned to the fishing rods. "My dad never took me out fishing, I was too young. I'd like to fish, see what he did all day. Could you show me how it's done?"

Jakub smiled, beckoned her over to one of the poles.

Dima gestured to George. "Would you care to try your hand at fishing?"

George thought a moment, then replied. "Perhaps in a while. I'm more interested in our travel. I've always ridden the land route, so this is all new to me. Perhaps I could trouble Artem to tell me about the river as we go."

Artem responded, "I'd be happy to." George joined Artem at the rear of the boat and they quickly became lost in a discussion on river currents and navigation.

Dima turned to Sturm. "What about you sir?"

"Fishing sounds good." Sturm walked over to Jakub. Oliver joined him.

Dima then turned to Tarek, "And you sir?"

Tarek peered out from under the hat, then shook his head. "I'm a bit haggard from last night. I'll just curl up and take a nap." He pulled the brim of the hat down and made a show of settling in for a nap. Underneath the hat, he listened.

Heather exchanged a look with Oliver and Sturm. Giggling, she mouthed, 'I bet.' They did their best not to laugh.

Along the port rail Jakub patiently showed the three landlubbers how to bait their hooks and get the line in the water without losing the worm. He warned them to make sure to not cross their lines as they set their poles into the brackets.

As they fished, Heather's curiosity over Sturm returned. "So... What is it like, living in a big city with your Gnome godfathers?"

Tarek had been nodding off, but now he perked up. He had little interest in the prattling of the barge crew, but anything he learned about George's guard may prove useful.

Sturm replied, "Actually, I live outside the city."

"Oh, on a farm?"

"It's more of a group of farms."

Oliver sat next to them removing the hook from a fish he had pulled in. He joined the conversation. "You're a noble, yes? So, the group of farms are your estate?"

Sturm nodded. "Yes, I live in the manor house. Next to it is the horse barn. A hamlet and fields surround it. There are a couple of outlying steadings where we have an orchard and a vineyard."

Oliver tossed the fish into the cooler, then turned back to Sturm. "What do you grow?"

"The hamlet has garden plots with beans, squash, and root vegetables. There are nearby fields that have lain fallow for years. We're clearing them to plant grain. Gnomes have settled in at the orchard and vineyards. The trees are mainly apples and walnuts along with a few hazelnuts. The vineyard had gone wild, but the gnomes are tidying it up. The grapes are a sweet red grape good for eating or wine. By fall, we expect to have excess harvest to take to market. That will be a first for us."

"Sounds like life there isn't so different than here. No livestock?"

"Just a small sheep herd."

Heather interrupted, "How many Gnomes do you live with?"

"I'm not quite sure. New faces keep popping up each time I return home."

"What? Really?"

"Perhaps, I had better start at the beginning." Getting nods, Sturm recounted the story he and Gnomes had created a decade ago. "Some time ago the Terter family lost their estate. I don't really know the details; it was before my time. When I was old enough, I went to the Academy at Socul. About all a knight without lands can expect is what he earns with his sword. When I graduated, I became a caravan guard. I've done well. I took my earnings and bought back the family estate. The buildings were in ruins, the fields overgrown." Sturm paused. The half-truths had been pasted together to protect him from who had sent his mother's executioner, and that executioner was within ear shot on the other side of the boat. Still, he felt bad for misleading Oliver and Heather.

Heather prompted, "So, how did you meet the gnomes?"

"First there were Gwiz and Gnumph. They were friends of my mother and are my godfathers. They've taken care of me after she passed. As for the other gnomes, well, they aren't welcomed in most places. My estate is a safe haven for them. Word spread. So now there continually are new faces. The effect on the estate is amazing. Every time I return home another building is repaired, or a new field is cleared. Some are skilled craftsmen: potters, carvers, and even a tinker."

"So, you live alone except for your godfathers?"

Tarek perked up again. His eyes had been drooping with listening to all the mundane farm details. Perhaps Sir Terter will reveal how many troops he had.

"Well, I have Mira."

"Oh, is that your girlfriend?"

Laughing, Sturm replied, "No, that's my puppy. And it's a he, not a she. You'd love him, he's a big ball of white fur. He looks like a bear cub. Chairs go flying as he runs across the room when we're playing. I'm trying to train him to save the furniture, but I'm not around enough. I have to spend a lot of time with the caravans."

That was when Tarek gave up on gleaning anything useful and gave into sleep.

Chapter 25: River Danu north of Bridgeport, 25th YOC, 17th Day of New Spring, 5 PM

The boat rounded a bend, and they had their first sight of Bridgeport. The city was an island, situated out of catapult range of either bank. The city was heavily fortified with three tiers of defenses. The lowest tier was at the upriver end. Five massive towers connected by 50-foot walls jutted up out of the water like the prow of a ship, splitting the river current to either side of a sheltered harbor. Each end of the row of towers was connected to the island by a gate house, with gates large enough to allow a merchant ship entry. The upper tiers were built to the same scale. A middle tier overlooked the harbor then circumnavigated the island on sheer cliffs rising from the water, defending the island from approach in any direction, including the harbor. The highest tier was on the island peak, on the back half of the island. Its towers overlooked the middle of the walls between the towers of the second tier.

Just downstream of the city was the bridge the city was named for. The span apexed 100 feet above the water, where it had a short cross connection to a city gate in the upper tier of the defenses. Each end of the bridge was set on a hill topped by a small castle. There was a village accompanying each castle, with a path down to wharfs on the river.

As the barge drifted abeam of the harbor gates, the vessels within were revealed: several barges; a hand of large versions of the lateen rigged caravels that plied the river; and two odd, square rigged, ships sporting a wooden tower at the prow and stern.

Sturm called out to Dima, "What are those? The ships with the tower at each end."

Dima looked to where Sturm pointed. "They call'em warships but they're just cogs with towers added on. They belong to the custom house and patrol between here and Venub. Not very good ships if you ask me. There's not enough sail for their weight, so they're as slow as a barge. The added weight also makes them sit low in the water giving them a deeper draft that gets them stuck if they stray from the main channel. But the towers sure look impressive, don't they?"

"Hey, we're going past the harbor. We're not going in?"

Dima shook his head. "If we went in there we wouldn't be out until morning."

"So how do we get in? And don't you have to pay a toll?"

"Well pull into the dock on the shore. You can take the road from the wharf."
Dima pointed out the road to Sturm.

Artem, as if taking a cue from Dima, leaned on the steering oar and the boat
turned towards the docks on the shore.

Dima continued, "There we go, heading that way now. So, the custom house is
at the wharf." Dima gestured towards a building flying a pennant with a balance
scale as its device. "We'll tie up for a bit, the custom's man will come to visit. The
druids don't have to pay a toll. So, all I'll have to do is share a drink with him. In
the meantime, Artem and Jakub will take the fish up to the market near the
bridgehead. They'll sell the catch there and buy dinner. Then we'll be on our way
in just an hour or two."

George interjected, "You'll not stay the night here?"

"No point to it. We'd have to sleep in shifts on the boat to protect our cargo. If
we're going to do that, might as well make time down river. The main channel is
marked with glowstone buoys. We'll be to Venub by morning."

"Very well then. Kian, Tarek, make sure you have all your equipment, and your
horses are ready to be led off the boat."

The next several minutes, the crew had no time to talk as they guided the barge
to the dock and tied it up.

George, Sturm and Tarek led their horses off the barge to the road and then
walked them up the hill to the market at the intersection of the road they were on,
the caravan route running southeast to Venub, the courier route to the east, and a
road to the bridgehead castles to the west. Oliver, Heather, and the two bargemen
carrying the cooler followed.

The market was a crossroads where a village had grown. The road from the
wharf to the northwest met the caravan route running southeast, the courier route
to the east, and the road to the bridge head castle to the west. The market was
busy with customers from Bridgeport mingling with vendors from up and down the
river.

George led his horse to a hitching post and lashed his reins to it. Sturm and
Tarek followed suit. George motioned to Sturm. "Go say your goodbyes, I need to
talk with Tarek a moment." Sturm bowed and walked over to where Dima and
Jakub had set down the cooler.

George pulled a folded letter from his pouch. "Tarek, I have something for you."
He handed it to Tarek.

"What's this?"

"It's the letter of completion, freeing funds for you to get paid when you return to House Cathar. Thank you for your service. It's too late for you to travel, so let me cover your night's stay here." George handed Tarek a couple of silver coins, enough for several nights' lodgings.

Tarek accepted the letter and coin, bowing with his best manners. "Thank you, milord. Where would there be a good pint along with the bed?"

George pointed to a two-story building in the village. "That's the hostel. They have beds, food, and ale. I hope you find the ale to your liking."

"Surely there are better establishments than that in the city."

"I'm sorry Tarek, but visitors are not allowed in."

Tarek eyed a young couple walking through the gate onto the bridge. He looked at the wagons further up the bridge. "What about them? Or the wagons?"

"Perhaps they live in Bridgeport or perhaps they're crossing to the other side. You can also cross the bridge, but you won't be allowed to turn into the city. That's just how it is."

Tarek was disappointed, there was a bounty for descriptions of the interior of Bridgeport. He allowed the disappointment to creep into his tone. "I would have enjoyed seeing the city. Perhaps another time. I hope you'll ask for me, should you need a guard again."

While George and Tarek were occupied, Sturm joined Dima and Jakub. Jakub took Sturm's offered hand and shook it with a smile and a wink.

Dima also shook Sturm's hand, but had to say a few words, "Quite the city, isn't it? Don't know that I'd be wantin' to spend much time in it. I'm used to the open river. I'd feel cramped and be afraid I'd get lost. Ah, anyway, I enjoyed our fishing. Hope you make it back to see us in Kunalas sometime. Take care!" Dima slapped Sturm on the shoulder. Dima motioned to Jakub, and they picked up the cooler and carried it over to an open market stall.

Oliver stepped up to shake hands with Sturm. "A pleasure. I hope we meet again. Safe travels." He motioned to Heather that it was her turn.

She hung back, pouting.

Oliver admonished her, "What ails you? Say bye to Kian, and let's take a look at the market before it closes."

"But, Uncle Oli, I really don't want to say bye yet."

"Well, the boat isn't staying the night so neither are you."

Sturm interposed, "Heather, it was a pleasure meeting you, but I don't want to deprive you of a wander through the market. You've never seen one."

Heather managed a weak smile. "You'll remember all I told you about the salve? Get that godfather of yours to read you the directions?"

"Yes ma'am."

"I really enjoyed the day with you. I hope you'll come back to Kunalas someday."

Oliver chuckled. "You mean like in two years?"

Sturm was confused. "Two years? What's in two years?"

Heather looked down and blushed. After a moment she tossed her hair defiantly as she looked up, then curtsied. "In two years, I'm of age, thank you much. And yes, if you come then, I just might let you court me." Heather suddenly turned and ran to the bargemen.

Oliver and Sturm grinned at each other. The shared grin disappeared as Tarek joined them.

"So, we're no longer in Kunalas. That means that oath thing is done, yes?"

Something in Tarek's tone made Oliver wary as he replied, "Yes, it ended a while ago as we left sight of Kunalas. Why?"

"The laws here are different. She's of age here. There are fifteen-year-olds with husbands and babies here."

"That's still not our way. In any case, she's not interested."

"She says that now, but I have a way with women. They always end up saying yes."

Anger crept into Oliver's voice, "Tarek, I don't know why you insist on this. Let it go. Leave her alone!"

Tarek grinned, his tone had a dangerous edge to it, "What are you going to do about it?"

"I don't think you'll like seeing what a druid can do!"

From behind Tarek, Sturm added, "I know you won't like what I'll do."

A cold tingle went down Tarek's spine. He hadn't noticed Sturm slip behind him. The kid was good. Tarek stepped forward past Oliver, then turned around to address both of them. "I guess she won't be here long enough for it to matter. "

Sturm locked eyes with him. "No, she won't."

Tarek abruptly turned and walked to his horse. He undid the reins from the hitching post and walked it over the village tavern, never looking back.

Oliver sighed with relief. "Thanks Kian. Fools like Tarek don't realize what a druid can do. That can start trouble which can rapidly get out of hand."

"No problem. It really wasn't about her. I don't think he was even really trying to start a fight. He was testing you. But next time it might be different. A word of advice for that next time, don't let an armed man so close to you if he's not your friend."

Oliver was taken back. "Why is that?"

"He can kill you before you can blink. Keep him beyond weapons reach and you have the advantage."

Oliver realized it was sound advice. Oliver was a powerful druid, but he had never been in a fight and had never thought on the reality of it. "I will keep that in mind."

Oliver pulled out a small wood carving on a thong. "As my thanks, let me gift you this token. Please, take it." Oliver took Sturm's hand and placed the carving into it. It was of a dog. "This will help you train Mira. Hold it in one hand while you pet him with the other. Think how much you love him. Then wear it anytime you are around him. When you want him to do something, concentrate on it, visualize what you want him to do. He will understand what you want. Likewise, you will also come to understand what he is telling you."

Sturm closed his hand around the charm. "Thank you. This means a lot to me. I'm sorry I have no gift in return."

"My friend, your advice was gift enough. It may save my life someday. I consider you druid friend. There is always a place for you at my table."

George walked up and held out his hand to Oliver. "It was great meeting you Oliver. Take good care of my friend Sylas."

"Of course. Nice meeting you as well. I should see to Heather. Take care all!"

George walked Strum back to the horses, then addressed Sturm. "So, still interested in learning Earthmagic?"

"Of course."

"Well then, let's go into the city. I hope you are prepared to study for quite a while. It's not easy to learn the basics, let alone to master magic. For some it takes years and for others it never happens."

Sturm bowed. "I will do my best." He was betting on a couple of ten day at most.

George unhitched his horse and led it to the gate. Sturm quickly unhitched Val, caught up, and walked at George's side. At the gate, the guards came to attention, and saluted. George nodded and they walked past the guards, through the gateway.

Sturm noted the stout defenses. The thick doors were 10 foot tall and reinforced with steel. The stone walls were several feet thick. As they passed through, Sturm realized this wasn't a castle, rather just a frontage. Even the tower at each corner was open at the back. Sturm queried George. "No walls on the backside?"

"No need for them. Come to the side of the bridge here. See how we're already over the water? No one is going to climb up behind the gate. Walls on the bridge side only make it harder to retake it, if we ever have to." George motioned for Sturm to continue up the bridge.

Sturm was struck by the enormity of it: an island turned into a city, the massive fortifications, a bridge that was a mile long. "Who built this?"

George shrugged, "We don't know. Our guild founder, Eldrin, discovered the city abandoned by man, though not by beast. It took some time to clear out what laired here. You're a trained warrior, surely you read of our heroes in the histories?"

"No sir, I never heard of any of this."

"No? I suppose they've purged the stories since so many of the heroes were MacMer clan, king's men. I suggest you look them up in our library, I think you'll find them interesting. There is also the story of how Eldrin repaired and remodeled the city and of his trials as the stone resisted him."

Sturm interrupted George, "Resisted?"

"The bridge and the city had magic in their stone, preserving them which also prevented modification until you learned the trick of it. It was different from any magic Eldrin had come across. He spent years studying it. When he was done, he had come to understand the nature of stone and magic in stone. He started teaching others and the guild was born."

"Eldrin did all that? I've not heard of him either. How long ago was that?"

"A couple of centuries, when the country was a kingdom, and the kingdom yet young." George leaned close to Sturm. "That story and the stone you protected are intertwined. There had been several such stones to cover such a large area. Only one still functioned when Eldrin discovered them. He studied them and learned how to create more stones, but his were nowhere as powerful or as enduring as the original. The one you saved is another ancient power stone, found in a land far to the west. I was excited when I found it. Yes, it would be useful in keeping the city and bridge strong but think what else we can do with it. Handling it those few moments during our trip..." George trailed off lost in memory of the power he had wielded.

After a moment George came back to the present and continued. "We normally don't allow outsiders into our city. That is why I turned Tarek away. We do make an exception for those we bring in as apprentices and for people proven to be friends to the Earthguild. You are both of those. So, come." George motioned Sturm on.

They continued to the apex of the bridge, where they stopped to catch their breath. Sturm took the moment to gawk at the view. He could see down river to where it branched into a delta.

George nudged him. It was time to go into the city.

The connection between bridge and city gate was fifty foot long. Immediately in front of the gate, the span was a drawbridge. Guards within the gate tensed as the two stepped onto the drawbridge. The guards recognized George, but they questioned him about his companion. It took George several minutes to convince them that Sturm was his apprentice, and the guards let them pass.

The guard sergeant watched George and Strum entered the gatehouse. He had served at the gate for 30 years, since before the revolution. Not once in that time had he seen a warrior brought in to be an apprentice.

Chapter 26: Bridgeport, 25th YOC, 17th Day of New Spring, 6 PM

George led Sturm down the passage that ran the length of the gatehouse, leaving the waning evening sunlight for the light of glowstone lanterns. Behind the gate house was a courtyard that was also an intersection. In the center was a fountain. A stable was to the left. Two story houses lined both sides of the roads. Glowstones hung from each doorway and paved the bottom of the fountain's holding pool.

Sturm looked up, holding a hand up to block the glowstones' glare from his eyes. He saw the roofs merge into a ceiling that arced overhead. It was darkly painted as a night sky. He looked closely at the buildings. They were not built from blocks of stone, rather they were carved out of the stone. Likewise, the road was carved from stone, with just enough texture to provide good footing. Sturm wondered if the stable stalls were also of stone. He didn't want Val to have to sleep on a stone floor.

Sturm's examination was interrupted as two horse handlers came out from the stable and met them. One greeted George's horse as if they were old friends. He quickly led the horse into the stable. The other came to Sturm and held out his hand. "Milord, if I may?"

Sturm handed over the reins and then followed them in. He was relieved to see the floor of the stalls had a layer of dirt and straw. He was further relieved as the handler assured him that he could see Val every day. He was advised of areas on top of the city where he could walk Val, or he could take Val down the bridge and exercise Val along either riverbank.

Saddlebags over their shoulders, George led Sturm to the fountain. He gestured to the statue in the fountain. "These statues serve as guides through the city. No two fountains have the same statue, and the statue faces towards the most direct route to the gate. Directions through the city are usually given from fountain to fountain."

Sturm dutifully took note of the statue. It was of a man in robes with a staff standing proudly. It had a plaque with a single word, 'Eldrin'.

George moved on. He stopped at the next intersection to give Sturm a chance to note the statue. This one was of a maiden sitting at the feet of another who was gesturing back the way they had come. The plaque read 'Twin Maidens'.

On they went, past several more plazas each with a fountain and a named statue pointing back the way they had come. Finally, they came to a cul-de-sac. The statue in the fountain was simply a large rock that glowed with changing colors. The wall on the far side of the cul-de-sac was carved as if it had vines twining around a massive stone door.

George walked to the door, laid his hand on the stone next to it. After a couple of muttered words, the door opened. He gestured Sturm in.

They entered a main hall worthy of a manor house. A chandelier hung in the center, with a multitude of small sparkling glowstones. Sconces with bright glowstones lined the walls. More subdued stones were on tables and stands scattered across the hall. Tapestry rugs ran down the center, their scenes beckoning to the back of the room.

People were gathered around a fireplace at the far end of the hall. They waved and shouted to George, welcoming him home. George took Sturm's elbow and walked him down the length of the hall to join the crowd.

George introduced Sturm, then George was surrounded and pummeled with questions about his trip. George tried to answer them all as he also arranged for food and a room for Sturm.

Sturm only half listened. He stared at the fireplace. The fire gave no heat, it was a glowstone that flickered as if was a fire. He had been around Gwiz's glow stones his entire life, but had never known how varied they could be, how beautiful.

George interrupted Sturm's reverie. He led Sturm through a side door, then up a spiral stairway. They climbed past several landings before George stopped. "Ah, here we are. This will be your home while you are here. I must go and put our stone away and provide a report to the guild leaders. That includes advising them of my new apprentice. Your dinner will be brought up shortly. You can explore as you please, just don't get lost. I will come by early tomorrow to start with your training. Have a good night."

With that, Sturm was alone.

He eyed his quarters. It was a single large room. A bed was to one side. Opposite it was a window with a desk placed to catch the light.

Sturm stepped to the desk and dropped his saddlebag over the back of the chair. He looked out the window and was transported from the city. Twenty feet below him were green fields and gardens. A couple walked leisurely arm in arm down a path. They stopped for a moment in discussion, followed by woman's laughter. Beyond them was the western branch of the river. To Sturm's right, the bridge curved down to the western bank. A breeze blew in.

He stood enjoying the breeze and the view. He mulled over what he had seen of the city. It was so unlike any other he'd seen.

Part 4: Just Rewards

Chapter 27: East Bridgehead Village, 25th YOC, 18th Day of New Spring, 7 AM

Tarek was up early the morning after his dismissal. He left his bedmate without waking her. His goodbye was a silver coin left on the nightstand. The coin was enough for several nights of play, though they only had the one. He didn't leave so much out of generosity; he wanted her to not forget their arrangement. Guards often talked to the women they slept with, he wanted to know what they said to her. The information may prove far more profitable than a few silver coins.

He didn't dally in the village. He had to report on his failure, that the stone had safely made it to Bridgeport. The first step in that failure had been the ambush of his caravan, sidetracking the stone from being delivered to him. Tarek needed to find out more which meant he needed to visit his trademaster in Barzan, before reporting in at Sulvi.

He rode hard, using the courier route. He bypassed Sulvi and pressed on down the caravan route. Entering Barzan, Tarek went straight to the Cathar compound. The gate was closed.

He dismounted and rang the bell hanging next to the gate.

After a few moments he heard shouting from the other side of the wall. "Just a moment, just a moment. I'll be right there."

The moments dragged. Tarek reached to ring the bell again when the peep hole on the door opened.

Bili peered out. "Master Tarek! Well hello, what brings you here? Hold on and I'll unbolt the door."

After a couple of clanks, the door swung open. Bili held the door for Tarek to lead his horse through.

In the courtyard, Tarek looked around. He snapped at Bili, "Where's Jurik? I need to talk with him."

"Jurik? Oh, I guess you wouldn't know. Sir Kian was here, oh, a ten day ago. He told Jurik that he was fired. So Jurik left."

"Jurik just took his word on it?"

Bili pointed to a scar in the wood of the door frame at head height. "That and the dagger that suddenly sprouted there next to his ear. That kind of persuaded him."

Tarek snorted and shook his head. "Where did he go?"

"I don't know. I haven't seen him since. My first guess would be his favorite tavern. Need directions?"

Tarek gave Bili a long look. The pleasant smile on Bili's face convinced him Bili wasn't being flip, just attempting to be helpful. Tarek let it go. "No, I've met him there before."

Tarek led his horse back out the door. Bili stared at his back a moment, shrugged, then closed and secured the door.

Chapter 28: The Oasis Tavern, Barzan, 25th YOC, 18th Day of New Spring, 8 AM

Tarek tied his horse up to the hitching post in front of the tavern and flipped a copper to the bouncer at the door. The man knew him and knew to watch his horse.

Tarek stopped just inside the door. He let his eyes adjust to the dark interior, then surveyed the room. There were only three patrons, already deep in their cups. Tarek walked over to the bar.

The barkeep looked up and smiled. "Tarek! It's been a while. Your usual?"

"Aye, I've been looking forward to it. It'll clear the road dust from my throat."

The barkeep made a show of pouring the ale into the clear glass mug, a bit of foam flowed over the edge and onto the bar top.

Tarek pulled out a small copper coin and let it fall to the bar next to the mug, then took his drink. After a couple of deep gulps, he set the drink back down. "Ah, that hit the spot. Say, my man Jurik was to join me. Have you seen him?"

The barkeep looked hard at Tarek a moment, then shrugged. "Jurik was last here a tenday ago, after he got tossed from his job with Cathar. Aren't you Cathar? What more do you want with him?"

Tarek decided to play nice. The barkeep was the only contact he still had in Barzan. "I didn't toss him. That Terter guy did, and he over stepped. I'm going to straighten it out. I need to tell Jurik."

"Oh, well in that case, yeah I know where he's at. He's camping outside of town. He's afraid to come into town in case Terter shows up again. He still likes his ale though."

The barkeep took a moment to look around. He spotted one of the kids he used as a runner. "Hey, Peylo, over here."

The boy ran up and bowed.

The barkeep lowered his voice. "Could you take this gentleman to see Jurik?"

The boy warily eyed Tarek then answered, "Yes, boss."

The barkeep nodded at Tarek. "There you go. Care to take a jug with you?"

Tarek chuckled; the barkeep didn't miss a chance for coin. "Sure, what is it, six pence?" Getting a nod in reply, Tarek pulled out the six small copper coins and set them on the bar.

The bar tender scooped them up. Moments later a full travel jug sat in front of Tarek.

Tarek nodded his thanks, then slid two more pence across the bar. "Here, have one yourself." Tarek motioned to the boy. "All right, let's go."

The boy was on foot, so Tarek also walked, leading his horse. The boy led him out the west gate and then south. They ended up at Jurik's campsite beside a stream. It was a pleasant spot under trees. The trees provided shade and also broke up the smoke of Jurik's small firepit.

The boy shouted out to Jurik and waved.

Jurik looked up and replied warmly to the boy, then noticed the man leading a horse. He tensed up, but relaxed when he recognized Tarek. "Oh, it's you. For a moment there I thought... Well, never mind that. What brings you here?"

"We need to talk. Best in private, I think."

Jurik nodded. "Peylo, thanks for bringing my friend. You need to run back to the tavern now, no delay. Right?"

Peylo hesitated. He looked back and forth between the two men. Tarek pulled out a copper coin and tossed it. Peylo plucked it out of the air, grinned, then sprinted away.

Tarek untied the jug from his saddle horn. He held it up for Jurik to see.

Jurik's eyes lit up and he smacked his lips. "Thank you master Tarek, for thinking of me. What can Jurik do for you?"

Tarek grinned as they sat down near the fire pit. He uncorked the jug, took a swig, then handed it to Jurik. "Well, first you can tell me what happened. Why aren't you over in the Cathar offices minding our mutual business?"

Jurik took the jug with a grimace, "Oh, that." He took a swig. "One of the mercenary captains came marching in, that Sir Kian Terter. He told me Lady Cathar had sent him and I was done. He was in charge of the caravan that got ambushed, so I knew he was under contract to her. He was mighty pissed off about all that. I didn't think it wise to argue with him."

Tarek knew Jurik was holding back a lot of details. It didn't surprise him, but it did irritate him. Tarek prodded, "You were scared of him."

Jurik flinched and looked away. "Er, no. Of course not. But I couldn't take the chance he was actually there on Lady Cathar's orders, could I?"

Tarek hid his disgust. Jurik was weak. Tarek had used that to intimidate Jurik. That plus silver coin was how Tarek had always counted on Jurik's behavior. Now he saw it was also a vulnerability someone else could use. He realized Jurik was no longer dependable. Tarek forced a chuckle. "I guess not." He held his hand out for the jug. "Was that after the caravan ambush or after the meet?"

"After the meet. Wait, how did you...?"

Tarek took a swig to hide his disdain. "I was with Lady Cathar when Terter returned from the meet, though I need clear up a few things."

"Sure, boss. What do you need?"

Tarek handed the jug back to Jurik. "First, why was the caravan ambushed? That wasn't the plan going in."

Jurik took a quick swig. "Well, I was talking with Rafe. He asked me about the special box delivery coming through. He knew all about it, so I thought we were working together again."

"Did it dawn on you that we don't normally ambush our own caravans?"

"Hey, that was before I knew about the ambush. When I found out, I told Rafe I didn't like it, it was bad business. He told me not to worry about it, the Fireguild was running things and that was that. I figured you were in on it."

"So, you don't know who was sent on the ambush? How many men were used?"

Jurik replied around taking another swig. "Nope."

"How did Terter set up the meet?"

"He walked into my office with a story of having the box and was willing to sell it. He was pissed about the ambush, and that made it expensive. He wanted a hundred gold for it. He gave me a time and place."

As much as Tarek was getting tired of hearing about Terter this and Terter that, he had to give the kid credit for brains. He'd suckered in not just Jurik but Rafe and a sorceress as well. "Go on."

Jurik took another swig from the jug, then set it down between them. "I told Rafe. That's all, I wasn't part of the meet."

"Why weren't you at the meet?"

"What? Then I'd be dead to."

Tarek suppressed a laugh. The thought crossed his mind that he'd prefer that Jurik had gone instead of Rafe. Rafe had been a good one to work with. "You didn't answer my question."

"Sorry, boss. Rafe told me it was Fireguild business and best if I stayed out of it. Seemed like sound advice."

"You know where it happened?"

"Yeah. The Lancour orchard. Old man Lancour found the bodies in his orchard a couple days after. He sent for the guard. They went out with a wagon and brought the bodies back."

"Did you see the bodies?" After Jurik nodded, Tarek prodded, "Well, what did you see?"

"Let me think. They were piled in a wagon, a real mess. There was Rafe. And then there was a woman. She wore some fancy, bright colored robes. There were also four men in armor."

Tarek prompted him. "What kind of armor?"

"Uhm... Heavy plate armor, real fancy like what the horsemen regulars from Ai wear."

"Were they from Ai?"

"I don't know. Maybe. They were 23rd. Isn't the 23rd in Ai?"

"You sure it was the 23rd?" The last Tarek knew, the 26th was in Ai.

Jurik nodded. "I counted the lines on the unit patch, two and three."

"Could you tell what had happened to them?"

"Well... Wolves had gotten to Rafe and the woman, so no for them. The soldiers... One was missing his helmet and his head was chewed up, so no for him as well. Two had a lot of dried blood down a lower leg, and the chain on the back of their knee looked parted. Maybe a sword cut?"

"And the last one?"

"Hm. He had a blood stain down his side. Couldn't see for sure, his arm was laid tight to his body, but I'd guess a cut to the armpit."

"Yes, that must have been it." Tarek felt like shouting with relief to finally get details out of Jurik, but after a moment the ramifications settled in, and he was very displeased.

Jurik could see Tarek getting upset. "Hey boss, what's that matter? Something I said?"

Tarek shook his head. "No. I was just thinking about what it meant. I'm wondering if Terter just walked up and sliced up the lot of them like they were nothing. That is not a pleasant thought."

Jurik's eyes got big. He took a long deep swig from the jug. "Wow. Yeah. I guess it was a good thing I didn't try to tangle with him, huh?"

Tarek paused a moment. Tarek's patience with Jurik was done. Jurik's usefulness was done. He stood up, forcing a smile. "Yeah, it was smart. I need to go now. Thanks for your help."

Jurik scrambled to his feet. "No problem boss. So, what now? Can you get me a job somewhere?"

Tarek patted Jurik on the shoulder with his right hand, and drew him close, while still smiling. "Don't worry, I have plans for you."

Jurik returned the smile, then a surprised look crossed his face. He looked down. Tarek had used his left hand to gut Jurik with a dagger.

Tarek pulled the dagger out and stepped back. Blood soaked Jurik's shirt as he slumped to his knees, then fell over. Tarek wiped his blade off on Jurik's pant leg, then returned it to its hidden sheath up his sleeve.

Tarek thought a moment. If he wanted to use that barkeep as his eyes in Barzan, it was best the body wasn't found, at least not while it could still be recognized.

While the corpse bled out, Tarek gathered up Jurik's things, and put them in a saddle bag. He searched the body. The only things on it that might identify Jurik was the belt pouch and boots. Tarik stripped them off and added them to the saddle bag. Then he threw the corpse over his saddle. He poured what was left in the jug over the blood, then kicked dirt and leaves over the puddle. He tossed the jug into the campfire, then kicked dirt over it as well.

Tarek took his horse's reins. He headed to a remote spot where the scavengers would take care of the body.

Chapter 29: Bridgeport, 25th YOC, 25th Day of New Spring, 11 AM

Sturm sat in his room. Esmeralda, George's journeyman, sat with him running him through drills. She was a tall blonde from Ostlig, on the east side of the Danu. Sturm liked her and her green eyes made him think of his mother's, even though they were lighter and didn't change shade with mood.

The window was open to let in fresh air. The window also let in the sounds from the gardens and the port, distracting Sturm. Strum was bored, so it didn't take much to distract him. They had given him a thin spell book with only five very basic spells: fix a crack in stone, cause a crack, strengthen stone, weaken stone, and make a stone glow. They put him through repeated drills using only the fix a crack spell.

Sturm had hoped to gain so much more from this. He knew the basics before he came. As for the spell, it was what George had used on Hemanji's glass. Having watched George do it, it was easy for Sturm follow the directions in the spell book to replicate it. It was also easy for Sturm to reverse the spell and had mastered it the first evening after his lessons.

Esmeralda brought Sturm's focus back to his practice. "Kian. I know this is tedious, but you are doing so well."

Sturm caught Esmeralda's eyes. She smiled and nodded encouragement. She had to be every bit as bored as Sturm, but she always had a smile. Sturm took a deep breath and made a show of focusing on the stone in his hands, looking into its structure and feeling the fracture inside. Then he summoned a trickle of magic force, leisurely shaped it, then released it into the crack causing the stone to meld back together.

George interrupted them with lunch, a tray of food and a cool pitcher of water. He set the tray down, then settled next to Sturm. "So, how goes the studies? What do you think Esmeralda, will he be ready to progress to the second spell soon?"

"He is very dedicated and has worked very hard. Yes, he is ready. Care to make a bet on how long it takes him to learn it?"

"Careful what you wager. Let's see, it took him only half a ten day to learn the first one, so another half for the second spell."

"I was thinking more like before the day is done."

"What? That fast?"

She looked over to Sturm. "Think I have the right of it?"

Sturm nodded.

George reached over to one of the remaining rocks with cracks and set it down in front of them. "Good, show me what you've got."

Sturm smiled. With a quick summoning of magic, the crack in the stone disappeared. As George was complimenting him, the crack reappeared, then disappeared and reappeared repeatedly. On the fourth time the stone disintegrated, the pieces glowed.

George and Esmeralda sat dumbfounded staring at the stone pieces. After a long moment, George looked up at Sturm. "It appears I need to apologize for the pace of your instruction. Most that we teach are young, and it would take them many tendays to learn how to fix the first crack, and several more ten days to repeat it without fail. I should have realized you would not need all the drills to create the discipline needed for consistent casting. What of the other initiate's spells?"

"Give me a couple more rocks and I'll do them for you."

"Ah... Well... You have certainly outgrown the initiate's book. I will find you an apprentice book before the end of day."

"That would be great!"

George continued in a different vein, "What are your expectations here? Your plans?"

"Well, I need to learn what I can, then get back to Vellar. My godfathers will want to know what happened to me, I need to put my caravan guard company back together, and there are things I need to do back on my estate." In his mind Sturm added, 'Including my promise to Gnump about that spider'.

"How long do you think it takes to master magic?"

"I have no idea. Why?"

"Esmeralda started when she was eleven and is but twenty now. I expect she will test for master at the end of the summer. Its extraordinary how fast she's come up to master level." He patted Esmeralda on the arm. "Don't blush like that. I'm only saying the truth." He turned back towards Sturm. "So, for her, a decade to get to the master test. Even then, few pass it the first try."

"I don't have that long. Perhaps, since I'm already an adult, it won't take so long?"

"Well, for your sake, I hope so. Have you thought more about what you may be facing when you return home?"

"You mean with the Fireguild?"

George nodded.

Sturm continued. "I don't really know what will happen. A lot depends on if they know I killed their sorceress. If they don't, then I'm just some guy who did his job guarding a shipment."

"So, perhaps you have nothing to worry about and you can just go back to business as normal?"

"I certainly have to go back to looking like business as normal. Meanwhile, I need to build up as strong of a position as I can. Even if the Fireguild isn't coming after me because of the sorceress, there will be something else sooner or later. They take what they want, they kill who they don't like, and they make it legal under the guise of the council. Yeah, there will be something else, you can bet on it."

George nodded. "Echoes of my words. Well, I guess time is wasting then. Let me go find that spell book for you. Enjoy the rest of your meal. Eat it all, stock up on energy, advanced casting will take it out of you."

Chapter 30: Bridgeport, 25th YOC, 25th Day of New Spring, Noon

George stepped out of the room and quietly closed the heavy door behind him. He turned around and was startled by a tall man in dark grey robes who stepped from the next room. George bowed deeply. "Master! Were you listening in?"

The man was tall and slim with the first streaks of grey in his shoulder length brown hair. He shook his head in mock rebuke. "Master? Really? I may have taught you the craft, but we have been friends for two centuries, and you have been a master in your own right for most of it."

"I know Eldrin, but I respect you and you are the guild master. It is only proper. But back to the question, did you hear?"

"Yes, I did. I am curious about this man. A warrior who is interested and even talented in magic. This doesn't happen very often. When is does, the guild laws require the warrior to lay down his sword." He shrugged. "Making it a law doesn't make sense n all cases, even if the general practice does. Years of study in a wizard tower is at odds for them to keep their melee skills honed and their bodies combat fit. That forces them to choose, but this man is different, isn't he? He doesn't intend to choose, and he seems talented enough to not need to."

"I know you had reservations for me to start with his training. He is already progressing to journeyman spells. Have you come around, or are you going to tell me to stop?"

"I'm still of two minds on it. Though it's silly to turn a typical practice into law, blatantly breaking the law could give them pretext them to react."

"React? The Fireguild already pushes hard without incitement and the others follow their lead or wring their hands and allow it to happen."

"George, I know how you feel. I've read your report several times. The attempt to steal our power stone was poorly done and smacks of impulse, not a larger plan. They had no way to know the significance of the stone. So how far should we really go in our reaction? Especially since they failed?"

"At some point they need reined in."

"Yes, but which point? Now? And how? We'd be facing the same coalition as a generation ago. That's much more than the Earthguild can fight alone. Who would stand with us?"

"You are a MacMer, the king's brother. Step out from hiding. The people will rise!"

Eldrin laughed bitterly and shook his head. "No."

"Is it because of Alernon?"

Eldrin glared at George a moment, then bent his head as he softly replied, "I suppose losing my son does factor in."

"It was a slaughter, pure and simple. News of the revolution hadn't reached him. He had no reason to think the regulars that met him were hostile. They never gave him a chance. How can you let that go without response?"

Eldrin straightened up. "George... How can I explain this to you? It wasn't just his loss or even the loss of his regiment. I faced reality. The king was dead, his heirs dead. Our clan was decimated. The regiments we could depend on destroyed. With General Nargoth disappearing a few years prior, it left only me. I'm no general. It was only by luck that I didn't die during that bloody time and was able to hide away here."

George attempted to interrupt, "Yes, but..."

Eldrin plowed on. "There was nothing left to fight with, and nothing left to fight for. All I would have done was get a lot of good farmers killed, if any actually would have followed me."

George tried again. "Yes, but that was then and now the Fireguild..."

Eldrin cut him off. "And the Airguild, and the Necromancers, and the Ecumenical Synod, and even greedy nobles give people new cause to rise up. I've heard your mantra before, but it is not enough for people to be killed over. And now? The MacMers are only history, and vilified history at that. As for what happened on the road from Barzan, most would view it as merely petty infighting between wizards' guilds. What do the common folk care about all that, other than to pray the fighting stays far away from their homes?"

George pointed at the room behind him. "That young man cares."

Thoughtfully, Eldrin replied, "Yes, he does. Though, with what he's already done, I'm not certain he's so common. Tell me, what did he do with his little demonstration? I couldn't see it."

"He summoned magic and then repeatedly alternated spells to mend and crack the rock. I believe it was four times before the rock disintegrated. He was as quick with the castings as any. The crack rock spell he taught himself from the book."

"Impressive. It makes me wonder though. Have you considered he may have some prior training? Most take months just to learn to read the runes but he picked them up on day one. Now he's jumped forward, much further than he should have."

George mulled the though around, then nodded. "He also approached summoning magic with surety novices don't normally have. So perhaps you're right. But what kind of magic? Do you think he is a plant, that one of the other guilds are trying to infiltrate us?"

"Were you able to confirm the Fireguild sorceress's death?"

George nodded.

"They wouldn't sacrifice one of their masters for this. I also don't see the other guilds crossing the Fireguild like that. So, I think no. Part of me is interested in knowing more, but as I think on it, the details don't really matter for any decision we make here. So, on to another thought. Have you considered what may have happened to that fire sorceress' spell book? The sorceress Sir Kian killed?"

"With his interest in magic, I expect he took it if he could. You don't think he can use it, do you?"

Eldrin laughed. "Of course he can. Magic is magic, and the runes are common to all the guilds. I found earth magic the hardest to learn. Sir Kian is picking up earth magic. Why not fire? However, he is likely to be less skilled with either as a result."

Eldrin paused, then made up his mind. "He needs skills to survive if they come after him. They are a common foe, and we can teach him skills he needs. I guess I've talked myself into agreeing with you. I'll even go you one better."

"What do you mean?"

"We also need to prepare for the day they come after us. I have been concerned by how few of us there are. Our footprint is confined to this city, limiting our applicant pool. And we're training new masters so slowly. We expect only three new masters this year."

George nodded, "Yes, but that is about what the other guilds are doing as well."

Eldrin corrected him, "That is what each of the four other guilds are doing. We're not facing any one of them, we're facing at least three of them, allied. So, we're quickly falling behind. We need to change how we do things."

"But how?"

"First, we don't have the luxury to take a generation to train a master. We need to learn how to do it faster. We can start with this Kian. In for a penny, in for a thaller! Don't give him an apprentice book, give him a master's. Make sure he fully understands each new tier of knowledge but push him. Keep him focused on useful spells, not all the esoteric stuff. He's not going to care about changing the color of a glow stone, and from the sounds of it he should be able to figure out how to make a stone hot. Take him as far and as fast as he's able to go. That will mean both you and Esmeralda are with him all day, every day. He seems willing enough, I doubt he'll baulk."

George nodded, "Will do. What about his sword?"

"He keeps it."

"Really? In spite of the law?"

"Yes. He'll need all of his skills to survive. Plus, I doubt he would relinquish it."

"And the fire spell book?"

"Yes, George, that as well. And here's the second thing. Esmeralda is already as skilled as a master; she just has to take her test. We both know she will pass it. Have her take it right after Terter is on his way home. Where is his home?"

George thought a moment, then responded, "Vellar."

"Perfect."

George was confused. "What do you mean?"

"Vellar is autonomous, not under the thumb of the Tionol and the Fireguild's manipulation of it." Eldrin paused and took a deep breath. What he was about to propose was momentous. "I want you to send Master Esmeralda to set up a new guild house there and teach any who come to her. She can continue to mentor Kian when he's around. If she finds any casters practicing outside the guilds, she is to work with them, help them, teach them even. I know, wildlings are outlaws, but no longer to us. If it works out in Vellar, then we'll send masters to other cities. There are those in the Highlands and in Ost who would welcome a counterbalance to the Fireguild."

George's eyes widened in surprise. "The other guilds will allow us to do that?"

Eldrin chuckled. "I'm not asking them."

"They will notice and react."

"Perhaps. It may take some time for them to notice, and they may choose to watch for a while to see if our experiment succeeds, which it might not. How many will come to us to learn? How many will be able to learn? It could end up a failure and the other guilds simply laugh at our efforts. We'll see."

"It could turn Vellar into a battle ground. What of your talk of dead farmers?"

"Vellar is the largest and wealthiest city in the kingdom. Sooner or later greedy eyes will turn its way. They are also more than just farmers. It's the second most fortified city in the country, second only to Bridgeport. If they choose to make a stand, they have a good chance of success. And they wouldn't be doing it for a lost MacMer cause, they'd be doing it for themselves."

Chapter 31: Cathar Estate, Sulvi, 25th YOC, 4th Day of Planting Month, 7 PM

Hemanji Cathar sat at her desk in a simple white shift. Her hair was tied back, and she was without makeup. She looked as young as her handmaiden Tej. She stared down at three ledgers sitting open on her desk. She absently nibbled on the feather end of her quill as she frowned at the numbers, looking back and forth between the ledgers.

A knock at the door disturbed her. Her frustration with the ledgers crept into her voice as she snapped, "What is it!"

Tej deferentially stepped into the office and curtsied. "Lady, Sir Kian Terter has arrived in the courtyard. The guards would like to know your orders."

Hemanji was surprised. It had been so long, she had come to believe Tarek's assertions that Sir Kian would be too ashamed to return. Tarek had told her that Kian had abandoned him and George during an ambush and had disappeared until Tarek had routed the intruders. Tarek even suggested that she should throw Kian out if he did show up.

She considered Tarek's suggestion. Tarek's story seemed at odds with other actions of Sir Kian. It wouldn't be the first time that one of Tarek's stories was slanted. However, even if Tarek's story was true, it had all happened after Kian left Sulvi in George's employ. It was between Kian and George. On the other hand, Kian's actions under her employ had indebted House Cathar to him.

She composed herself and made her decision; it was only proper to treat him as an honored guest, listen to his story, even give him his reward for the services he had provided her. Luckily, Tarek was off on another commission so she wouldn't have to argue with him about it.

"Thank you, Tej. I'm sorry I snapped at you. Bring Sir Kian to my antechamber. Tell him I will be with him in a few minutes. In the meantime, have the servants bring food and wine. I will need some time to dress before I meet him."

Tej curtsied. "Yes Lady Cathar." She quickly left the antechamber.

Hemanji looked at herself in the full-length mirror, did a final adjustment to her bright purple sari. Another look, then she centered the white opal pendant in her cleavage. A moment more of critical appraisal, then she nodded – done.

She stepped through the doorway and past the curtain into the antechamber. Her eyes swept across the room noting the white tablecloth and the purple stemware next to a purple decanter. Her gaze crossed to tarry on the warrior standing next to the table.

She evaluated him. Sturm's armor was still covered in road dust. She wondered if he owned any other clothes than that armor coat. It was all she ever had seen him wear. She looked up to his face. He looked weary and hadn't shaved for a few days. Then her gaze was captured by his eyes. Today they were olive green. How could eyes change between as many shades as his did?

Sturm nodded to her, and half bowed. "Lady Cathar."

She nodded in acknowledgement. "Sir Kian, it's good to see you again. We had expected you two tendays ago. I hope nothing inconvenienced you?"

"Just the opposite. George fulfilled his promise to try to teach me magic."

Hermanji mulled over his response. That had been the deal struck between Kian and George. It was a plausible explanation but was it true? "What did you learn?"

Sturm first impulse was to impress her but then his common sense kicked in. Anything he showed her would get back to Tarek. He decided it was safest to downplay things. "Poor George! He tried very hard to teach me, but about all I could do was cause a rock to crack and then repair it. He tried to tell me how great I did in the short time we had, but I think he was only being polite."

Hemanji was distressed by his reply. Had George taught Kian, or had he not? If Kian had learned magic, it would prove Tarek wrong. It also would make Kian more useful to her than Tarek. "You are too modest. Please, show me your spells."

Sturm hesitated. How much should he reveal?

Hemanji saw Sturm's hesitation. "Well? Have you told me true?"

Sturm realized he needed to provide her some proof of his tale. "I'll need a few rocks."

Hemanji rang the small bell, summoning Tej.

Tej bowed her way in. "My lady? How may I serve?"

"Could you fetch us a few rocks?"

"Rocks, my Lady?"

Hemanji nodded, then turned to Sturm, "Does it matter what kind?"

"Not as long as they don't already have any magic to them. I probably couldn't do anything with them if they did. Rocks from the courtyard would be fine."

"Tej, you heard him."

Tej bowed, wondering about their sanity yet obedient. "Yes, my lady. Immediately!" She turned and left. She quickly returned with four big rocks. They were as much as she could carry.

Sturm took them from her. "Thanks, Tej. These are perfect."

Tej smiled in relief, then quickly bowed her way out before they thought up some new fool's errand for her.

Sturm examined each rock then handed them to Hemanji. After she had examined them, he took them and set them in a line on the floor.

Sturm took several deep breaths as if he prepared for a major physical effort. He scrunched up his face and waved his hands while he made sounds like a fake magician in the marketplace. He put on a show for nearly half a minute. When he saw Hemanji getting bored, he cast his spell and the first rock cracked with a pop.

Hemanji sat up, startled.

Sturm grinned. He repeated his show on each rock.

Hemanji clapped her hands. It was true, he knew magic. "Please Kian, now show me how you make the cracks go away."

"I will try. This is far harder than making the crack in the first place. Let me concentrate."

Hemanji stared at the rock.

Sturm waited a few moments to keep it from looking easy, then cast his spell and the crack disappeared.

Hemanji clapped. "Oh, do it again!"

Sturm repeated it with the second stone, then faked failure on the third, and then did it again on the fourth.

Hemanji applauded each success. "I am so pleased Kian. Really! You say it is nothing, but it's very impressive!" His magic would be useful, she just had to figure out how to best use it. She would have to keep it secret from Tarek until then. She took a moment to imagine Tarek's consternation when she revealed it. A wide grin spread across her face.

"I am glad milady is pleased."

Hemanji's thoughts returned to Tarek's story. Things had not gone as Tarek had portrayed them. How great was his lie? She fished for the answer. "I was wondering... Tarek said you were ambushed one night. He said you two were split up. What happened?"

Sturm was caught by surprise. He had so enjoyed showing off for Hemanji that he had forgotten about Tarek. He wondered if Tarek would walk in on them any moment. He decided it was best to get the confrontation over with. He forced his voice into a pleasantness he didn't feel. "Perhaps he should join us, and we can compare our journeys?"

"He left a couple of days ago. Some new commission for the council."

"Oh, doing what?"

"I really don't know. We have done so many of them over the years I don't keep track of the details anymore. They're lucrative and as long as they keep us in the council's favor, I don't ask questions."

Strum wasn't surprised by her response. There were many who would follow the same course. Sturm wasn't one of them, there were some contracts he just wouldn't do. Like, he wouldn't go kill a lone elf woman armed with only her belt knife.

Hemanji interrupted Sturm's thoughts, "Tell me about the night ambush."

Sturm hesitated. He preferred to know what Tarek had said. Glaring differences with Tarek's accounting would be trouble. "Why don't you tell me what Tarek told you and I'll fill in details from that."

"Sir Kian, please don't be coy, just tell me."

"I don't know what happened on Tarek's side after we had settled in for the night. George warded himself into a comfy nook and sent us to take care of ourselves. We didn't stand watches."

"I understand. I don't need you to tell me what Tarek did, only what you did."

"Well, I went and hid nearby where I could hear if anything happened. Eventually I woke up to the sounds of intruders in the camp. I headed towards George to protect him but then spotted our horses were gone. We weren't going anywhere without them, and George appeared safe behind his ward, so I went after the horses. I found them with the intruder's horses, so I ran theirs off and I moved ours. When I returned to camp, it was quiet. I stood guard in front of George's ward. Moments later George dispelled it and joined me. Not long after, Tarek rejoined us. Then we quickly left."

"I see. So, there was no fight." Irritation flared within Hermanji. Tarek had lied to her.

"Tarek said he ran them off, so perhaps he had one."

"Yes, perhaps. How was the rest of the trip? Where did you end up?"

"The road didn't lead to where we expected. We ended up at the druid enclave on the Danu River. They gave us a boat ride down to Bridgeport."

"Tarek made a brief mention of the druids. Simple farming folk, quite boring, yes?"

"No, I wouldn't say that at all. They're good people. I enjoyed their company, not boring at all."

"Oh, well, I suppose different perspectives and all." Hermanji wasn't actually interested in the Druids. However, Bridgeport was another matter. "So, on to

Bridgeport. Tarek told me they don't let many strangers within the city walls, so he wasn't able to get in. Very mysterious, I wonder why?" Hemanji picked up her wineglass and sipped from it, looking at Sturm over the rim. Men found it an alluring look. She used it to hide her expression as she waited for his response.

Sturm wanted to tell Hemanji all the wondrous things he had seen there, but then overruled himself. George had told him outsiders were not to know any details. "Sorry, but I didn't get to see much of the city. I spent my time stuck in my rooms struggling to learn spells. I wish I had seen more. Perhaps I'll be able to return someday."

"Well, when you go, take me with you. For all the extent of my trading routes, I have never traveled beyond Sulvi or Ai. Exploring the mystery of Bridgeport would be an adventure."

Sturm knew that he'd never be able to take her, though there was an appeal to it. "Yes, it would. But I can't make such a promise. I don't know when, or even if, I'll be able to return there. In the meantime, if you'd like to visit somewhere beyond the triangle, you could always visit Vellar. I have an estate outside the city."

"Oh, so you've done well for yourself. Perhaps I will. Maybe in the winter when trade is slow. In the meantime, I have something for you." Hemanji picked up the bell and this time rang it twice.

Tej carried in a long, narrow package wrapped in oiled cloth. She set one end on the ground, waiting Hemanji's orders. It was a bit taller than she was.

Sturm stared at the package, mystified.

Hemanji smiled. "I promised you a reward. I looked for something fitting for a warrior. Please open it."

Sturm took the package from Tej. He unrolled the cloth, revealing a bowstave and a quiver filled with arrows. While the war arrows were what any smithy could make, the stave was unique. He was familiar with staves that were a straight piece of wood. This stave had a double curve to it and was made of numerous thin layers glued together. He put his hand on it and was surprised to feel a tingle of magic. He was amazed by the gift. "Lady Cathar, I am... I am overwhelmed and grateful. Thank you!"

"I was told this is Elvish. It is said they make the best bows. Please, string it. Test its pull."

Sturm hid his consternation. He had little ability with a drawn bow. The instruction he had was mostly with a cross bow, and that was years ago. "Milady, this is a very special bow. It's not like the others I have seen. I think it would be wise if I learned more about it before even stringing it." He also preferred to experiment with the bow in private where she couldn't see how inept he was.

Disappointed, Hemanji replied, "But you do like it?" Getting an enthusiastic nod in reply, she continued, "Good. I really am very grateful for what you did. Not only with the box, but also concerning Dukar. You averted a trade war. I lost my father in the last one. I fear what could happen in another one."

"I'm sorry, how did he pass?"

"The trade war was widespread. Many died, much profit was lost. The heads of the cartels met to come to terms to end it. There was a betrayal, fighting. My father died with the other cartel heads."

"But Dukar is still around."

"Dukar was on the sideline of the war, non-aligned, so not at the meeting. At the time I thought he waited like a vulture. Perhaps I judged him too harshly."

Sturm thought about his meeting with Lord Dukar, the feel he had for the man. "You know, I think he didn't want to lose anyone to it. He cares about his people. But if someone started something with him, he'd finish it."

She nodded, accepting his statement.

Sturm continued, "So, what happened? Did your father have no guard?"

"He did, Tarek and several others."

"How was it the bodyguard survived when the man they guarded didn't?"

"The first hint of trouble was my father being killed. All Tarek and our men could do was to exact revenge and then fight their way out."

Sturm wasn't satisfied by the story. It clearly showed in his expression.

"Don't be judgmental. We lost some of our men. Tarek was wounded."

Sturm realized she had accepted the story, so he had no choice but to move on. "Then what happened?"

"It was only with Tarek's help that I was able to hold the cartel together. The other two cartels fell into pieces, the pieces fighting it out with each other. Eventually we ended up taking over most of their trade routes."

"And Tarek backed you?"

"I am the only heir. And, well, we had a relationship. I mean even before the war started."

Sturm's expression hardened as he thought; what a convenient situation for Tarek.

Hemanji misinterpreted the look. "You're judging me, perhaps you're right. It wasn't a great idea, but at the time we started I was only 15, a girl. I was impressed with his looks and his strength. Then after my father died, I had no idea what I was doing. I leaned on him heavily."

"Only a girl." Sturm didn't realize he repeated her words out loud. His thoughts had gone back to Tarek's behavior toward the druid girl, Heather. There was a repeated pattern of nefarious behavior.

Hermanji again misinterpreted Sturm's reaction. "Kian, I am only 23 now! I work hard at looking older than I am, so I am taken seriously during meetings. Even so, even now, it really helps having Tarek in his armor standing next to me."

She continued, "The relationship is over. I grew up. Also, we have differences of opinion on how to run the cartel. His way is short sighted, we might make profit short term but long term we'd lose. It's not simple, like for you. I don't see an enemy, pull my sword, and go charging in."

"It's not that simple for me either. I had to sort through available contracts for what would be best for my company. Then I had to make sure we survived them." He bit back the though of how the last contract had turned out.

"Ah! You understand, yet I could never explain it to Tarek. It came down to one of us had to be in charge. I realized that as long as I was sleeping with him it wouldn't be me. So, I had no choice. That was the end of it. But he sometimes forgets, presumes too much, either in running the cartel or in where he intends to sleep at night."

Sturm wondered if Hemanji was as much in control as she thought. Would the guards outside have reacted the same if Tarek was around?

Hemanji stepped over to the decanter and refilled their glasses. Smiling warmly, she handed Sturm his glass. "Enough of all that. Here, let's toast."

Taking the glass Sturm raised it. "To what?"

"To us, of course. Just don't make Tarek's mistake and forget who runs this cartel."

Chapter 32:   Sulvi, 25th YOC, 5th Day of Planting Month, 6 PM

Tarek was nearly to the gates of the Cathar estate when a man stepped out from the crowd. Tarek's hand instinctively went to the hilt of his sword as he pulled up his horse.

The man waved. "Tarek! Good to see you back my friend. You look thirsty."

Tarek knew the face. His hand came away from his sword. "I am at that. I'm about to gag on the road dust."

"I'm heading to the Wailing Wench. Why don't you join me for a pint?" The man disappeared into the street traffic.

Tarek kicked his horse into motion. The man wasn't his friend, he was a messenger. The invitation was a summons. It wouldn't be wise to keep the boss waiting.

He was in the Cathar compound only long enough to toss the reins to a stable hand and detail him to take care of the horse.

It was a half hour walk, winding his way through the streets, to the seedy district the Wailing Wench resided in. The tavern's street-front was of battered wood that looked like it had seen one bar fight too many.

Tarek's boss had come to favor it for meetings since they started the trade war. Tarek made it a point to be a regular, meeting with tradesmen or guards in the back room for a few pints. The meetings with his boss were lost among all his other visits.

He pushed through the door into the common room, then stopped to look around. He spotted a few of the regulars. He forced a smile and returned their nods. He also noted several unfamiliar faces. They watched him, evaluated him. He didn't need to know them to know what they were, or who they belonged to. He had been one of them once. They ensured no one made it to the backroom door if they weren't welcome.

He wove a path towards the back. He traded a quip here or slapped a shoulder there with men he'd drunk with in the past. As he passed barmaids, he flirted with them; his hand wandered where it shouldn't have, but the women gave him no rebuke.

He paused a moment to enjoy the music. A woman sang, accompanied by a man plucking the strings of a buzuki. He smiled at her, she smiled back. He had slept with most of the women at the alehouse. Perhaps he'd sleep with her again tonight, assuming his meeting went well. If it didn't, he wouldn't be sleeping with anyone.

He continued to the last table in the back, next to the door. The two men didn't stop their conversation. One nodded to him almost imperceptibly, his confirmation to enter. Tarek put his hand on the doorknob, opened it, and stepped in.

A man with short white hair and beard sat at a table with a jug and two mugs in front of him. He wore a jerkin and pants, nothing fancy but well kept. A leather cap, common to the working class, sat on the table next to him. He appeared to be a tradesman ready to relax after a long day, except for the eyes. The eyes were intent, considering. The eyes gave lie to the warmth of his greeting. "Ah, there you are my friend. Glad you could make it. Please sit and join me for a drink."

Tarek closed the door behind him and sat down across from the old man. He braced himself as the old man closed his eyes briefly in concentration, then with a wave of his hand and a word the room seemed to waver and twist around Tarek. Tarek shuddered; his stomach threatened to rebel. He took several deep breaths to recover.

The wizard slid a mug over to Tarek. "There we are, safely warded. We can speak freely now."

"Yes, milord, thank you." He took the mug, made a toasting motion, then took a good gulp from it. Tarek would normally be more cautious, but if the wizard wanted him dead, poison is not how he would have done it. Also, the wizard always had the best ale, even in a dive like this and this time was no different. Tarek smacked his lips in appreciation.

The wizard smiled indulgently. "Ah, I see you still fancy this brew. Good, good. Now then, do you have a stone for me? A story for me? Both, I hope?"

Tarek sat a bit straighter. "Well... No stone, but a story, yes."

"I'm disappointed in you Tarek. We went to great lengths to get that stone. Instead, all I have is a missing sorceress, and many questions."

Tarek had seen others who had to account for a failure. Few fared well through the experience. Tarek needed to quickly deflect focus to who had initially caused the series of failures. Tarek watched the wizard carefully for his reaction. "She isn't missing. She's dead along with her four guards."

"What? How did that happen?"

Tarek smiled inwardly. Normally the wizard already knew at least some part of what Tarek was reporting on, leaving Tarek on uncertain ground. This time the wizard didn't already know. Tarek had an edge. "The caravan bringing the stone to Sulvi was ambushed. Something you might know something about?"

The wizard locked eyes with Tarek. His gaze bored into Tarek.

Tarek mildly returned the gaze with an eyebrow raised in question. After a few heartbeats, Tarek worried his question had overstepped.

The wizard finally replied. "I had nothing to do with the ambush."

That was good news to Tarek, it made it easier for him to make the sorceress the scape goat. "That would explain why it was so poorly done."

"What happened?"

"The caravan was guarded by Sir Kian Terter, and a hand of guards he had put together. He survived the ambush and delivered the stone to Lady Cathar who gave it immediately to the Earthguild wizard George. Too bad they didn't stick to the original plan. I could have intercepted the stone in Sulvi, and it would have simply disappeared lost somewhere in transit."

"Did the sorceress die in the ambush?"

Tarek shook his head.

The wizard sipped thoughtfully from his mug a moment, then nodded. "Continue."

"After reporting in at House Cathar, Terter returned to Barzan. He correctly guessed the Cathar trademaster was involved, not that it was hard to guess. Terter met with him, made an offer to sell the stone. The trademaster didn't realize the stone was in Sulvi, so he set up the meeting. What happened there?" Tarek paused to shrug. "Only Terter and the dead know for certain."

"Your trademaster was a fool. I assume you tied up that loose end?"

Tarek nodded.

"Good. Can you make a guess on what happened?"

"The sorceress brought with her the local Dukar trademaster and four troopers of the 23rd. The bodies were not found until several days afterwards. I didn't see them myself, but the description indicated sword wounds for the troopers. Animals had gotten to the sorceress and the trademaster. I got no specifics beyond that."

The wizard frowned. "Its hard to accept that someone with her skills was just cut down by a sword."

"Perhaps an arrow caught her? I don't think magic was involved. There was no report of fire in the orchard where she was found. The clothes on the corpses weren't burnt."

"Tarek, not all magic is that obvious." The wizard paused in thought for a moment before he continued, "I think perhaps you're right and no magic was used. But does it mean he is so skilled with the sword or that he has many allies and is capable of a clever ambush?"

Tarek didn't reply. He knew it was a rhetorical question.

"What of their equipment?"

Tarek was at a loss. He hadn't thought of that question. He wasn't certain what was important to the wizard. His mind whirled, he tried to remember every word Jurik had said. After a moment he pieced together an answer. "The guards were still in their armor, I'm not certain if the Barzan authorities returned it to the 23rd. I have no details on the sorceress."

The wizard was not pleased with Tarek's answer. He didn't need things like the sorceress's spell book floating around unaccounted for. Spell books were dangerous things if a wildling wizard ever got their hands on one. He was sure someday it would come back on them. He didn't bother to mask his irritation. "Why did you not investigate this any sooner?"

"That was during the time I was on the way to Bridgeport."

"Ah, yes. Your trip. So, was Bridgeport the intended destination or only a way point? Did the stone make it there?"

Tarek hesitated; he was back on uncertain ground. Did the wizard already know about the trip? It left Tarek guessing how much he could shade the truth. "Yes, the stone made it to Bridgeport, and I believe that was its final destination."

With a hint of amusement, the wizard asked. "You believe?"

"The wizard carrying the stone said so. It makes sense."

The wizard sat back. He rested his elbows on the chair arms and brought his hands up in front of him, fingers forming a steeple. "So, tell me about your trip."

Tarek proceeded warily. He had seen that pose from the wizard before. It outwardly appeared to be contemplative but was actually that of a snake coiled to strike. "I wasn't able to be alone with the wizard. He brought Terter with him. Terter always had his eyes on me."

"So, you didn't even try to take it?"

"I did try. I had an ambush set up, but the wizard suddenly changed our route just as we got to it. My men followed and made a try that night."

"But they failed."

"One of them was killed and the horses run off before they could even start."

"How did that happen?"

"It had to be Terter. The wizard was behind a ward."

"Terter, Terter, Terter." The wizard paused for a moment, thoughtful, then with a wave of his hand, "Continue. Details. How did your man die?"

Tarek squirmed a bit as he replied. "Hard to believe, but there had been no struggle. He was taken by surprise and cut down by an assassin's stroke to the neck. He never had a chance to make a sound, let alone put up a fight."

The wizard stared at Tarek.

It dawned on Tarek what he'd just said.

The wizard leaned back, then quietly but with a tone that set a chill down Tarek's spine asked, "An assassin's stroke? Where would he have learned that? I thought we had eliminated the other assassin groups. You sat here five years ago, in this very room, and told me to my face that the trade war was over. You assured me the assassins were dead."

Tarek bowed his head as he responded. "Yes, milord. I did say that. And we've had five years of quiet without any sign of assassins at work, other than our own, as a testament to our success. As for an explanation, I can only pose a theory."

"Ah, a theory. You have come far from the cocky street blade I first met. Please, do tell me your theory."

"I found out what I could about Sir Kian Terter. He seems to just be another knight, but he was trained at a sword academy located at Socul which ..."

The wizard finished Tarek's sentence. "Is located near Havlok, which is where the first group of assassins we eliminated worked from. I was not aware of an academy at that sleepy village."

Tarek nodded. "Yes, milord. I had heard of that academy before but didn't know its location."

"You need to look into this academy."

"Yes milord."

"How long ago did he graduate?"

"I don't know." Tarek squirmed under the wizard's stare and made a guess, "He is young, so maybe a couple years ago. We took out the Havlok cell maybe seven years ago. He would have been only an apprentice when that occurred."

"And here he is now, a shadow of the night, killing trained blades without making a sound. Yes, perhaps we missed a young pup who has grown up."

The wizard thought for a moment, then continued, "But perhaps this could be useful."

"What do you mean?"

"Never mind, continue your story."

Tarek was worried. He had missed vital associations pointing to Terter being assassin trained. He needed to provide something worthwhile to the wizard, and quickly. He glossed over the trip after the night attack, quickly got to the broken bridge. Tarek knew what happened there would be important to the wizard. He interrupted his narrative to pique the wizard's interest. "It was at this point that I saw what the stone can do."

The wizard sat forward, immediately diverted. "Really?"

Tarek nodded. "Yes. The Earthwizard went to reconstruct the bridge. Initially, he cast with aid of his staff. It was slow going. It took him several minutes to bring a single block of stone up from the gully and join it to the bridge. At that rate it would have taken him all day to finish. That would have given my men enough time to catch up. Then he took out the stone. With it he commanded all the fallen stones to fly up and rebuild the bridge in but moments."

The wizard became lost in thought. He mumbled more to himself than Tarek, "A stone of power. We suspected it was something important, even unique, but that? And now it's at their guildhouse, our opportunity lost. Yet, perhaps, there is some good in this. Perhaps their defenses are faltering..."

The wizard focused back on Tarek, "Relax, I know you wouldn't know. Continue."

Tarek took another long drink of his ale, emptying his mug, then resumed with how the road ended unexpectedly at Kunalas. He detailed how he had to swear to the druid's pax. He hated the pax oath at the time, but now it gave him a good excuse for not having a chance at the stone until it was too late at Bridgeport.

The wizard lifted his mug only to find it was empty. He picked up a small bell and rang it, but no sound came out.

Tarek reflexively flinched. When he had been a door guard, he could hear that bell and would have to jump to the summons. It was quite annoying. Luckily, that was a thing of the past.

One of the men from the table outside entered. The wizard handed him his mug. "If you would be so kind. Tarek, another?"

Tarek was relieved. The wizard wouldn't have offered if Tarek's employment was about to be terminated. He nodded as he handed the man his mug.

"Two then." After the door closed the wizard continued. "So, this brings us to Bridgeport. I presume they didn't let you in."

"No, but I did enlist someone to cozy up to the guards and send us information."

"Another woman for coin?"

Tarek nodded.

"You put too much stock into your seductions. So, what then?"

"I rode to Barzan to find what I could and to tie up the loose end. Then I returned to Sulvi...."

The wizard finished for Tarek. "And then I had another commission waiting for you. How did that go, anyway?"

"No problem. I killed one peasant leader with the other leader's knife. Then I planted the bloodied knife where it would be found. I even left a little trail of blood to it to ensure that someone would find it. Eventually it was a neighbor's dog. Any sort of solidarity that village had against their lord has disappeared."

"You are sure they blame the one you framed?"

"I watched them lynch him before I left."

"Good, that should get them back to growing and milling. You'll get your pay after we have that confirmed. Perhaps you haven't lost your edge after all."

"What do you mean by that?"

They both paused, as the guard returned with the full mugs.

After the guard bowed his way out and the door had closed, the wizard answered. "There is the failed mission with the stone, and then with Hemanji..." The wizard let his voice trail off, waiting for the reaction.

Tarek was caught off guard. The wizard enjoyed his little head games, and they never turned out well for who he played them on. Tarek kept his tone neutral as he asked, "What about Hemanji?"

"Oh, you wouldn't know yet, would you, just getting back? Well, while you were gone Sir Kian came through town and stopped off to see her. She rewarded him for a job well done."

"With what?"

"Oh, just an elven made bow and - oh yes - herself. You need to do something about that soon, or she may have you sleeping in the streets."

Tarek was more worried about the wizard than Hemanji. His position at House Cathar was part reward and part assignment. Hermanji was just a piece of fluff he had controlled for years. However, if the wizard though he no longer controlled her, the wizard might remove him. Tarek came to an ugly realization that the wizard had eyes within the Cathar manor, but who? "How did you come about this news?"

"Not your worry, Tarek. I know I send you off on many different commissions. You can't be there all the time, so I have additional eyes there to cover your back."

Tarek doubted that it was to help him in any way.

The wizard continued, "I can see you don't like my little secret. Don't worry yourself over it. I insist. Don't try to find out who they are. I think they can be so much more effective if left undiscovered. Don't you agree?"

Tarek didn't like it, but he didn't have much choice. The wizard had him on a leash. He nodded his agreement.

"Good. So, let's see. There was your commission, job well done and all that but nothing really to glean from it either. One doesn't learn much from their successes, especially when your opposition are such novices. Then there is the stone. It slipped through our fingers. I suppose that the sorceress' overenthusiasm is what really caused the problem. Pity. I thought she was more competent than that, and I rather liked her even though she was Fireguild."

The wizard took a sip from his mug then continued, "On the other hand, there is this Sir Kian Terter. If not for him, her ambush would have been a success. If not for him, your ambush would have been a success. If not for him, your hold on House Cathar would not be threatened. This makes Sir Kian Terter a very interesting young man. Maybe I should hire him?"

The wizard watched Tarek, enjoying his discomfort. Then he drained his mug and set it down. He smacked his lips mimicking Tarek's reaction earlier. "It really is a good brew, isn't it? We're done here. Finish your tankard, enjoy your ale. I hope I'll hear back from you soon on the Socul academy. Make sure Kian is not part of a larger problem. Perhaps I will have another commission for you when you get back."

The wizard stood up, then waved his hand.

The room again did its dance around Tark, causing him to shudder again.

The wizard smiled in amusement. He picked up his cap, set it on his head, then walked out of the room.

Tarek allowed himself a sigh of relief. His stomach was flipflopping, but he was still breathing.

He took a few moments to let his stomach settle as he thought over the meeting. Hemanji's distraction with Terter was worrisome. Other than that, the meeting was pretty much a wash. The wizard was not pleased, and Tarek had not escaped without the punishment of being tasked without talk of payment. He hoped the wizard wasn't serious about hiring Terter. The kid could be competition, competition Tarek would prefer to eliminate. Though, on second thought, the pretext of hiring him might allow Tarek to set him up for a terminal failure. It was something he could think on during his journey to Socul.

Tarek emptied his mug and went to the common room. Only the day regulars were still there, sprawled around their drinks too drunk to leave. It was a bit early for the night crowd. The woman was still singing.

Tarek caught the eye of a serving wench and ordered three drinks: his, one for the singer, and another for her buzuki player.

He settled in where the singer could see him. After that meeting, he needed to do some unwinding and she would do nicely. He'd deal with Hemanji on the morrow.

Chapter 33: Vellar Main Gate, 25ᵗʰ YOC, 6th Day of Planting Month, 10 AM

Sturm dismounted short of the Vellar main gate then walked Val the rest of the way. He was in no hurry. He still mulled over his decision to come to Vellar instead of turning up the lane to his estate.

This was his first visit to Vellar since his mother's death. The city both drew him and repelled him; childhood memories of growing up with his mom competed against the memory of her blood on the street. The latter had always outweighed the former and he'd avoided returning. He'd been able to get away with that decision, using Gwiz as his proxy for any business in the city.

This duty Sturm couldn't pass on to Gwiz. Sturm's men had lived in the city. Now he would meet the families for the first time - to tell them their men weren't coming home. He couldn't even delay it. If his men had survived, their return was due. The families would start to worry and perhaps suffer hardship. Sturm carried not only the wages due but the wergild payment. It wouldn't bring his men back, but it would help with keeping a roof over the heads and food on the table for their families.

He reached the gate guards. They wore the same livery and breastplate over chainmail armor Sturm remembered from his childhood. The one on the right was too young to have been one of the guards back then, but the other one could have been. He nodded to them. "Good morning gentlemen."

They grinned back at Sturm. The elder half bowed. "Good morning to you, sir. May I be of aid in your business today?"

"Yes, you can. I need to pay wergild for some men lost guarding a caravan. I never had to do this before and am not certain where to start."

"Ach! It's been years since we've had one come through with wergild, not since the trade war. My sympathies. It's a hard day for all concerned, I can tell you that. I'd suggest, as a first step, you put up that fine war steed in the stable over there."

Sturm's eyes followed as the guard pointed out a structure over by the caravan campground. It was unguarded. "Will my horse be safe over there? We also need to make sure people give him plenty of room for their safety." Val was good around people, that was part of his training. However, saying otherwise might make people stay away from Val.

"They always ask that. You can hire a man to watch your horse. There's normally off duty constables hanging around looking for such chances of coin."

"I'll do that. How much do they expect?"

"Oh, a copper penny. Maybe two if it's a long day." The guard turned and looked through the gateway. He gave out a shrill whistle and waved his arm. A young man in the leather jerkin of a constable jogged up.

"Problem?"

The guard laughed. "As if you'd be a lot of help if there was. No, don't get in a huff, I'm just messing. Here's a chance at coin. The lord here needs his horse watched. Interested?"

The constable clearly was.

A few minutes later, Val was under the care of the stable and the watchful eye of the constable. Sturm returned to the guards.

Again, it was the elder guard who provided Sturm with guidance. "So, all squared away? Good. Then you'll need to go to the custom house on the north side of the plaza just the other side of the gate."

That made sense to Sturm. The custom house was where Gwiz had done business in the past. He probably needed to deal with the same old man Gwiz had. He didn't look forward to it. To hear of it from Gwiz; the man's mind wandered, and everything took a coin or several to do. Sturm entered the city following the guard's directions.

The plaza was much as Sturm remembered though some details had changed, such as the Willful Wench was now the Frothy Mug. The tavern had been only one story, now it was three, making it one of the tallest buildings in Vellar, nearly half as tall as the outer walls behind it. He took a moment to remember his younger version who had been so interested in the wenches there, only to be turned away for having no coin. He had coin now. For a moment he toyed with the idea of going in and seeing if the wenches were as pretty as in his memories. He laughed at himself, any excuse to delay! Instead, he turned towards the custom house.

As he wove his way through people and vending stalls, he spotted the theater stage where he had regularly met his childhood friends. He paused to look for a familiar face, then shook his head. His old group were all grown up and gone, replaced perhaps by their younger siblings or cousins. He was now one of those odd travelers walking into the city watched by the kids. He wondered what tales they were imagining about him.

Sturm had stayed in one place too long. A vendor descended on him, plying leather goods. "Surely the warrior needs a new belt for his sword. I have fine sturdy belts, with beautiful tooling. Perhaps new boots? I have the finest in the city. Come, look."

Sturm attempted to wave the man off, but couldn't get a word in, as the man extolled his wares. Sturm backed away. The vendor switched to a tale of his starving children and how he needed to sell his goods to feed them.

Sturm turned to escape, only to bump into another vendor. He bounced off the man and kept going, weaving his way between booths. Each vendor tried their best to get his attention, but he buried his head and pressed on.

He managed to make it to the custom house without any purchases. He stepped in and was suddenly surrounded by quiet. There were only two people in the large room. They were bent over scribe tables going over scrolls with long feather quills in their hands. Both were near Sturm's age. There was no sign of the old magistrate.

The closest one noticed Sturm. He stood up and strode over to Sturm hand out, a welcoming smile on his face. "Good day sir! I am Gregori Krol. How can I help you?"

Gregori was of average height, with the dark hair and brown eyes so many in Vellar had. He was well kept; hair brushed, and his short beard neatly trimmed. He wore a doublet and breeches. The doublet had an extensive needlework pattern that spoke of quality, not ostentation, that could be from either uptown or downtown. The man's smile was genuine as was his handshake.

Sturm immediately had a better feeling for how the day would go. "Pleased to meet you Master Krol, I am Kian Terter."

"Please, just call me Gregori."

"Alright, and I am Kian."

Gregori waited expectantly as Sturm tried to formulate what he needed. Finally, Sturm blurted out, "I'm here to pay a wergild."

"Oh, who did you kill?"

"No, that's not what I meant. I run a guard company. I lost some men. I'm here to pay what is owed per contract, to their families."

"Oh, you mean Umowny Posmiertny Wynagrodzenic."

Sturm stared at Gregori a moment, then laughed. "I have no idea what you just said. I couldn't even pronounce it. Who the heck would call anything that?"

At the far table, the scribe raised his hand. "I would. That's the proper legal term."

Sturm hesitated, then replied, "Well, no one around the caravans calls it that. Its wergild, or even blood money, not Umow... Whatever you said."

Gregori nodded his head thoughtfully. "Ah, I see. I have to admit, you're right. It is a mouthful. If you spoke the old kingdom language it would be less imposing. It simply means a contractual salary payment for a death."

Sturm shrugged.

Gregori grinned. "Yes, you don't speak the old language. No one does anymore, except for us and then its only for legal matters. We really need to join the times don't we! So, wergild has come to mean not only a judicial penalty to recompense for killing someone but also a contractual one for death in service. Yes, I'll have to suggest updating our legal terms at the next city council meeting."

Sturm cleared his throat, time to get on with it. "Will I need to see the Head Magistrate for this?"

"What? Oh, no. You can talk to my assistant if you'd rather."

"Oh! You're the Head Magistrate? I thought he was an older man."

"You must be thinking of the last magistrate. He died two years ago. Sad story. He lived like a pauper. If he had spent a bit on wood or charcoal to keep his home heated, he might not have been taken by pneumonia. And it was so unnecessary. When the city cleaned out his shack, they found enough coin tucked away that he could have lived in a villa uptown."

"My condolences." Sturm wasn't particularly moved by the story; the old man had lived the way he had chosen. As for the coin, it confirmed Gwiz's suspicions that the fees had been pocketed.

Sturm wondered if Gregori's fees were more than the old man's. Gregori didn't look to lead a pauper's life. No matter the fees, Sturm needed to press on. "So, what does the law say about this Umow..." Sturm struggled, trying to pronounce the legal phrase.

Gregori rescued him. "Wergild. We'll use your term. What we need are the terms of your charter. Do you have your guard company registered here? If so, we can pull our copy of the charter. Or do you have that with you?"

Sturm was overwhelmed. "Registered? No. We're not registered anywhere, there's no charter. All I have is the contract we had from House Cathar."

"Do you have that with you? May I see it?"

Sturm pulled out a couple of folded over pages and handed them to Gregori.

Gregori carefully unfolded them and then read them over, talking to himself as he did. "Let's see then. Caravan from Barzan to Ai. Ah, here is where the payments are stated. Good. Yes. Oh, and here is the receipt, signed by both parties. Very good."

Gregori handed the papers back to Sturm. "I have to hand it to House Cathar. They know how to write a contract. Short, to the point, and they didn't miss a thing. Yes, then. The contract covers it, and the receipt shows they have already paid it to you. So now it's up to you to distribute."

Sturm nodded.

"Good! Then no problem. You'll need a witness of course, and a receipt in triplicate for each payment. One copy filed here, one for House Cathar, and one for you."

"Witness?"

"Yes, most anyone will do. Just not another of your employees, or a family member. In the case of a contract like this, it would help if the witness could read so they could ensure the contract was fulfilled as written."

"I... I have no idea where to find one."

"It's all a bit much isn't it? Especially after all you've been through. Well, we can provide the witness, either of us will do." Gregori turned to the scribe, "Danylo, would you like to get a bit of fresh air with Kian? Or would you rather stay with what you're doing?"

"Stay. This accounting is a mess. If I leave it, I might as well start over again. I'm even skipping lunch."

"Oh, it's that time, isn't it?"

"Yes, sir. You're doing it again."

Laughing at himself Gregori confessed to Sturm, "I get so focused on what I'm doing, I miss what time it is. The clock is only the next building over, how do I not hear the chimes? Come, let's go. I'll stretch my legs, get a bit of lunch. Danylo, want me to bring you anything? I'll treat."

"Oh, yes sir! Thank you, sir! I have a fancy for the soup at Kranz's. His booth is just the other side of the barracks. I think this is the day he does his sausage soup. You should try it, sir."

Gregori grabbed a bag and loaded it up with a writing pad, ink, and quills. He hooked two lunch pails to the bag's carry strap, then he ushered Sturm back to the plaza. "The closest are listed as Sally's, so I suggest we start with them. It said the two men had no one designated for payment. What did you want to do with their payment?"

"Yes, Emilio and Mirka stayed there. I need to see if they were with anyone, settle their tabs. Is there anything more I should be doing?"

"You mean under the law? No. Since there is no one designated, you could simply keep the money. You have no requirement to pay their bill, though it would be nice to tell the innkeeper that they no longer need their rooms."

"It doesn't seem fair to not pay their tab."

Gregori broke into another of his smiles, "Very good, sir! This way. It's on the other side of the bridge in new Downtown."

They walked down the eastern edge of the plaza. They passed the Frothy Mug and several other well-kept establishments. Then they came to the river running through the city. Crossing the bridge was like entering a different city. The area was called 'new Downtown' since it was the latest add on to the city, but it looked old. The buildings were run down, so were the people. Sally's was the first building on their left. The front of the building was a bar that served through an open window to the street, with a drop-down shutter that could be bolted in a moment's notice. An older woman leaned on the sill, showing a lot of cleavage. At her age, it wasn't a good look.

Sturm nodded. "Good day ma'am."

She smiled as her eyes danced. "Oh, you're a pretty one. Looking for a room? You can share mine, at a cut rate!"

"Er, no ma'am. I'm here about Emilio and Mirka."

"Oh? Who are you then? What do you want with them? I don't let just anyone harass my guests."

"I need to speak to the proprietor and settle their bill."

"Well, that would be me. I'm Sally. Why don't they do it themselves? Oh, wait. I see. They passed, didn't they?"

Sturm nodded.

"They were good guests. They never got into a fight. Not them."

"Yes, they were good men. Did they share their rooms with anyone, leave you the names of anyone to contact?"

She shook her head. "No, and no. So sad! Here, let me get my book, and I'll see what they owe."

She popped inside a few moments, then returned with a small ledger. "They haven't paid for the last month. So that will be a silver gulden, I mean lion, or equivalent two ounces silver for each."

Gregori interrupted, "Sally, really? You're lucky to get a copper farthing a day. After a month that's not even an ounce, so even a copper lion is an overly heavy charge let alone in silver."

"Oh? And who are you?"

Gregori bowed. "Chief Magistrate Gregori Krol, at your service."

Her eyes widened, and she bowed. "I am sorry, milord. I'm only trying to make an honest profit so I can pay my taxes."

"Sally, this gentleman doesn't have to pay you a farthing. Please don't take advantage of him."

Sally looked down sheepishly, then back up to Sturm. "He's right. A copper lion, for both of them, would be fair."

Sturm paid the coin, and she led them to the rooms. There was little left behind. Sturm consigned what there was to Sally to dispose of as she saw fit.

Next on the list was Hamza. His address was several blocks into the warren of houses in the new Downtown section.

The woman there was upset with the news, then composed herself before calling for her husband. After introducing them, she hurried off to do a chore leaving them to settle up with him. A silver penny later, the smiling and bobbing man waved to them as they left.

Sturm walked down the street lost in thought. After a few moments he shook his head.

Gregori asked, "What is it?"

"Oh. I don't know. I just thought... Hamza had talked about that woman a lot. I thought maybe they were..."

"A couple?"

Sturm nodded. "Guess I got it wrong."

Gregori shrugged. "Maybe not. Sometimes people love who they cannot have." He grinned mischievously. "Then again, maybe there is something that the husband doesn't know?"

Sturm grinned in return.

Next on the list was Cade. He and his woman, Uzza, rented a house only a few blocks over from where Sturm had grown up. The buildings here were older than on the south side of the canal, but of better construction with stone walls for their first floors.

Sturm was flooded with memories. The shops in the buildings were mostly unchanged with the same wares and the same shopkeepers. He saw half remembered faces, older and weathered. Sturm worried he'd be recognized, but they looked past him to Gregori. Sturm was just a guard, whereas the man he was with might be a customer.

They came to the address and knocked at the door. A dark-haired woman answered. She was a local, prettier than most. Her hair was meticulously done up.

She dressed like one of the serving wenches in a tavern. Sturm remembered Cade had told him that's where the two had met.

Sturm explained why he was there. She stared at him a moment, then demanded, "So, where's my coin?"

Sturm winced. She seemed to care as much about Cade as a rock. Sturm wasn't certain she deserved the money, then realized it wasn't a judgment call for him to make. Cade had wanted her to have it. Sturm needed to honor that. He handed her the large silver coin and two small gold coins and left, leaving Gregori to take care of her signing off on the payment.

The last on the list was Ned. Sturm had dreaded this stop the most, Ned had a daughter.

They traveled several blocks west to one of the nicest downtown neighborhoods. A deep breath, then Sturm rapped the knocker on the door.

The woman who answered the door was another local, but decidedly different from Cade's woman. She had a pleasant face, with a tired smile. Strands of her dark hair fell loose from her simple tieback. She brushed them away from her face as she nodded in greeting. "Good day gentlemen."

Sturm glanced down as a little girl's face peaked around the door. He quickly focused back to the woman. "Liana?"

"Yes? Do I know you?"

"No ma'am. My name is Kian Terter."

"Oh, my husband works for you."

"Yes ma'am..."

"So, where is he?"

"Well, I'm afraid I have some bad news."

The woman's gaze bored into Sturm. She ordered the girl, "Nayeli, go, get your uncles."

The girl hesitated, curious about the strangers. Liana frowned. "Now young lady!"

Nayeli pouted, but Liana wasn't having any of it and shooed Nayeli off. Once the girl had disappeared into a back room, Liana turned back to Sturm. She noticed the man standing behind Sturm. "Who are you?"

Gregori bowed. "My name is Gregori. I am the magistrate of the city. I'm here only as witness."

She turned back to Sturm. "He's not coming back, is he? That's why it's you and not him that's here."

Before she could say more, two men came to the door. They introduced themselves as Ced and Fred. Ced was the one who asked, "Well, what is it? Nayeli says you have some news about Ned?"

Sturm remembered when Ned first told him about his brothers. They had a good laugh over the names and how Ned's mother came up with them. Right now, it wasn't so funny. Sturm opened his mouth but was interrupted by Liana before he got a word out.

"This isn't business for in the street. Come inside." She shooed Ced, Fred, and Nayeli back in, leaving the door open behind her. Sturm and Gregori followed.

Much of the first floor of the house was a large common room, with a kitchen to the back. There was a work area for a seamstress to the right. A loom sat in mid project. A small table was near it with a dress laid across it, along with a small basket with sewing materials. Several testaments to the seamstress' skill were about the room: embroidered cushions on the furniture, small tapestries on the walls. They gave the room a hominess.

The others had already sat down, one chair remained open. Neither Sturm nor Gregori made a motion to sit in Ned's chair.

Liani put a protective arm around Nayeli. "So, tell us. Not too detailed mind, not for her."

Sturm nodded. "Yes mam. We were on the trail to Sulvi and settling in for the night. I was still out doing a sweep, so I didn't see how it started. I heard a fight and rode back as quick as I could. We ended up killing the ambushers, but Ned fell in the fight."

Liani demanded, "Why did you survive and not him?!"

Sturm looked down at his feet. He had asked himself the same question. He gave her the only answer he had. "Just pure blind luck that I was still on my horse, and their swords didn't reach me."

Nayeli finally understood and burst into tears. She buried her head on her mom's shoulder. Liana tears flowed as well as she rocked her little girl.

Ced fought through tears to choke out, "What did my brother die for?"

"There was a special cargo, carried in secret, hidden even from us. It was important to who owned it, and to who wanted to steal it. Was it worth it? I cannot say. It was delivered to the rightful owner, our contract completed..." Sturm trailed off, knowing his words were of no comfort. He couldn't face them any longer. He reached into the wergild wallet and pulled out all the coins in it. He didn't bother to split out Liani's share from what was left. He knew she'd need it all. He laid the handful on the table; four large silver and eight small gold coins. He mumbled something about pay and wergild then choked up. He shook his head and fled the house.

Sturm didn't go far. He sagged against a building. He stared down at the street cobbles, numb inside.

A few minutes later, Ced and Fred ran up to him.

Sturm flinched expecting them to attack, but they stopped short.

Ced held out his open hands. "No, we're not here for that. You didn't do it to him. No grudge, right? I've got to know though. Did you get who did it?"

Sturm nodded.

"I don't mean who attacked you. I mean who sent them."

"I found who ordered the ambush. I killed them. Any other details, well... Probably best you don't know."

Ced started to protest but Fred put his hand on Ced's chest. "Let it go. It's done."

Fred then turned to Sturm. "That Gregori fella told us how much the contract said should be paid. You left a lot more coin on the table than you had to. You mean to do that?"

"Yeah."

Fred looked Sturm over a moment, then nodded. "Thanks." He grabbed Ced's arm and led him back home. They passed Gregori as he walked up to Sturm.

Gregori handed Sturm several folded over papers. "Here are your copies of the payment receipts and my witness for the payments. I have the city's copies and I'll file them back at the custom house." He looked Sturm over, concern in his eyes, "You alright?"

Sturm shrugged, then nodded.

Gregori sympathetically slapped Sturm on the shoulder. "I know that was hard, but we're done now. I'll walk you back."

As they walked, Sturm was quiet and looked troubled. Gregori let him be with his thoughts for a block before he started a discussion. "So... What now? Back home?"

Sturm glanced sidelong at him, nodded, then focused back to ahead of them.

"Is it far?"

"An hour ride, maybe."

"Oh, you're local. Which hamlet are you from?"

"Not a hamlet, the Terter estate. Northeast of Vellar."

"Really? I was under the impression it had been abandoned. Would you be the lord there?"

Sturm nodded. "I bought the estate under your predecessor. Last year or two, I've been working on bringing it back from ruin."

"What are your plans for it?"

Gregori had successfully diverted Sturm. The next several minutes were occupied with talk of crops and how to bring in tradesmen needed to make an estate successful.

They made it to the plaza. Sturm stopped walking when he spotted a familiar produce stand. His thoughts jumped to the last time he'd seen Fallon; the last few moments before his mother's death, the apple to be paid for next time. Well, it was next time, and payment was long overdue.

Gregori stopped with Sturm and waited patiently. When Sturm's attention wandered back, Gregori grinned. "I lost you there for a moment. Perfectly understandable. Would you care to join me for lunch? Danylo is entirely right about Kranz's. The fare is really quite good."

"No, I think I'll just grab a couple of pieces of fruit from the stand over there, for the ride home. Thank you for your help today and all your advice."

"No problem. Anytime. I have one more thought for you. Since you're a local noble, you're a member of the city council. There is an open seat waiting for Lord Terter. You should come to a meeting sometime and occupy it. Some of us haven't set foot out of the city in years. Your experiences with what's happening on the trade routes would be invaluable to us. After all, trade is the lifeblood of Vellar."

"I'll think on it."

"That's all I can ask. Either way, come see me the next time you're in the city. I'd like to hear how you're getting on. Best of luck." Gregori shook Sturm's hand before he left.

Sturm stared a moment a Gregori's back. It dawned on Sturm there had been no talk about fees. All in all, the magistrate was not what Sturm had expected.

Sturm reached into his purse and pulled out a coin at random, an old silver thaler. There were few of those still around. He grinned and remembered the price on his music box all those years ago. He had thought it a fortune back then. Now that he thought on it, he never did go back for his payment.

He walked up and flipped the coin to Fallon, who caught it.

Fallon bowed. "Good day milord." He looked down at the coin in his hand, and his eyes widened. "Milord, what is the coin for? I'm afraid I don't have change for such a large coin, even if you were buying all on my cart."

Sturm grinned. "An apple."

"You play with me. As you can see, I have no apples. Tis not the right season for them." He held the coin out to return it to Sturm.

Sturm waved it off. "No. You already gave me the apple years ago. I owe you."

Fallon scratched his jaw a moment, then shook his head. He looked Sturm over, then locked eyes. After a few moments, he nodded. "There was a lad once with eyes like yours. Sturm?"

Sturm broke into a wide grin. "Aye Fallon. Good to see you!"

Sturm stepped around the stall to shake Fallon's hand. Their handshake turned into a bear hug.

Fallon was near to tears. "I can hardly believe it! You're back, you're alive! I'm so sorry about your mother. But look at you. You're looking good! Doing well?"

Sturm stepped back and nodded. "I've been doing guard work on caravans."

"You hire on with the magistrate?"

"No, I just had some business that he helped me with. You know him?"

"Not really, but he's starting to get a reputation. A good reputation. You know you could do worse than to hire on with him."

"Well, I have to say my first impression agrees with you. But I don't think he needs a guard."

"I wouldn't be surprised if soon he might."

"Why do you say that?"

"I've been hearing talk. People are saying he'd make a good next mayor."

"Oh, and the current mayor might remove the competition?"

"No. The current mayor is old, and sick. Rumor has it he won't last long. He may even step down and retire. After he's gone, we'll be electing a new one, but you must be breathing to win. There are a couple of nobles who might go for it, but the one the magistrate really needs to watch is this guy sent by the Tional..." Fallon trailed off. He could see Sturm's attention had wandered.

Sturm eyes had gone to the street that led to where his mom had been murdered. His mind replayed the events of that day.

Fallon followed Sturm's stare. "What are you looking at? That's just the road to the warehouses. Oh, that's right. That's the road your momma went down just before she was killed. I never did understand what she was doing down there but she seemed in a hurry to get there."

"Sorry. I need to go down there and have a look."

"You know she isn't buried there. She's in the cemetery outside of town."

"I know. I've been to see her. I just... I think if I see the alley in daylight, maybe I'll stop seeing it in my nightmares."

"Ack, you were there when she died! You poor lad. Well, you do what you have to do. I'll see you next time, right?"

Sturm flashed a smile. "Right!"

Strum retraced his steps to the corner where he had watched his mother executed. The scene replayed in his mind. He saw Tarek's killing stroke. He saw Tarek flee. He saw her lying dead. He saw her blood on the pavement.

He looked beyond his memories to the empty alleyway and the stone buildings. The bodies and blood were long gone. He saw nothing that hinted to him why it had happened here.

Perhaps it wasn't a place of her choosing? Tarek would know. Sturm filed the question away for latter.

He turned to get Val and go home.

Part 5: Protecting His Own

Chapter 34: High Meadow North of Manor Terter, 25th YOC, 7th Day of Planting Month 3 PM

Gnumph clawed his way up the last few feet of rocky slope to where it leveled out, becoming the high meadow. He was cussing a blue streak. He had scraped his shin and it was throbbing.

He sat down and pulled out his canteen. He poured water over the wound, rinsing away the blood and dirt. He decided to heal it, so it wouldn't get infected. He gathered power. Healing flowed into the scrape. The wound closed over, and it quit throbbing.

He took a swig before he capped the canteen and put it away. He sat a few moments regaining his composure, admiring the view as he did. The hillside fell away to the forest below. Gnemaley's steading was lost among the trees, but the Terter manor house and its surrounding fields were visible. Gnumph fancied he could even make out the walls of Vellar in the distance.

Gnumph reminded himself that the view wasn't why he was here. He was here to fetch Sturm. The time had come to go after the giant spider threatening the Gnemaley's steading. A group was gathering at the steading this evening and then getting an early start in the morning.

Gnumph stood up then stretched to his tippy toes trying – and failing – to look over the grass. He scratched at his beard in dismay at the prospect of wandering back and forth across several acres of high grass to find Sturm.

A dull boom and rising smoke to his left caught his attention. He eyed it anxious that the meadow was on fire. As he stared at it, the puff of smoke lazily drifted upward and dissipated. Anxiety changed over to curiosity. What had caused the smoke? Was it Sturm? He headed to his left.

Gnumph came across a rock nearly as tall as a gnome. He scrambled on top of it. He had a clear view and spotted Sturm next to a scorched patch in the grass. Sturm was consulting a book set on a makeshift stand thrown together from field rocks. Sturm looked up from the book, focusing on his hands as he made motions like he was making a snowball. A ball of fire formed between his fingers. He tossed it. It landed in the middle of the scorched patch and exploded. Another puff of smoke rose in the air and dissipated.

Gnumph snorted a laugh. Well, that explained the noise and smoke. The boy had come to play with the spell book he had looted.

Gnumph hopped off the rock and continued towards Sturm. He was to shouting distance when there was the sound of a large beast charging through the brush towards him. He braced himself for the worst. Even so he was nearly knocked over by a large white pup.

Mira jumped up and down and repeatedly licked Gnumph on the face.

Gnumph's first attempts to get Mira to sit were ignored, but eventually Mira behaved. "Good boy Mira!" Gnumph rubbed the pup's ears. Mira moaned in pleasure. The pup wasn't even half grown and already as big as Gnumph.

Gnumph walked past Mira to Sturm. "So, there you are. Its quite a hike to up here. What have you been doing with yourself?" He gestured towards the stand. "I see three books there. I recognize your mother's book. I saw you using the second to cast fire. Is it the one you took from the sorceress?"

"Yes." Sturm picked up the book and showed it to Gnumph. The scales on the cover shimmered in the sunlight between red, orange, and golden yellow.

Gnumph was impressed. "Ah, very pretty. Thick too. Many spells in it?"

Sturm nodded. "It's a master level book. Not only are there a lot of spells, but different techniques for advanced forms to give them added range, added power, added effects. What I was casting was only a beginner's version of one of their primary spell effects. I still have a lot of work to get to the advanced forms."

"Well, don't burn down anything important by accident. What's that last book?"

Sturm carefully set down the fire spell book then picked up one with a cover of grey stone. He handed it to Gnumph. "This is my reward from the Earthguild."

Gnumph examined the cover. "Ah! Not nearly so pretty, is it? But earth has always been unassuming and fire flashy, to pardon the pun. Hey, what gives? The cover is stone, but it's so light! How did they do that?"

"I haven't a clue. It's probably a spell in there somewhere."

"It's thick. Is it also a master's level book?"

"Yes."

"You must have gotten on well with the Earthwizards."

"I studied under George, the master that I had ridden with, and his journeyman Esmeralda. They were great, I liked them. But, At first, it felt like I was wasting my time. The spells were dumb. Create a crack, make the crack go away. And I had to do them, and do them, and do them."

"You were bored to tears?"

Sturm nodded. "I did my best to hide my spell ability, to not raise questions. Eventually I couldn't take it anymore and I rapidly pounded a stone with the spells until it disintegrated."

"Did you give yourself away?"

"They didn't seem to care. They gave me this book and really increased the pace. Our sessions turned grueling, lasting well into the night. I learned more than I had imagined possible, and it's only a peek at the full power of magic. Even so, Earthmagic seems pointless, no better than parlor tricks."

Gnumph snorted a laugh. "I know I say that about Gwiz's minor spells, but the truth is they're quite useful. I'm sure Earthmagic is useful as well."

"Perhaps, but I don't see it. They're not like in the old stories where a wizard could do anything with a snap of their fingers. The earth spells are so limited in effect and casting anything more significant than a crack in a rock just takes so long. You have to completely concentrate on it, immerse yourself in it, and slowly bend the rock to your will. That's why I'm working on the fire magic. Its quick to cast, just a matter of learning to control forming and aiming it."

"Don't turn your back on the earth magic. It's your imagination on what to do with it that limits, not its power. Like the book being so light. What if you could make a load of stone weigh so little? Men in the quarries and masons at the other end will be praising you."

"It doesn't win battles."

"No, but the walls they build might. What about when you made that stone disintegrate? That could be useful in the right time and place with someone else's walls."

Sturm shrugged. "Perhaps. And I'll admit there is one spell that caught my eye. It embeds a spell within a crystal."

"You mean like Gwiz's light stone trick?"

"No, that is an effect put on a stone. These are spells put inside waiting to be triggered. Just think, if I could put something from the fire book into a crystal arrowhead, I could shoot it far beyond the distance I can cast."

"There you go, imagination at work."

"I'll have to do a lot more than just imagine in order to create one. I have to work both a fire and earth spell to do it. For that matter, I'll need to get a lot better at making arrows. That one afternoon session at the academy was a lot of years ago.""

"Was the stone you transported something like that? Something that holds a spell?"

"I think it's something different. It holds magic power. George used it to magnify his spells."

"No wonder the Fireguild wanted to steal it."

"George thought they didn't even know what it was, and they tried to steal it just because the Earthguild seemed interested in it."

"That puts fire and earth at odds. From the way you talk, sounds like you're on the weaker side if it comes to a battle."

Sturm shrugged. "I didn't choose a side, I just ended up with earth. We'll have to see how things play out."

"Just as long as you're able to look at yourself in a mirror the day after. Ach, well, I'll trust your judgement on that. So, the book was from the earth guild. Did Hermanji reward you as well?"

"House Cathar gave me a bow." Sturm pointed over to a strung bow leaning against the stand. Next to it was an empty quiver.

"Pretty bow. I've not seen that kind of workmanship. What is it?"

"Elven."

"Is the bow all the reward you got?" Gnumph waggled his eyebrows, then chuckled as Sturm turned red. Gnumph pointed to the bow. "Doesn't that thing need arrows?"

Sturm was relieved with the change of subject. "Yeah, it came with arrows, but I used them all. I kept overshooting the target and the arrows are lost out in the brush."

"I thought you know how to use a bow. Didn't you take bow at the academy?"

"I did. The original bow master taught vertical bow, but he disappeared early on. His replacement taught cross bow, so I only had a few sessions using a vertical bow."

"So, it's going to work out for you."

"What do you mean?"

"You'll get plenty of practice making arrows."

"Ha. Funny. There is also one more thing." Sturm pulled out the dog charm then continued, "I got this from a druid."

"A druid? Where did you... Eventually you are going to have to sit down with us and tell the whole story of your trip. No, I mean it, and soon. So, what do we have here? It looks like a small carving of a dog or wolf." Getting a nod from Sturm he continued, "Is it a charm?"

"It's to help me train Mira."

"Ha! He needs it! So, show me."

Sturm took the charm back and held it as he thought for a moment visualizing Mira walking over to him. Then he called to Mira. "Come."

Mira trotted over. Sturm gave him a hug and a "Good boy!"

Gnumph snorted and shook his head. "That is no test, I taught him to come months ago. Try something he wouldn't normally do, something I haven't already taught him."

"Alright, what?"

Gnumph thought for a moment looking around the pasture. "Hmmm. How about have him go to that berry bush and back?" Gnumph pointed to a bush 20 feet away.

Sturm turned to Mira. Again, he visualized what he wanted done. Then he pointed to the bush. "Mira, go to the bush and back."

Mira looked at Sturm a moment then trotted over to the berry bush. He sniffed it, lifted his leg to mark it, then turned around and trotted back.

As Sturm hugged and praised Mira, Gnumph laughed. "Wow, that's pretty good. It's like he understands what you say now."

"It may be even more than that. One time I got him to do something without saying a word."

Gnumph grinned. "I wonder if we can do that with the rabbit that gets into my vegetable patch. Maybe he and I can come to an understanding?" Gnumph's grin faded, "Or how about spiders? Right about now, that would be really useful."

"You mean giant spiders? Yeah, I talked to Gnemaley on the way up here. She mentioned they spotted some new webs in the trees east of here."

"So why aren't you over there sorting it out?"

"Because I'm here trying to figure out a better way of dealing with it than just beating on it with a sword."

"So, have you?"

"Ah, no. The fire spell would be useful, but I don't have it under control yet. It's suppose to roll to its target, instead it drops where I toss it."

"Well, you're out of time. Gnemaley is hot to go after what made the webs. She is worried about how they're coming closer to her steading, and not just because of the livestock. She's concerned about the young gnomes."

The thought of gnome children being hunted and eaten by spiders caused Sturm to start packing. "Give me a couple of minutes to get my armor on, and we'll go find it."

"Well, actually I was thinking tomorrow."

"What? Now you tell me to wait?"

"Yes. Gwiz is brewing up a super strength anti-venom potion. He expected to be done with it in time to meet us at Gnemaley's for dinner. He's also bringing a couple of stout Gnome volunteers. Since we really don't know what kind of trouble we'll be walking into, think a bit of help might be good?"

"Of course."

"Alright then. So, let's not be late for dinner."

Sturm's packing didn't take long. The big things, the stand and the archery target, he left for the next time he came to practice. The spell books he carefully wrapped in a padded cloth and slid into the travel bag he had taken from the sorceress. All the odd bits of gear around his camp, and even his bow, followed the books. He lifted the bag. There was a bit of a heft, but it was nowhere near as heavy as it should be.

Gnumph eyed the bag. "I hope you're not expecting me to carry that."

Sturm called Mira over, put a harness on him, and attached the bag.

Gnumph took a close look the rig. "Isn't that the harness Gwiz made? He was looking for it. How does Mira take to it?"

"A little trouble at first. Once I used the charm to get him to understand what I wanted, he put up with it. Now, I think he likes it."

"Well, if he'll take a pack, you think he'll let me ride him?"

Sturm gave him a dirty look. "Er, no. Come on, let's not miss that feast."

Chapter 35: Gnemaley's Steading, 25th YOC, 7th Day of Planting Month, 5 PM

Sturm and Gnumph clambered down the hillside and entered the forest below. As they neared the steading, neatly pruned berry bushes replaced the wild undergrowth. Trees were surrounded with two-foot-high fences marking truffle gardens. A young gnome, with a piglet on a leash tending one of the gardens, pointed them to the path to Gnemaley's tree.

The path ended in a shaded glade; tall trees arched high overhead. These trees had wooden house fronts no taller than Sturm, with gnome sized doors. In the glade was a fire pit, with a goat roasting. The smell of roasting meat mingled with several other tantalizing aromas.

Gnemaley, in her pink elder's cap, appeared from around a tree. She was followed by two gnome lads, adult in size but too young to have earned their caps, carrying boards. She pointed out a spot for the lads set down their boards.

Sturm hailed them, "Evening Gnemaley."

Gnemaley curtsied. "Welcome milord." She nodded to Gnumph. "Cousin."

Sturm nodded in acknowledgement, but he wasn't comfortable with her genuflecting. He was used to a 'I'm on it boss' in the caravan, not the obeisance. "Please, Gnemaley, there is no need for that."

"Lord Kian, I know that I do not have to, but I want to."

"But why?"

"Because things are so different here. Other lords require bowing and scraping to them, while taking every turnip we have in taxes or rent. That is, if they let you live on their land at all. No, Lord Kian, I am serious. Things have gotten so horrible since the revolution. I've had to move twice since then. Now, I've found a home and I'm grateful."

"But I have done nothing."

"Well, you just keep doing nothing and you'll have hundreds of grateful gnomes. So, sit and have some ale while we get things ready."

"I'd rather help. What can I do?"

Gnemaley started to protest, but a stern look from Sturm caused her to relent. "If you insist. There are tables to set, torches to put up." She gestured to gnome lads. "Go with my boys. They know what needs done."

Gnemaley turned to Gnumph. "What? Need a special invitation?"

Gnumph opened his mouth to reply, but she didn't give him the chance. "You're just family you know, so hop to it. I'll bring out some pints of ale when you're done."

The mention of drink brought a smile to Gnumph's face. He quickly followed Sturm.

The glade quickly filled with four tables, thirty-two gnome chairs, a log for Sturm to sit on, and ten torch sconces. They were still pouring lamp oil into the sconces when Gnemaley showed up with the pints of ale. As she handed out mugs, Gwiz appeared on the far side of the glade accompanied by two gnomes and a pack mule.

Gnemaley called out to Gwiz. "Ah, just in time for ale!"

Gnumph snorted, "Suspiciously so. Who's that with you?"

"This is Drel and Kjel."

Gnemaley handed the last of the mugs over to Gnumph then went over and embraced Drel. "I heard you were thinking of moving here. It is so good to see you again. It's been what, three years since the sling competition? We need to have one here, it was such fun!"

Drel laughed. "Fun for you, you won. You embarrassed the lot of us."

"Oh, now, now. You did very well yourself. If I remember right, it was only a couple of point spread." Gnemaley turned to Sturm. "Lord Kian, don't let Drel fool you. He's very good with the sling."

Drel stepped over to Sturm and bowed. "Milord. I want to thank you for letting me stead in the old vineyard. I promise you sir, we'll get you a bumper crop this fall. You mark my words!"

"I look forward to your wine." Sturm turned to greet Kjel. "Thank you for coming. Are you another slinger?"

Kjel hesitated, then he yammered out a couple quick sentences in gnome.

Sturm held up his hand. "Hold on, that's too fast for me to understand. Do you understand human language?"

Kjel held up his hand with a small space between thumb and index finger.

"A little bit. I see. That's the way I am with gnome. I can understand it better than I can speak it. Tell you what, I'll talk to you in human, and you talk to me in gnome. We'll each talk slowly. Deal?"

Kjel nodded.

"Good, so let's start over. Do you use a sling?"

Kjel shook his head no.

"What do you use?"

Kjel stood up tall and proudly announced, "Kuanker." Seeing a lack of response from Sturm, Kjel added, swinging his hand up and down, "Bam, bam. Kuanker!"

Gwiz, laughed and translated, "Cudgel."

During the discussion Gnumph stepped over to the mule and looked over the packs. "Gwiz, what have you packed on this poor beast? How long do you think we'll be out there?"

"I'm only bringing the essentials; food, gear to cook it in, the potions I made, and a tarp incase the weather closes in on us. I already have Sturm's tent, so I thought it prudent to have something for us gnomes."

Gnumph corrected Gwiz. "Sturm's tent is only for here, for tonight. We're not going to be camping out. So, we can leave most of this and just backpack the rest."

"If we have the mule, why not just bring it all?"

Gnumph countered, "If we don't need the mule, why bring it and put it at risk? What if the spider gives us problems? We might end up having to either defend the mule or leave it behind."

"Oh. I guess you're right. We'll leave the tarp and cooking gear. But we can bring the rest. Most of it we can stuff into Sturm's fancy magic bag."

Gnemaley interrupted, "A magic bag? Really? I've never seen one of those. When will Sturm arrive? Do you think he'll let me look at it?"

Gwiz glared at Gnumph.

Gnumph's eyes widened as it sank in what he had said.

Sturm mentally shrugged. He had hidden his name in fear after his mom's execution. After all these years, he had finally met her executioner and it turned out they never had a clue he existed. There was no reason to still hide his name, though he needed to keep the Terter name. Sturm broke the silence. "Gnemaley, I'm sorry for the confusion. Sturm is my name from when I was little. And yes, of course you can look at the bag. It's over there by Mira."

Gnemaley looked over to Mira. He was asleep sprawled on his back, laying across the strap of the bag. "Aw, he's sleeping on it. I won't disturb him. I'll look latter after he's up and about."

Gwiz interjected, "Sturm can show it to you when we repack it for the expedition. So, Sturm, what's the plan for tomorrow?"

Sturm was caught off guard. "Well, I don't know. I thought you had it figured out."

"I did some preparations, like making up the potions against the spider poison, but that was it."

"Yeah, Gnumph told me about those. They'll be good, if they work. I mean, it's not a normal spider."

"These aren't for a normal spider. I took some of the ram's blood and worked from that. So, it's based on the essences of this spider's poison. It should work."

Gnumph interrupted, "What do we do with it?"

"Drink it."

"I figured, but wasn't that ram paralyzed by the venom? Isn't that what spiders do? So, if I'm paralyzed how am I going to drink it?"

"I had the same thought. So, I came up with a backup. I figured if the spider could inject the poison, I should be able to inject the antidote. So, I made myself a fang. I based it on those push cylinders we made to apply glue evenly. Let me show it to you."

Gwiz pulled out his apparatus; a small hollow wooden cylinder with a push rod filling it. Attached to the end of the cylinder was a wooden needle with a tiny hole drilled lengthwise. "See. You put the potion in the cylinder, put the rod behind it and push it." Demonstrating it with ale, he shot a stream a couple of feet.

"I guess it might work. I just hope I'm not the one you experiment on."

"Don't get bit by the spider and you won't be. So, there you have my day. What about tomorrow? Who all is coming?"

Gnemaley volunteered, "I'll go with you. I can show you where the webs are, and it will give you a second slinger."

Drel objected, "Wait. With Lord Kian, Gwiz, Gnump, Kjel, you and me that makes six. Six is an unlucky number."

Kjel pipped up in gnome, "Five is luckiest!"

Sturm had never believed in numerology. "Going into a fight, I'd rather have more than less. I am not dropping someone just to get to a lucky number."

Gnemaley nodded, "I agree. I can ask Vzin to come. He is a boar hunter. That will make seven which is almost as lucky as five."

Drel had a new objection. "What good is a boar hunter when we're hunting a spider?"

Gnemaley patiently explained, "Have you ever been on a boar hunt? No? Well, first you need to understand that these are wild boar and not a farmer's pig. These are bigger, they have tusks, and they're mean. Vzin actually uses their mean streak against them. When he finds a boar, he goads it to charge him, then he sets his spear and hopes the boar impales itself on the spear. That takes courage, and that alone makes him a worthwhile addition. Also, he is the only one who might come. The others, including my sons, are staying here to defend the steading."

Drel visualized facing a boar a moment then shuddered. "Good point."

"No more objections? Good. I'll be back in just a minute."

The group waited while Gnemaley walked to a home a few trees over. She knocked on the door. In response, an older gnome popped out his head. They exchanged words. He disappeared back inside, then emerged a few moments later carrying a spear. The shaft was 5 foot long, the spear head was two foot long with a sturdy cross guard. The spear was disproportionally long for a gnome, and Vzin had trouble getting it out his door.

Gnemaley led him over to the group. "Gentlemen, may I introduce Vzin."

Vzin bowed and proudly showed off his boar spear. There were several moments of head bobbing, exchanges of names, and a round of 'pleased to meet you'.

Sturm, perhaps being less versed in Gnomish courtesy or perhaps just the most impatient, redirected things back to the endeavor at hand. "Great. We've got ourselves to a lucky number. What about the spider?"

Gwiz answered, "Spiders normally tend their webs. So, I suggest we start with the nearest one. If its not tending it, burn the web and to the next."

Drel remonstrated, "Are you sure burning is the best? We don't want a fire to get out of control."

Gwiz reassured him, "We'll be careful to keep it a controlled burn."

Drel wasn't done with his objections. "Hm, alright. What about the dog. You decided to not take the mule. Wouldn't the same reasons apply to the dog? We don't need to be worrying about him either."

The gnomes looked to Sturm for his response.

Sturm didn't like it, but Drel had a point. Even with the charm, Mira was just a puppy and was easily distracted. "You're right Drel. Mira will stay behind. I'll leave him to guard here, he can understand that. Anything else?"

Sturm looked around, but there were no further objections.

One of Gnemaley's boys came up and whispered in her ear. She smiled and replied to him. "Yes, go to the neighbors and have them bring their dishes."

She turned back to Sturm, "The meal is ready milord. Let me get you another round of ale as we bring the food out."

As the meat was carved, dozens of gnomes emerged carrying platters of food. These were side dishes: freshly roasted shelled nuts, steaming white and orange roots, early spring peas, and mushrooms as big as Sturm's fist. Along with the platters, fresh bread with herb butter and a small honey pot appeared on the table.

A round of goat cheese was set on the table. Pitchers of ale also appeared, and mugs were filled.

The gnomes settled in. Every chair at the tables was filled, plus a few gnomes had brought their own stools and were sitting to the side.

Sturm sat down on his log at the head of a table. Mira sat down next to him, eyeing the meat platter. Sturm put several slices of meat on a plate for Mira and set it on the ground behind him. Then he loaded up a plate for himself.

After dinner, the Gnomes played a pantomime game of guess the animal. They were very good with their impressions. Sturm was able to recognize each animal, but was never fast enough to get an answer in.

Several mugs latter, pantomime gave way to singing. The verses were in gnomish, and Sturm had trouble following the stories, but the tunes were merry. Sturm found himself tapping in time to the music.

Sturm reached down and scratched Mira's belly, getting a contented moan in reply. Sturm raised his mug toasting the end of a song. As the next song started up, it came to Sturm that this was the first time since the caravan ambush that he was able to take a deep breath and let go of things, if even just for the moment. These were his people, and all was well. On the morrow, he would go out and make sure it stayed that way.

Chapter 36: Gnemaley's Steading, 25th YOC, 8th Day of Planting Month, Dawn

Sturm fought a dozen spiders, each the size of a horse and with Tarek's face. He dodged and swung his sword. Something grabbed his boot. He couldn't shake it off. He twisted but was wrapped up in spider web. He rolled and... woke up.

He was in his tent at Gnemaley's steading. There were no spiders. The webbing around him was actually his blanket. He looked down to his feet. Gnemaley stood at the tent flap. Just outside of the tent lay Mira, head on his paws, watching Sturm.

Gnemaley curtsied. "I'm sorry milord, but I tried to wake you gently as I could." She gestured to Mira, laying outside the tent. "Your tossing and turning chased him out of the tent. Nightmare?"

Sturm sat up. The world swam around him for a moment, his head pounded. Sturm grimaced.

Gnemaley continued, "Ah, and a bit hungover, are we? I'm not surprised. You were really drinking it up like a gnome last night. I'm glad you so liked my ale. Here, have some of this, it's good for what ails you." She picked up a steaming mug she had set on the ground and offered it to Sturm.

Sturm took a moment to focus on Gnemaley, and the steaming mug in her hands. He carefully reached out and took the mug with both hands.

She took a step back, put her hands on her hips, "Go on then, drink some. It's not ale, but a remedy. Some even say it tastes good."

With another grimace over the thought of ale, Sturm tentatively sniffed. He was pleasantly surprised by the aroma of chicken soup with hints of mushrooms. He took a sip. A rosy warm glow spread through his body. "This is good, and I'm starting to feel better already. What is this?"

"It's just an old family recipe. Gwiz, for all his potion lore, doesn't know this one but I can share it with him when we get back. After all, he's family."

Sturm was at a loss. Back? Back from where? Then he remembered what was planned for the day. The spider they hunted would, hopefully, not be as horrendous as his dream. "How are the others? Are they ready to leave, or do I have a bit to get myself sorted out?"

Gnemaley laughed. "Gnomes get hung over too. Drink the rest of that mug, then get your things together. The others should be ready when you are." She turned and left the tent. Mira came in and curled up next to Sturm.

Sturm gazed out the tent flap as he absentmindedly scratched Mira around the ears. He saw one of the gnomes still sat at the table, face down on a plate. Sturm watched as Gnemaley brought a steaming mug to the gnome. She prodded the gnome a couple of times, with only a vague mumbled response. She pulled him back by his shoulders until he sat up straight in his chair. It was Drel, a smear of whatever was on the plate stuck in his beard. Gnemaley prodded him another time with the same lack of response, so she held his nose until his mouth opened and poured in a sip of her concoction.

Drel sputtered and his eyes opened. "Wha...?"

She handed Drel the mug and only said "Drink!" before she turned and walked away.

Sturm grinned, then remembered his mug. He drained it with a few gulps. He quickly felt ready to face the day.

He reached around Mira and pulled out his chainmail coat. He tossed it out the tent. His helm and weapon belt followed, then his magical bag. Right after he tossed it, he remembered he needed to empty it to make room for the supplies Gwiz wanted to bring. With a mumbled curse, he dragged it back in. He pulled out the bow, the empty quiver, the spell books, a cloak, a water bag, a food wallet, a medical herb wallet, then odds and ends. He shook his head over the size of the pile as considered what to do with it.

Mira leaned over and sniffed at the food wallet.

Sturm grinned, opened the wallet and gave Mira the jerky strips still in it.

Sturm returned to considering his pile and realized he wouldn't take any of it. The bow with an empty quiver was useless. He wouldn't have time to look things up in the spell books, so they were also useless. He did need to make sure the bow and the books were put somewhere safe. He tossed the empty bag out, on top the armor. He wrapped the books in his blanket and then set them and his bow just outside the tent.

Sturm crawled out of the tent. Mira stayed behind, happily chomping on his jerky treats. Sturm gave Mira's ears a parting scratch. "Alright big guy, you can stay and finish them. I have a few things still to do. You wait here."

As Sturm stood up and stretched, Gwiz wandered up. Gwiz spoke around a frayed willow stick he was using to brush his teeth. "Morning. How are you feeling? Did Gnemaley get some of her morning-after broth into you?"

Sturm nodded. "I'm good, it did wonders." Sturm tossed him the bag, "There you go. How long before you're packed? I'd like to get rolling in short order."

"Well look at you. A few sips of Gnemaley's restorative and you're roaring to go. Give me a few minutes and I'll be ready." Gwiz took the bag and walked away.

Sturm went about getting his armor coat on and then went over to the fire pit. He grabbed a stick and stirred the embers, bringing them back to a small flame. There was still some meat on the goat. He carved off a slice and held it over the flame to reheat it. The smell of the goat meat brought Mira out of the tent. The first slice went to Mira. Sturm sliced off more for himself.

Gnemaley brought him a pot of tea. The others, one by one, joined them.

Drel was last. He made it a point to give Mira a wide berth. He glared at Mira as he ate. Finally, he interrupted the breakfast small talk and gestured towards Mira. "I thought that wasn't coming with us."

Sturm first reaction was irritation, Mira was not a 'that'. Then Sturm realized there was something more going on than just rudeness. "Oh, you're afraid of him."

"Am not."

Sturm chuckled. "Yes, you are. I can see how Mira being bigger than you would be intimidating, but don't worry. I said he's staying here, and he is."

While they talked Kjel walked over to Mira, offered his hand. Mira sniffed it, then nosed it. Kjel petted Mira on the head, then Kjel interrupted the conversation. "Can I ride him?"

Drel's eyes were wide. "Are you crazy?!"

Sturm stifled a laugh. "Kjel, if he lets you, you can ride him when we get back. Deal?"

Chapter 37: NE of Gnemaley's Steading, 25th YOC, 8th Day of Planting Month, Earl Morning

Sturm and the gnomes hiked through the forest. It was cool under the forest canopy. Birds flew back and forth, chirping while on their business.

Sturm was the only one in metal armor, with his chainmail coat. Gnumph, Vzin, and Kjel each wore a sleeveless leather jerkin over their normal attire. The jerkins were thick and afforded some protection to the chest. Kjel also had a targe, a small wooden shield, that protected his small body as well as a standard round infantry shield would a human. The other three were in their normal daily attire.

Gnemaley walked alongside Sturm, showing him the way. Several times along the way she pointed out where she planned some project.

Gwiz was close behind. He carried the magic bag stuffed with anything he could fit through the mouth of it. In spite of everything in it, it was not onerous to carry.

Gnumph and Kjel were next. They carried a pole from which a fire pot hung.

Drel stayed close to them. He didn't carry any of the gear. He had made sure everyone knew how important it was he kept his hands free so he could use his sling properly.

Vzin was the lone rear guard. He was a solitary sort, a bit odd by gnome standards. The other gnomes seemed pleased with where he was.

They came to a huge web strung across a game trail. The strands were much thicker than any spider web should be and probably could net a deer.

Sturm wondered how big the spider was that matched the web. He prodded the web and waited with his sword ready. Vzin and Kjel stood to either side of Sturm.

There was no sign of the spider.

Gnump pulled out tongs, extracted an ember from the firepot, then applied it to the web. The web caught quickly. Some of the nearby trees were singed but the fire didn't spread to them.

They waited a bit longer, still no spider. There was a collective shrug and Gnemaley led them to the next web. It had a bird trapped and cocooned.

Gwiz cut it out of the web and examined it. Though it was limp, it still breathed. He retrieved his antidote potion from the bag and attempted to pour a few drops into the bird's beak. The liquid dribbled out. He took his fang and carefully injected a small amount into the bird. He cooed to it, urging it to wake and move. The bird stirred then struggled in Gwiz's grasp. Gwiz released it and it flew off. Gwiz looked around at his companions, grinning. "See! It works."

Sturm wiped grime from his face, this web had been smoky as it burned. "That's good news. I still hope we won't need to use it. We're done here, where to now?"

Gnemaley responded, "The place we found the ram is just ahead. This way." She led them further north.

There was no web at the location. They searched around for a web. Vzin was the one to spot it. He motioned everyone to silence and waved them over.

The web had a fawn tangled in it. A spider, a good foot across, was busy enveloping the fawn into a cocoon. The spider didn't notice their approach.

Kjel growled and charged, swinging his cudgel. He sideswiped the spider. The spider's exoskeleton caved with a crunching noise. It tumbled and lay twitching where it landed. A second blow ended the twitching.

The fawn stopped struggling, fixating on Kjel. It was wild eyed, ready to panic at the least excuse.

Kjel spoke softly to it, holding out his hand for it to sniff. Then he gently petted it as he extricated it from the webbing. It was a sticky job. He got as much on him as he got off the fawn. Done, he stepped back.

The fawn stood trembling. Suddenly it turned and bolted, strands of web trailing.

Drel chuckled. "That wasn't as hard we expected, and with two rescues to boot. We'll be back in time for dinner."

Gnemaley sharply corrected him, "Really? You think that was it? The spider was big, but it was having a hard time dealing with a fawn already trapped in the web. You think it could have ambushed and subdued a ram without a web? No. We have some work ahead of us yet."

Drel's face clouded up, but before he could reply Sturm interrupted. "Has anyone noticed something odd about the lay of the ground? Imagine it without the brush. There is a flat swath much wider than a deer path, more like a road, leading towards the mountains."

Drel pointed to the distant mountains. "Up there? We wouldn't make it that far in a day. Not in a week. And we're not here to do random exploring. Let's find that spider and go home."

"Well, what I'm noting is, we followed up this old road from the last web. Maybe the roadbed will lead to another. Anyone have a better idea?"

No one replied, so Sturm continued, "Its close enough to the midday meal. We'll eat now, then continue on. The return trip is downhill and a lot quicker, so we've got several hours yet to finish this. If we don't, we'll have to come back. Especially since it seems to have babies."

Drel's jaw dropped, "Babies?"

Sturm pointed over to Kjel's kill. "Babies. Normal spiders have many at a time. We can't assume this was an only child."

Drel grumbled, "Oh, you're just full of good news, aren't you."

They ate their meal, then pressed on. The road wound between hill tops as it slowly climbed.

They found another web. It had several old kills cocooned. They burned it and moved further up the road.

The trees gave way to a meadow. Sturm called a stop. His gaze followed the roadbed, aimed at a cleft in the mountains to the north. He suspected the cleft opened to a pass through the mountains. He was drawn to finding out where it led to.

Gwiz stepped up next to Sturm. "So where now? No trail of webs here in the open. Do we need to go back down and hunt around?"

Gnumph humphed. "I don't think so. Look over there." He pointed to the left, at a break in the ridge. Trees covered in webs filled the break. Then he pointed to a stone block ahead of them. "And a marker as well."

The marker was a three-foot-high obelisk with glyphs on three sides. One set of glyphs faced them, another towards the mountains, and the third towards the break in the ridge line. The glyphs were weathered beyond readability.

Strum was intrigued. "So not only do we need to go to over there for the spiders, but something interesting may be there as well."

Drel interrupted, "Interesting? Ha! Scary, dangerous, evil even is what comes to my mind."

Gnumph, ignoring Drel, agreed with Sturm. "True, there may be some ruins over there. Who knows what we might find."

Drel refused to be ignored. "That's what worries me!"

Sturm shrugged. "It's where we've got to go. Let's take a break, eat and drink something." They didn't really need a break, but Sturm hoped the food would distract Drel.

Chapter 38: Foothills of Highland Mountains, 25th YOC, 8th Day of Planting Month, Afternoon.

They followed another overgrown road from the marker to the break in the ridgeline. Beyond the ridge was a sheltered valley filled with a forest. The trees were sickly, covered with webs choking the life out of them. Old, dried, webs full of forest trash and husks of captured prey intermingled with fresh, sticky, webs. Gwiz, Gnumph, and Sturm huddled and discussed their course of action.

Gwiz shook his head in dismay. "This is a lot different than the forest below. Down there it was individual webs, widespread. The trees were healthy and full of water with little fire hazard. Here, I don't know."

Gnumph snorted. "Yes, you do. It would take nothing to lite up the whole valley."

Sturm interjected, "That may be just what we need to do. How many spiders are there? How can we be sure we've gotten them all?"

Gnemaley had been staring at the trees, heartbroken at their condition, but Sturm's words got her attention. "Burn the forest down? No!"

Sturm replied, "Look, if we don't, those spiders will breed and keep coming out. Remember your worries over your children and livestock? This has to be delt with."

Gnumph pulled on his beard thoughtfully. "Sturm, are you still interested in what that marker might point to?"

Sturm nodded.

Gnumph continued, "We don't know what that might be, or what a fire might do to it."

"I hadn't thought that through, but you're right." Sturm mulled it over a moment. "I give. We'll hack a path in following the old road and see what we're dealing with." He turned to Gnemaley, "We might not burn it now, but I still think we'll end up with no choice. For now, we'll see."

Gnemaley went into a pout but didn't argue.

Sturm pulled out his sword and started chopping at the webs blocking their way.

Vzin stepped next to Sturm and joined in. After a few moments they figured out how to work together and got into a rhythm.

It was hard, sweaty work. The dried webs were tough, but they parted after several strokes of a blade. The fresh webs were worse. They stretched and yielded and also clung to hand or blade. Pieces that fell to the ground stuck to the warrior's boots and then picked up trash from the ground.

Gwiz stepped up to help, pulling his dagger. He quickly realized it was useless. It was a stabbing dagger with no real edge to it. He disgustedly sheathed it. He considered using his magic, perhaps a spell to neutralize the stickiness.

Gnump poked Gwiz with the firepot pole. "Here, grab this. Let's go."

"Give me a moment. I might have a spell for those webs."

Gnump chuckled. "Really? And how many castings will it take? Will you run out of forest before you run out of magic?"

"I'd like to do something..."

"Save it for when it's really needed. For now, take the pole. Gnemaley and Kjel can watch the sides, Drel the rear."

Gwiz grumpily took the pole muttering about his druthers. The others fell in as Gnump had suggested and they followed Sturm and Vzin.

Twenty feet in and the trees stood further apart. The webs were less dense, with gaps between the trees. Sturm exploited the gaps where he could, at times traveling tens of feet before returning to chopping.

He quickly lost track of the old roadbed and all sense of direction. The only landmarks were the next tree ahead. He couldn't steer by the sun; it was obscured by a canopy of webs overhead and the things the webs held. Their backtrail was lost to sight as they wandered around obstacles. He called a halt. "Sorry all. This isn't working out. I'm afraid we'll lose our way. I think we'll have to go back."

Gnemaley stomped her foot, "No!"

Everyone turned to Gnemaley.

"If we go back, you'll just burn the forest."

Gwiz set down the pole. "Everyone hold on. I think I have a solution." He rummaged through his pockets, then he produced a small box. "Ah, here it is. This will take care of it."

Gnemaley was dubious. "What does that do?"

"It has a magic needle in it that always points north." As he spoke, Gwiz flipped open the box. He pointed to the direction the needle was aimed. "That is north. We initially headed northwest."

Sturm shook his head. "Why didn't you tell me you had that?"

"Why didn't you tell me sooner that we had a problem? Come on, let's go."

Chapter 39: Valley of Webbed Trees, 25th YOC, 8th Day of Planting Month, late Afternoon.

The afternoon became a blur of cut a web, push it to the side, clear the web off your weapon then off you as well, step to the next web, repeat. Repeat. Repeat.

The forest became darker, more ominous. The trees creaked.

Everyone was on edge. Drel was the most vocal about it and got on everyone's nerves. For him, every creak was a portend of an attack, each bush or pile of rubbish held a spider ready to pounce.

Sturm stopped for a break. Under his armor, he dripped with sweat. He was tired, irritable, and his patience with Drel was gone. "Drel, enough."

For perhaps the hundredth time Drel asserted, "I'm sure I saw something."

Sturm resisted the urge to cuff him, then said with a forced patience, "Is it anything different from the last hour or so?"

"Well, no. But I hear things moving around out there."

Gwiz interrupted, playing peace maker. "I'll swap with you and take rear guard. Will that be better?"

Drel looked uncertain for a moment then nodded. "It'll have to do."

Vzin cleared his throat, getting their attention. He rubbed his right shoulder while rotating his arm. "I need a few minutes. This spear isn't meant for cutting. My shoulder is killing me."

Drel suddenly yelled, pointing to their backtrail. "Look! I told you!!"

Three spiders on strings of web slowly dropped to the ground. They were of the same size as the one they had killed earlier. As soon as they hit the ground they charged.

Drel fumbled around in his pouch for a stone, while continuing to tell everyone how right he had been. Gnemaley was more focused and got the first stone off. It struck the spider square, with a solid thunk to it. The spider flipped backwards and laid twitching, goo oozing out of the hole in its face. Drel's shot a moment later took a second spider with a similar kill shot.

The third spider was upon them before they could get another shot off. Kjel met it with a sweeping blow that rolled it and knocked it backwards. It righted itself and came at him again. It was moving slower, dragging a couple of its legs. Kjel swung again, scoring a solid hit to the body, crunching the carapace and killing the spider.

Drel was shaken by the encounter. "That's it. I'm done. Time to go back."

"No!" Gnemaley looked at Drel angrily. "I'm not giving up on this forest that easily."

Drel looked to Gnemaley, then down their trail, then back to Gnemaley. He really wanted to go back to the sunlight. He then looked around at the rest of the group.

Sturm was expressionless, staring over Drel's head like the discussion wasn't happening. Gnumph and Gwiz stared at Drel with impatience. Kjel grinned, proud of his victory. Vzin simply picked up his boar spear and turned back to the webs. That action overruled anything more Drel could say. The party moved forward.

Chapter 40: Valley of Webbed Trees, 25th YOC, 8th Day of Planting Month, Evening.

Sense of time disappeared. Sense of how far they progressed disappeared.

The webs became fewer, older, the distance between greater. The party's progress became quicker, but to where?

Drel's complaining stopped them again. "I'm hungry. Isn't it dinner time? Can't we take a break?"

Gnemaley agreed. "I'm hungry too. I agree, break time." She looked around at the others.

Vzin sighed, grounded his spear, then leaned against it wearily favoring his sore shoulder.

Sturm also didn't argue. He cleared the web from his sword, sheathed it, then flexed his sword hand repeatedly to loosen it up.

Drel quickly dug into his travel pack and pulled out a small loaf of bread. He warily eyed the forest around them as he bit into the loaf.

Kjel pulled out a handful of hazel nuts. He offered them around. When he came to Gwiz, he eyed the box. "Does that box tell you how far we've gone? Feels to me like we've crossed the valley three times by now."

Gwiz chuckled. "No, Kjel. This points to where north is, but not the distance either in front or behind."

Drel interrupted, talking around a mouthful of bread. "I think it's time to turn back. It's starting to get dark. We're surely not going to stay overnight in this forest."

Gnumph handed Drel a water skin. "Here, drink some water before you choke on that bread." Then he turned to the rest. "In truth, I was thinking about that also. Do we want to spend the night here, or outside the valley?"

Drel added, "I haven't seen any birds, deer, or even rabbits."

Gwiz wryly observed, "Well, there are spiders here you know."

"That's my point. There are spiders here. They don't fear us. They don't have any food. I don't know that I'll wake up tomorrow if I bed down here for the night."

Gnemaley sighed in defeat, "I hate it, but I have to agree. We need to go back." She knew that likely meant they'd end up burning the forest.

Drel was relieved. "Finally, some common sense. The way is cleared, we could come back another day."

Sturm shook his head. "Nope."

Drel demanded, "Why not?"

"How long would it take them to spin more webs and block the way again?"

Drel opened his mouth to retort, then closed it. It obviously wouldn't take long.

Sturm continued, "So, we leave only to come back and start over again. if we're going to do this at all, we need to just keep going."

Vzin broke in, "Continue to where? I've been cutting on these webs, working as hard as you milord, but I'm not seeing we've gained anything by the doing. I'm getting to feel like Drel. It might be time to turn back. While we can."

Gwiz scratched his beard, thoughtful, then repeated himself, "There are spiders here."

Everyone turned to him.

He looked around. "There are, but where are they? We haven't seen any since that last break we took."

As if his words were a cue, Kjel pointed, "There's some now."

Spiders were on their back trail. Some dangled down from the branches overhead, others came around undergrowth. A few were twice as big as any they'd seen.

The spiders scurried towards them.

Sling stones flew. They had little effect on the larger spiders but proved effective against the smaller ones.

Sturm stepped forward swinging his sword at a larger spider. It was an awkward side sweep as the spider hardly came up to his knees. His blade bounced off the main body but his follow through caught a leg and tore it off. The loss of a leg wasn't much of an inconvenience to the spider. It rotated to face Sturm. Sturm didn't get a second swing as a mace crashed down on the spider's body. Blue goo gushed out as the spider was flattened.

Sturm did a double take. Gnumph wielded the mace. Sturm had never seen Gnumph with a weapon before. Another spider came at Sturm, grabbing his attention.

The spider was on Sturm's off hand side. He rotated and chopped down, cutting through where the front and back segment met. Surprisingly little goo oozed from the wound and the spider's legs were all attached to the front segment. It rotated towards the source of the attack.

Kjel jumped forward and swung his cudgel. The spider's face caved in, and the spider dropped. Kjel's victory shout echoed from the trees.

Sturm pivoted back and forth looking to engage the next spider. Instead, he saw the gnomes doing victory jigs between the smashed corpses. It only lasted a moment before a couple more of the little spiders appeared on the back path.

Sling stones dispatched them. Then more spiders dropped on the path, easily twice as many as the first fight.

Gwiz called out to Sturm. "We can't go back now. Forward. Quickly! You and Vzin lead the way, break a path. We'll hold the rear but get moving."

Sturm dodged his way through gaps in the webs and underbrush where he could. When blocked, he frantically slashed through where there was the least to cut.

The gnomes stayed close on Sturm's heels. They called out as they spotted spiders pacing them on their flanks.

The party was brought up short by a cliff wall. They were at the far end of the valley.

Sturm turned around and faced the spiders. "Everyone, backs to the cliff."

A three-foot-wide spider dropped on Sturm's back and sank its pincers into him. The weight and pain knocked him face down. Sturm struggled to get up but was slammed across the back forcing him flat again. Spider goo covered his back, as the broken spider body fell off. He struggled again to push his body up but numbness spread through his arms, and they refused to obey him.

Suddenly he was rolled over. Gnumph held Sturm's head up as Gwiz forced his mouth open and dribbled liquid in.

Sturm sputtered and choked. His brain seemed as numb as his body; his thoughts were disjointed. Even so, he realized they must have given him some of Gwiz's potion. He forced himself to swallow what he could, while he could. The little he got down allowed him to move, but his mind couldn't quite grasp why he should or to where. Sturm was surrounded by a frantic fight, but all he could do was watch.

Spiders rushed in. A few were met by stones, shattering carapaces. Others were met by Kjel and Gnumph, their weapons were a blur crumpling spiders around them. It wasn't enough, there were too many spiders.

Gwiz threw the fire pot at a web covered tree. The clay pot shattered; bits of smoldering punk scattered igniting webs. Flames rapidly spread across the webs and into the trees. Spiders scurried to avoid the flames.

Suddenly Vzin was next to Sturm, urging him to his feet. Sturm stumbled and almost fell, his legs wobbly underneath him. Vzin steadied Sturm, then dragged him forward.

Sturm's mind struggled to make sense of what was happening, as they fled along the cliff wall. It seemed they ran for a lifetime, then suddenly they were in a cave.

Sturm found himself sitting, watching light flickering from the cave mouth. He saw Drel and Gnemaley in silhouette, desperately casting stones into the light. He couldn't understand why someone would cast stones at light. Then Gwiz joined them and threw handfuls of fire at the light.

Sturm giggled. What would fire do to the light? Especially Gwiz's spell that was only good for starting a winter fire in the fireplace, though the flames were pretty.

Gnumph knelt next to Sturm. He checked the bite on the back of Sturm's neck. He turned Sturm's head and looked Sturm in the eyes. Sturm looked back but he wasn't focused.

Gnumph muttered, "This won't do." He dug through the magic bag and pulled out a water skin and a jar of salve. "I hope this is as good as the druids say it is." He put some of the salve on the bite on the back of Sturm's neck, put a clean cloth over it, and shoved Sturm's hand on it to hold the cloth in place.

Gnumph pulled a cup out of the bag. He spooned out a dollop of salve with his fingers and tossed it in the cup then mixed in some water. He held the cup to Sturm's lips. Sturm feebly tried to take the cup. Gnumph tilted it for Sturm, urging Sturm to drink. Some of the concoction spilled, but Sturm swallowed most of it.

Gnumph looked up as Gwiz and Gnemaley joined him. "What's going on out there?"

Gwiz wearily replied, "Nothing but fire out there now. How's Sturm doing?"

Sturm mumbled something, but Gnumph talked over him. "I don't know. That was a big spider and it looks like that potion of yours wasn't up to it. He is dazed and his limbs are weak. I have some of the druid's Isatis salve on him and in him. I'm good with cuts and bruises, but not so much with poisons. Any ideas?"

Gwiz replied, "Maybe he just needs more potion to counter a stronger poison? It shouldn't hurt him."

One eyebrow raised, Gnumph queried, "Shouldn't?"

"You have a better idea?"

"I already tried that."

"Then help me get him to drink it."

Several minutes later Sturm's eyes came back into focus. He looked from Gnumph to Gwiz to Gnemaley. Gnemaley was crying. Sturm was touched. "Gnemaley, there's no need to cry. I'll be alright."

She glared at him. "You're not what I'm crying about. I'm crying for the forest. You got your wish. It's burning. The whole forest is burning!"

Sturm looked to Gwiz, "What is she talking about?"

"We ran out of options. I threw the fire pot to distract the spiders while we grabbed you and made a run for it. You could say it worked too well. The fire swept across the webs and the forest caught. It drove some of the spiders on our heels. This cave was safe haven for them as well as us. We had a desperate fight to keep them out of the cave. My fire spells forced them back but also added to the forest fire. Looks like its spread will go all the way down the valley." Gwiz turned to Gnemaley. "You need to understand, there was no choice."

She responded, "I know, and I know you just don't get it. You city gnomes have lost your roots, how could you understand?"

Gnumph rebutted, his tone gentle, "I do get it. I know what you grieve for. You see the trees and think of your steading and how you live with a tree as your home. You see your animal friends living there with you." His tone hardened, "That is not how this forest is. Do you not see? The animals are long gone, only the spiders remain. The trees are already dead, even if you could still see some leaves on the tallest ones. The forest is done. So, give over. If we live through this, you'll have the chance to come back and plant a new forest. I'll even help you."

She lowered her eyes and nodded. "You're right. I'm sorry."

Gnumph replied softly, "Believe me cousin, so am I."

Kjel tapped Gwiz on the shoulder. Gwiz looked up. "What is it?"

Kjel bobbed his head respectfully. "I apologize for interrupting. I don't suppose you have a torch in the magic bag. I think I saw some carvings on the walls, and I'd have a better look at them."

Gwiz dug through the bag and came out with a torch and a small bottle. He drizzled some liquid from the bottle over the working end of the torch. Then he handed the torch to Kjel. "I need to rest a bit before more castings. See if you can light it outside but watch yourself."

Kjel nodded thanks and grabbed the torch. He passed Drel and Vzin at the cave mouth and disappeared outside. A moment later he returned waving a lit torch with a grin on his face. "Works good!"

Gwiz rolled his eyes, then waved Kjel on. "Let us know how far back the cave goes, but don't wander too far. Come back at the first sign of trouble."

"Sure. See you in a bit."

They watched as Kjel walked along the cave wall; torch held high. The torch light revealed figures scratched on the wall, but they left it to Kjel to figure out what the figures meant.

Sturm addressed Gwiz, "Is there a particular reason you want him to stay close?"

"You're not really with it yet, are you. Alright then, do you remember how the spiders showed up both times we stopped, and then they nipped at our heals driving us in this direction? I'm thinking we were herded to this cave."

Gnemaley snapped, "To bad you didn't think of that before we ran in here."

Gwiz didn't meet her eyes as he replied, "Actually, I did. I just didn't see we had a choice."

While they talked, Kjel worked his way towards the back of the cave. His torch got a good distance away, then disappeared. This went unnoticed by the others, as they continued their discussion. A few minutes later the torch light reappeared, and quickly headed directly towards them.

Gnemaley finished the point she was making, "So while I've seen spiders build traps where the soil permitted, and I have seen them put webs across openings, I really don't think there is any reason to think they nest in this cave."

Kjel stepped into the light of the fire, interrupting their conversation. He forced himself to speak slowly so Sturm would also understand his gnomish. "I think they may be pets, living in someone's house, and that someone might still be home." Having their full attention, Kjel explained. "The cave narrows down and turns a corner. Past the corner it turns into an arched passage and worked stone. There are lots of carvings of people and the large spiders. Around another corner there was blue light."

Gwiz interjected, "So, you were spooked by a blue light?"

"No. It was hard to make out what was in the passage. I saw a statue, I hope it was just a statue, of a huge spider that was part human. Then I saw a big shadow moving behind it and I returned as you told me to."

Childhood tales of forest demons, part human and part spider, sprang out of Gnemaley's memory. Her reaction was immediate. "A forest demon? It's time to go home, and quickly!"

Gwiz disagreed, "We can't. It will be hours before the forest fire burns down and we can make our way out."

Gnemaley forced her mind past stories of forest demons destroying gnome settlements and feasting on the inhabitants. "I see. Of course, you're right. But what should we do?"

Sturm struggled to his feet, swayed a moment, then straightened up. "I don't know anything about forest demons, but I don't fancy sitting here waiting on whatever made that shadow to figure out a plan."

"You sure you're ready to go?"

"No, but I'll have to do. Get Drel and Vzin, then we move to Kjel's passageway."

Chapter 41: Cave in the Valley of Spiders, 25th YOC, 8th Day of Planting Month, late Night.

Gnumph pulled a torch from the bag and handed it to Sturm. As he reached in for another Kjel handed him his saying, "Take this one. I need this hand for my shield." The others deferred on the torches, and then the group fell silent.

As the silence drew on, Sturm realized the gnomes were waiting on him to give the word. "Oh, right then. Let's get on with it before the torches burn out. Kjel, show us the way."

Kjel led, pointing out the primitive stick figures of people and spiders. Sturm struggled to keep up, each step was an effort. The mix of spier venom and antidote made him want to lay down and sleep. Gwiz kept pace next to Sturm, worriedly watching Sturm. Gnemaley followed, wide eyed. Gnump walked along with her, whispering reassurances. Drel and Vzin hung further back, grimly guarding the rear.

At the first corner, they stopped. Again, the gnomes seemed hesitant to move forward. Sturm motioned with his torch, "Alright Kjel, keep moving." The two of them stepped around the corner.

As Kjel had described, the cave like passage suddenly transitioned to an arched hallway. The figures on the wall also transitioned from primitive scratched stick figures to a skillfully chiseled mix of people and spiders.

Sturm and Krel advanced to the next corner and stopped. Krel whispered, "A peek around this corner is as far as I got."

Sturm adjusted his grip on torch and sword, then lunged around the corner leading with his torch. Kjel and Gwiz followed him. Kjel sprinted the steps to the far side of the hall. Gwiz filled in the center.

A huge spider was ten feet from them, at a four-way intersection of corridors, spinning a web across a side corridor to the right. Another corridor to the left was already covered over. The strands were thicker than what they had cut through in the forest, as thick as their thumbs. The spider paused to stare at them, its eyes glowed red in their torch light, then it rotated away from them to lay another strand of web. Gwiz cast a ball of flame and hit the spider square on its spinneret.

The spider jumped and screeched. It scurried through the open hallway, a strand of flaming web trailing behind. The flame also caught the strung webs, and quickly spread. Thick black smoke coiled into the intersection, filling it. The blue light made the smoke glow eerily. The smoke continued to build and rolled their way, filling the upper half of the hall.

The three backed to the corner. The smoke followed. Sturm's back bumped into the wall. He slid into a squat, looking under the smoke.

Kjel nudged Gwiz in the arm and pointed down the hall. "You did him a good one! I didn't know spiders made noises like that!"

Gwiz laughed and replied, but Sturm quit paying attention. His focus was grabbed by the stonework on the walls. Carved stones were inlaid on each wall forming a relief sculpture of a spider body. The left and right walls were mirror images. The upper body disappeared into the smoke, but from what he could see, the spider was much larger than any they had faced. The body and leg segments were individual polished onyx stones. Off-black stones were fitted between for the joints.

Moments crept by and the smoke thinned. Its lower edge drifted upward to chest height for Sturm, revealing the rest of the spider body but where Sturm expected a spider face a human torso in onyx extended upward into the smoke. As the smoke continued to clear, it became apparent the human torso was a woman's form in a bodice or perhaps a fitted breastplate. Her hands extended in front of her as if receiving something. The arms were done in a dark grey stone with a grainy texture. Her hair cascaded down her back, done in intertwining strands of white, cream, and grey glass. Finally, the last of the smoke cleared, revealing her face.

Sturm was transfixed. She was beautiful. Her cheekbones and ears looked vaguely of his mom. Her fangs and glowing red eyes gave her a feel of danger, an aura of evil. Sturm was both drawn to her and repelled.

Gwiz startled Sturm back to his surroundings. "She looks elven doesn't she. Other than the fangs and such. Everyone, come around the corner, you've got to see this!"

Gnumph slid in next to Strum, "Wow..."

Gnemaley rounded the corner and caught sight of the sculpture across from her. It was the demon from her stories! She gasped and involuntarily stepped back, bumping into Vzin.

Vzin put his hand out to her shoulder to steady her. The touch caused her to startle again. She stepped forward, then sidled along the wall so the others behind her could step into the passage, staring at the figure as if it were about to pounce. As she came even with the figure, she felt her back slide across raised stones. She looked behind her. Spotting the matching figure behind her, she flew to the corner throwing herself into Gnumph's arms. She buried her face on his shoulder.

Gnumph reflexively wrapped his free arm around her. He patted her on her back and spoke quietly into her ear. "Cousin, they're just rock. Sculptures put there by who knows who, and who knows how long ago."

Muffled and between sobs, she replied, "But... but... what if she's still here?"

"What makes you think she ever was here? You're making a very big assumption. Every time you carve a bear or a badger, is it standing in front of you?"

"Well... No. But what if she is here?"

"You are not a gnome child of the stories. You are also not alone and lost in the woods."

Gnemaley drew strength from his confidence. She pulled herself together and nodded. "You're right, of course. When we meet her, we'll face her together and kill her."

That wasn't quite the point Gnumph wanted to make, but anything further was cut off by Sturm as he gathered everyone close.

"Alright. The smoke has cleared. It's time to move forward. Let's be quiet as we do this. The spider, and whatever else, is waiting for us now. Let's try to hear them before we walk into them."

They advanced down the hall to the intersection. Pillars bracketed each corridor opening. Web strands were sculpted on the pillars extending from the floor up their entire length and then extended across the ceiling to intertwine at the apex.

Blue glow stones dotted the ceiling, placed like cocooned prey within the web. The blue light was dim, leaving things indistinct. Their torches provided better light, though only over a short distance.

After a moment's hesitation, they decided to continue down the main corridor and follow the spider. Puddles of flaming goo provided a trail down the hall.

Twenty paces down, the passage opened to a large room. There were several worktables, each with shelves and hooks. Next to one table, a copper hammer hung from the wall along with copper punches lined up on a shelf under it. At another table were obsidian shears and needless. The shears handles were of wood, dried and cracked speaking of great age. There was no working materials and no finished product.

Gwiz wondered why anyone would use copper or stone tools when steel was so much stronger and durable. He stuffed the tools into his bag for later examination.

The hallway extended beyond the room. Sturm urged the gnomes down it. He didn't want the flame trail to burn out.

They passed two more workshops, then there were several side passages. A quick peek revealed empty living quarters. The only hint of who had occupied the rooms were beds of a size between what a dwarf or a human would sleep on.

Sturm didn't tarry and led them further down the hall to where it opened on a large common room with an arched passageway in the middle of each wall. The trail led across to the arch in the far wall.

Sturm led them across the room, taking in details as he went. On either side were rows of tables with chairs, the seating height a couple of inches short for a human. The sound of trickling water came from a back corner where there was also a fire pit. Copper pots and skillets hung on a copper rack bolted to the stone wall next to the pit. Ashes were in the pit from a fire long burnt out. A vent was over the fire pit, too narrow for even a gnome to fit through.

The table at the far end of the hall was the only one not cleared. It had nine place settings, four on either side and one at the head of the table. Each setting consisted of an unadorned plate, utensils, and a cup decorated with figures fired onto the clay. Each cup was upside down on the respective plate.

Sturm stopped to pick up a cup and examine it. The figure was of a forest demon, with a man's torso. Sturm quickly set the cup back down. He wasn't sure which was worse, the Tarek faced spiders of his nightmare or what was on the cup.

Kjel pulled at Sturm's sleeve. Sturm responded, "What is it?"

Kel tapped his ear and pointed down the passage.

After a moment, Sturm heard what had caught Kjel's attention. A soft thumping sound came from the passage the trail led to.

A shared look, a nod, and they moved forward into the passage. The trail of flaming puddles extended far beyond their torchlight, disappearing into the haze of blue light.

Sturm flinched as a glow stone flew past his shoulder. It landed then skipped far down the passage. Sturm looked back to see where it had come from.

Gwiz sheepishly shrugged, "I want to see what we're walking into."

"That's a good idea, just warn me next time."

The white glow down the passage brought clarity from the blue haze. They moved forward with added confidence. When they came up to the light stone they paused. The thumping noise was still ahead of them, more pronounced. Gwiz picked up the stone and tossed it again.

They continued down the trail past occasional empty side rooms. Occasionally the flame trail led to a wall, where there was a smear of flame a couple feet above the floor. Then the trail continued down the hall.

Three stone throws down the hall, the trail turned into an opening to the right. The thumping came from the opening.

Sturm peeked around the corner.

The spider wandered about in a room, dragging it spinneret along the floor leaving droplets of flaming goo behind it. It came to the far wall, twirled, and slammed its spinneret into the wall with a thump. It rubbed the spinneret against the wall leaving a smear of flames.

Sturm drew back into the hallway. He shared with the gnomes what he had seen, ending with, "Its time to put it out of its misery, but how to do it? I'm thinking with it being so big, our blades aren't going to do much to its shell."

Vzin interjected, "The joints. While I had little luck stabbing through the shell of their bodies the joints were still vulnerable."

"You're right." Sturm turned to Kjel, "Aim for the legs."

Kjel bounced up and down, ready go. "Got it, break the legs." He eagerly waved his cudgel.

Gnumph mimicked Kjel with his mace. "I can help with that. Sturm, I know you're still dragging but we'll get it done."

Gnemaley jumped in, "The legs are probably too hard for us to target with our stones. We can instead go for the head, maybe even take out its eyes. Right Drel?" Gnemaley looked expectantly at Drel.

"I don't know..." Drel inadvertently met Gnemaley's gaze. His tone changed, "I mean, yes. We can stay back here and keep it distracted."

Gwiz piped up, "What about me?"

"Keep an eye on the hallway. If something comes at us from behind, you're our best bet to hold it off long enough for the rest of us to react. Now, let's go."

The four swarmed into the room. Sturm and Kjel to the right, Vzin and Gnumph to the left. Slings whirled and stones flew into the room bouncing off the spider's head.

The spider flinched and backed until it bumped the far wall.

Sturm and Kjel attacked from the sides. The spider turned from side to side, its fangs snapping in response. Then a stone took it in the eye. It hesitated, dazed.

Vzin seized the opportunity and poked his spear into the remaining eye. Gnump stepped in, his mace came down between the eyes, cracking the chitin armor. A second blow sank deep into the spider's head. The spider's legs twitched, it lost its footing and the body dropped to the floor.

Drel did a little victory jig. Kjel and Vzin jointed him.

Gnumph was about to join them when he noticed Gnemaley staring down the unexplored portion of the passage. "What is it cousin?"

She glanced at him, then back down the passage. "I fear what's down there. The demon will be far worse than that spider. Mark my words."

Sturm gathered their attention, "I don't know that there are any demons here, but she's right that we're not done yet. This room isn't the spider's lair."

Gwiz agreed, "Aye, no sign of a hatchery."

Drel grumbled, "But where do we look? This place is huge. Don't tell me we're going to go down every side passage to make sure nothing else is here."

Sturm replied, "If that's what we have to do, that's what we do. For now, we'll continue down the main hall." Sturm saw Gnemaley hesitate. "You with us?"

She took a deep breath, then nodded. "For my children and my grandbaby on the way, aye, we need to finish this."

Two stone throws down the passage was another archway. Sturm and Kjel stepped through the archway as Gwiz recovered his stone.

The warriors tensed, readying for an attack. Sturm stood with his torch forward and his sword back, ready. Kjel's brought his shield to just below his eyes and balanced his cudgel on his shoulder ready to swing. Gnemaley peered past them and stifled a scream.

The demon of the entry sculpture stood before them in the center of the room, ready to attack.

Gnumph and Vzin jostled their way next to Sturm and Kjel, forming a line across the archway. Drel reached into his pouch and pulled out a stone for his sling. Gnemaley followed his lead.

Gwiz hissed, "Wait." His glow stone flew past their battle line. It hit the floor a few feet in front of the demon, bounced up, and clacked against the demon's leg. The stone dropped at the demon's feet, illuminating the demon from below. The white glow from below made her face look more menacing than before.

The demon didn't react.

Gwiz laughed with relief. "Ha! It's only a statue."

Sturm shook his head, irked for falling for the optical illusion.

Gnumph clapped Sturm on the shoulder. "Don't be hard on yourself. The statue is masterfully done, and the blue light robs enough detail that we were all taken in."

"Yeah, I guess you're right." Sturm looked around the room. He saw a large passage directly across the room with three smaller ones on either side. "This way." He led them to the large passage.

Frescos adorned either side of the passage entrance. Small figures of dark-skinned elves with white hair bowed in supplication to the passageway.

Gnemaley took one look at the fresco and backed away, shaking her head.

Gnumph touched her shoulder, getting her attention. He whispered, "Remember the grandbaby."

She stared at him a moment, before weakly responding. "We have six other passages to explore. Could we at least go down this way last?"

Gnumph turned to Sturm. "What do you think?"

"One passage is as good as another, so why not. We'll start with the nearest on the right and work our way around. We'll need a rear guard in case something comes from the other passages. The best spot for them to hold would be the mouth of the passage we're exploring. It will give the slingers an open field of fire. I'd have two melee with the rear guard as well, Vzin and Kjel you stay back with them."

Drel wasn't happy. "You're splitting us up? That's a recipe for disaster!"

"If you see spiders call for us. If the passage extends far, we'll call for you. If we run into trouble, we'll run back to you. Gwiz, Gnumph, you're with me. Let's go."

The passage led to a workshop for alchemy or distilling. Clear glassware containers sat on the countertops with glass piping connecting them. Bottles of different sizes lined the shelves. Some bottles had disintegrated stoppers and only a residue was left in the bottom. Bottles with glass or metal stoppers were still full, but their contents had separated leaving layers of colored liquids or particulates.

Glittering particulates in a bottle caught Sturm's attention. Sturm reached for the bottle to get a closer look, but Gwiz slapped his hand away. "Don't! You don't know what it is. Old alchemy agents can be unstable."

Further search found a closed tome on a shelf, its backing brittle with age. Gwiz gingerly wrapped it and packed it for examination later.

They rejoined their rear guard, then moved to the next passageway. This passage ended in a dorm room. Wooden bunk beds for a score of people lined the walls. The wood was dry and cracked. There was no bedding or mattresses. There weren't even any chests to store personal effects.

The moved to the next passageway. It was a short hallway ending at a door. It was the first door they had come across.

Gnumph pondered, "If none of the rest of the rooms had a door, why would this one?"

Gwiz responded, "Maybe it's their jail? A place to hold prisoners?"

Sturm chuckled. "Why would they need that? They could just web anyone up into a cocoon."

Gwiz volunteered, "I'll check the door for traps and magic just to make sure." After several minutes of examination, he scratched his beard. "No magic. I also can't find the lock, let alone if its trapped."

Sturm did his own examination with the same results. Exasperated he exclaimed, "Enough of this." He lifted the latch and gently pulled. Gnumph stepped back, Gwiz winced.

The door didn't move.

Sturm yanked on the door. The door hinges squealed in protest as the door opened a few inches.

As Strum braced for another yank, Gnumph laid his hand on Sturm's arm, "Wait a second." He pulled out a small bottle of oil with a narrow wooden spout. He applied the oil to the hinges.

Sturm shook his head in disbelief, "You brought penetrating oil from the workshop. And you gave Gwiz grief for what he packed."

"Well, yeah. All that camping gear, really? But little things like this? You never know when you might need it."

"What else did you bring?"

"Just a bit of this or that. Whatever looked like it might be useful and would fit in my pockets."

Sturm tried the door again. It still squealed, but this time it opened the rest of the way. Inside was a large room, filled with empty wooden racks. The wood was dry and cracked.

Gwiz tilted his head back and forth in puzzlement. "What would this have been?"

"It's an armory." Sturm pointed to various racks as he continued, "Those racks are for swords, and those for spears. Those over there are for armor, helms, and shields. Look, there is another door in the back. Gnumph, you have more of that oil to get us in there?"

That door was also hard to open, but the oil worked its trick. Inside were reinforced, widely spaced, shelves. Some sort of storage room, but empty.

Gnumph observed, "Looks like the place was cleaned out long ago."

Storm replied, "We still have four passages to check out, come on."

Back at the main room they gathered their rear guard and crossed to the first passage on the left side. Gnemaley warily eyed the statue as they passed it, as if she expected it to spring to life at any moment.

The three passageways each led to identical courtyards. Each courtyard had three rooms attached. These rooms had been living quarters. At each room entrance was a waist high stand with a carving of the forest demon illuminated by a glow stone with the same blue light as in the passageways. Within each room was a bed with bedding and shelves filled with personal belongings. Each room also had a wardrobe, within were finely tailored clothes of a strange style. The clothes were so fragile that they fell apart when touched.

One of the nine rooms was larger, with an adjoined study. Each side of the study nook had shelves with scrolls and tomes. Centered to the back was a scribe's stand. A tome lay open on the stand with lines of runic script half filling the left page. Next to the tome lay a worn carved bone stylus and a bottle of dried ink.

Gwiz cast a cantrip to detect magic, but none was revealed. He gently lifted the right page, revealing blank pages after it. He let the page fall back and looked at the writing. "This isn't a language I'm familiar with."

Sturm looked over Gwiz's shoulder. "Hmm. Some of them look like mom's elf runes." He pointed to a rune on the first line. "That one looks like 'last'. Two lines down is one that could be 'food'." He pointed to several others, calling them out. Unfortunately, he was only able to make out a few randomly located across the page.

Gwiz went to the tomes on the shelves, checked each for magic, then peaked inside. Each had runes that were just as indecipherable as the first.

Gnumph still stood at the entryway, scratching his beard as he looked around the room.

Sturm addressed Gnumph. "What are you thinking?"

Gnumph shrugged. "It's a puzzle. Why are there rooms for an entire community but only these nine rooms were occupied?"

"I don't know, maybe the last passageway will give us answers." Sturm turned to Gwiz, "You done? We need to move on."

Gwiz eyed the artifacts on the shelf. "Give me a moment. I'm going to take these to study." He cleared the scrolls and tomes from the shelves and packed them in the magic bag. Then he came to the open tome on the stand. He gently closed it, but the back binding cracked anyway. With a sigh he pulled out a cloth and wrapped it around the tome to hold it together, then packed it as well.

They returned to the main room.

Drel startled as they came out. "Oh, it's you. About time. What took you so long? I think we're about to be attacked."

Vzin chuckled, "If we are, it won't be much of a fight."

Drel gave Vzin a dirty look.

Sturm looked back and forth between them, then asked Vzin. "What are you two talking about?"

Vzin gestured towards the unexplored central passage. "A couple of small spiders, not even as big as my hand appeared from there. One came this way. I stomped my foot, and they all scurried out the passage we came in. They could be outside by now."

Sturm saw Drel working up a rebuttal. Sturm was exhausted and didn't want to deal with any more from Drel. "Drel, it doesn't matter. Look, we need to go down that last passage. There may, or may not, be something we have to face. I mean something a lot worse than a few baby spiders. Let's just get it done, then we go home. Come on."

Drel was left grumbling but had no real objection.

Sturm headed down the remaining passage, Gnemaley lagged behind. Her gaze flicked across the murals of the dark elf supplicants. She closed her eyes a moment, then took a deep breath and exhaled as she mouthed 'for the grandbabies'. She nodded to herself, stood straight and shoulders back, then grimly caught up to the others.

The final passageway was 20 feet long divided into two sections by pillars. Each section had a carved relief scene of dark elves with white hair and forest demons, their upper bodies matching the dark elves. One scene showed the elves bringing animals to the spiders to be cocooned. Another scene showed demons directing the elves as they built three stone pillars under the trees. A third showed demons leading armed elves as if off to battle. The final one involved a male elf, a female elf, and a forest demon. Each scene was accompanied with runes in the same script as was in the book they had found.

Sturm looked over the runes hoping that with the associated pictures he'd be successful, with much the same results as with the book. He recognized the most runes in the final scene, but with enough gaps to leave their association ambiguous. If put together one way, the runes indicated celebrating a mating or wedding. Read another way it was about an offering, though it was uncertain if the couple was making an offering or they were the offering. Sturm stared at the runes as if by force of will he could wring meaning from the runes.

Sturm jumped as he felt a hand on his arm. He looked down at Gnump.

"Still not making sense?"

"Yeah. It's frustrating."

"Let it go for now. Maybe what's further in will sort it out."

"You're right. Sorry about the stop." Sturm moved forward.

The passage opened to a large amphitheater; its far walls lost in the blue lighting. The first dozen feet was a landing before the floor fell away to form step seating. The landing and the first few rows of steps were covered with spider eggs. Most of the eggs were torn open. Those that were intact were in scattered clusters.

As they took in the scene, a spider tore its way out of its egg sack. It was the size of a human hand. It noticed them and came over to investigate.

They readied their weapons, startling the spider. It fled, escaping down the passageway.

Vzin looked from the passage back to the eggs. "I don't fancy fighting all these when they're big." He stepped over to the nearest intact egg and stomped it. The spider inside crunched, blue ichor squirted through the egg sack and oozed.

Sturm moved to another cluster and stomped. Kjel, Gnumph, and Drel quickly followed suit.

Gwiz and Gnemaley hung back, watching lest a spider mother came to defend her brood.

Sturm followed the egg clusters down the steps until he smashed the last egg. He checked on the gnome's progress. They were also done. Blue ichor covered the landing and the gnomes' boots. The ichor glowed in the blue lighting.

Sturm looked across the room for more eggs. His gaze traveled down the steps to a stage at the far end. Several feet separated the base of the stairs and a stage. Several dark patches were in the gap. Another dark patch was on the edge of the stage. Details were lost in the haze from the blue lighting.

Gnumph walked over to Sturm, leaving a trail of blue ichor. "Do you see more eggs?"

"I don't know, maybe. There is something down by the stage, but I can't make out what it is. I'm heading down there, come on."

Going down the stairs was awkward for Sturm. Each level, he had to take two short steps forward and then a steep step down. The gnomes didn't have much of a problem, they simply sat at the edge of the step and then dropped down.

They discovered the dark patches were desiccated bodies. There were nine in front of the stage, in undergarments, kneeling with heads bowed. They likely had stood between five to five and a half foot tall. They had pointed ears, giving them an elvish look though their skin was dark and their hair white. Next to each body was a small pile of possessions; a neatly laid out black chainmail shirt, a helm, and a weapon. The chainmail shimmered iridescently in the flickering torchlight. The helms were of copper and appeared to be ceremonial with the fronts formed into fanged faces. One of the weapons was a black obsidian sword, the rest were maces made with copper.

The body on the stage was of human size and the ears were of human shape. He lay on his back with his legs dangling over the edge of the stage. His steel chainmail coat was unfastened and spread open revealing a puncture mark on his chest. There was no sign of struggle, his sword was still in the sheath.

They were startled by a woman's voice coming from a dark archway at the back of the stage. No one understood her words though Sturm thought they sounded elvish. He replied in elf, a simple greeting and a 'who are you'.

She replied. The tone was quizzical, the words were still unintelligible.

Sturm tried again. She tried again. After several back and forths, it was obvious they simply could not communicate.

She called out, changing her tone. Now it was pleading, seductive.

Sturm felt drawn by it but resisted.

Kjel stepped towards the stage mumbling something about 'needing to save her'. He was oblivious to everything around him.

As Kjel started to climb onto the stage, Gnemaley grabbed him, pulling him back. He tried to shrug her off. She swung him around and slapped him. A hard, stinging blow.

Kjel angrily shoved Gnemaley away, his hand reached for his cudgel. His expression changed to surprise followed by concern. His hand lowered from the weapon. "I'm so sorry. I don't know what I was doing. What is the matter with me? Am I crazy?"

"It's the demon's voice. Don't listen to her. Come away from there." Gnemaley led Kjel away from the stage.

The voice continued pleading.

Gwiz plugged his ears with is fingers and started to loudly sing one of the songs from the previous night's feast. The others quickly joined in. It was hard on the ears, Drel was every bit as off key as he had been while drunk, but it cut through the glamour of the demon's voice.

After a couple of verses the pleading ended. The gnome's responded by stopping their singing and waited.

Claws scrapped on stone and a forest demon scuttled out to the edge of the stage. She towered over them, menacing. Her spider body was far larger than any of the spiders they had fought. The black chain mail on her woman's torso glittered in the torchlight. She glared down at them and made an imperious gesture towards the ground uttering a single syllable demand.

Sturm and group involuntarily backed away, readying their weapons.

Sturm scrutinized her for vulnerabilities. It dawned on him this was not the demon of the sculptures. She wasn't in a platemail like bodice. While she was taller than Sturm, she was shorter than the statue by maybe a foot. Also, her features differed from the statues, though her fangs looked just as demonic. He called out to the gnomes, sharing his observation.

This was not the response she had demanded. She jumped down to bodies on the main floor, causing the gnomes to scatter. Sturm backed up two steps, holding the torch forward. She grabbed the obsidian blade from the ground. She swung it at Sturm.

He reflexively blocked with his torch only to have it slapped out of his hand. Sparks scattered as it arced over to the steps and landed.

The obsidian blade rapidly came back at Sturm. This time he blocked sword on sword. When the blades met, pain seared through his hand and up his arm. The force of the blow knocked him down, his sword flying from his hand. He rolled with the blow, out of her reach.

Vzin darted in and thrust his boar spear. Sparks flew as his blade skittered across the chainmail. Vzin jumped back, out of her reach, to gather himself for another attack.

She turned on Vzin. With her empty hand she summoned power and directed it at him. A single syllable released the spell and Vzin crumpled.

Gwiz gathered his own spell, a protection, but Vzin was already down. He hesitated, holding the spell ready.

She saw the magic gathered around Gwiz and cast a spell at him. He released his spell at the same time. The two spells collided, swirled, then dissipated.

Sturm pushed himself up frantic to rejoin the fight, only to have his sword arm give out. It was still wonky from the jolt of pain. With a growl he rolled to standing, drawing his off-hand dagger.

Drel loosed a stone, but it was rushed with little speed behind it. The demon saw the stone, snatched it from the air, and threw it back. It whizzed through the air and smacked Drel in the shoulder. He staggered backward, bounced off the bottom amphitheater step, then landed hard and laid still.

Gnemaley's stone flew fast and low, striking the demon in the knee of the second leg on the left.

The demon shrieked and stumbled. She summoned magic to cast at Gnemaley but was interrupted by Kjel charging her from the other side.

The demon saw Kjel's motion. She lashed out with a front leg, slamming Kjel on his shield. The force of it split the wood and spun him around causing him to trip and topple. He awkwardly struggled to get back up. The demon stepped forward bringing her sword up to finish him. Gnump stepped forward trying to shield Kjel.

Sturm didn't give the demon the chance to finish her action. He charged her and jumped on top of her spider body.

Gnumph saw Sturm's charge and threw his torch up at her face to distract her. The demon focused on the torch; her sword swatted it away.

Sturm landed on her back. He raised his dagger high. The demon reacted, twisting at the waist. Her spider legs clacked on the floor as she rotated in place trying to confront what was behind her. She ignored a stone that grazed her cheek, drawing blood.

Sturm plunged his dagger into her neck with all the force he could muster. The mithril blade shattered its way through her vertebra until it was buried to its hilt.

The demon screeched. Her arms and legs went limp. Her twisting-rotating motion turned into a roll as her legs collapsed.

Sturm flew from her back. He landed and rolled a few feet, stopped by the bottom amphitheater step.

The demon ended up on her back, her body twitching. Gnumph stepped forward and smashed her head with his mace – then again and again, each blow more furious than the last, until the twitching stopped. He stepped back panting, wild eyed. As his panting eased, he heard Kjel's whimpering. Gnumph's expression turned to concern. He knelt next to Kjel and examined him.

Kjel laid on his back, his shattered shield over his body. His lower arm, still tangled in the shield straps, was broken.

As Gnumph was focused on Kjel, Gnemaley stepped over to aid Drel. He laid moaning and nursing his shoulder. She helped him stand up.

Meanwhile, Gwiz bent down to Vzin. He exclaimed, "Thank the gods! He's still breathing, but its shallow and ragged. He's just staring. Gnump, come help."

Gnumph said a few words and waved his hand over Kjel's arm temporarily removing the pain. "Don't move until after I get back to you." Then he joined Gwiz. "I've got him, you check on Sturm."

Gwiz moved over to Sturm. Gnemaley and Drel jointed him. Gwiz bent down and put his hand on Sturm's shoulder.

Sturm opened his eyes.

"Sturm, you alright? That looked pretty wild when she threw you."

Sturm chuckled, "Yeah, I'm fine. I learned a long time ago how to get off a rearing warhorse, that wasn't so different."

Gwiz snorted and gave Sturm's shoulder a rough but affectionate shove. "You gave me a fright!"

Sturm struggled to sit up. His sword arm still wasn't cooperating. "Sorry. My arm took a good jolt when the swords met. That wasn't normal. Maybe there's magic to that obsidian blade. It's worth looking at." He moved to stand up.

Gwiz stopped Sturm. "No, you sit and catch your breath. It looks like you're going to have to carry Vzin out."

"What about the sword?"

"I'll take care of it. I'll also go see what that archway at the back of the stage leads to. See if you can get that arm working."

Sturm acquiesced. "Alright. Anyone see where my sword landed?"

Chapter 42: Terter Manor House, The Master's Suite, 25th YOC, 11th Day of Planting Month, 8 AM.

Sturm woke to the sun streaming into his bedroom. His weariness was gone, as was the numbness to his arm, but he felt battered from head to toe. He shifted, but found he had trouble moving. The covers were tucked under him on one side and a snoring Mira was stretched out next to him on the other. Sturm worked an arm out then reached over and gave Mira's ear a rub.

Mira stretched and moaned. His paw pumped the air.

Sturm wiggled free from the covers. The ear rub turned into a game of Sturm's hand darting in to continue the ear rub, and Mira's paw batting away Sturm's hand. Sturm repeatedly won through to Mira's ears. Mira retaliated by rolling over and standing over Sturm, licking his face. This time it was Sturm's turn to block Mira's attentions. Things quickly turned into a larger wrestling match that lasted several minutes before Sturm called a truce and had Mira get off the bed.

Sturm swung his feet off the bed and reached over to the nightstand for the dog charm. He paused as he noticed a signet ring and a book next to the charm. Those had not been there when he went to sleep.

The signet ring had the Terter bull's head crest inscribed on its face. Nobles often had rings like this to stamp wax seals. Sturm wondered if the gnomes had commissioned it for him.

Sturm turned to the book. The cover bore the Terter heraldry - the bull's head in gold on a blue and red patterned background. Sturm opened the book and read the first page. It proclaimed this was a journal belonging to Baron Haval Terter. The word 'Baron' was angled from the name, the letters scrunched, as if it had been inserted. Sturm's curiosity was piqued. He knew nothing of the Terters. He skimmed through several pages describing a young man's life on the Terter estate before the revolution. He came to where the Haval's father, Eduard, disappeared in the chaos of the revolution leaving Haval in charge of the estate. After that, the entries depicted Haval failing as he tried to manage the estate. Midway through the book, Haval came up with a desperate plan to go into the mountains.

Mira, bored with the inattention, nudged Sturm.

Sturm petted Mira. "I need to read this. Come, let's sit outside where the light is better."

Sturm walked through double doors to his balcony. The view overlooked his estates rising up to the mountains. He sat down on his rocking chair and returned to the book.

Mira again nudged Strum for attention. Sturm petted him on the head then motioned Mira to lay down. Mira circled a couple of times, then settled in at Sturm's feet. Sturm returned to reading. He read through to the last entry, then set the book down and stared at the mountains. His thoughts were interrupted by Gnumph joining him.

"Hey Sturm. Up at last! You slept around the clock and then some. Here, I brought you some of Gnemaley's restorative." Gnumph set a tray, with a steamy bowl and a chilled tankard, on a table next to Sturm.

"Thank you. I was going to come down and get something to eat but was distracted by this book." Sturm took the bowl and spooned in some broth. He felt a warmth flood through him reminiscent of Gnemaley's restorative. It tasted a bit off though. "You said Gnemaley made this?"

"No. She gave Gwiz the recipe and that's his effort. He's still downstairs fussing over the pot."

Sturm wrinkled his nose. "Well, Gnemaley's tastes better!"

"Yeah, for all that he makes those fancy potions I prefer my own cooking and Gnemaley puts mine to shame. Anyway, get it down, then I need to take you downstairs."

"Is there a problem?"

"Like something Gwiz and I couldn't handle?" Gnump chuckled. "No."

"Is it the boys? How are Drel, Kjel, and Vzin?"

"Drel is still nursing his shoulder like its broken even though it was only bruised, and I healed it yesterday. Kjel is just the opposite. I set his broken arm and mended it, but he's trying to do too much too fast."

"And Vzin?"

Gnumph shrugged. "No change. Luckily, he's still breathing but he can't do much else. I'm concerned that a few more days without water and he'll die of dehydration. We're at a loss for what to do."

"Did you try some of the spider antidote?"

"Sturm, this is from a spell, not a spider bite."

"So, you didn't try it. You should. You never know, and what's there to lose?"

"Perhaps. I'll talk with Gwiz about it. In any case, that's not why I came up here. Gwiz finished going over what we hauled out and has approved most of it to be handed out."

"Great! I can't wait to get my hands on that sword."

"Well, unfortunately, the sword is one of the things he didn't approve. There is an inimical magic to it."

"But did you see what it did in combat? When it met my blade, it shot pain up my arm, and I couldn't keep ahold of my sword. It also left a gouge in my sword edge. It must slice through plate armor like butter. A blade like that would give me a real edge."

"Yeah, I saw. However, think about it a moment. A sword that inflicts pain. Who would make a sword like that? What else might it do? There is a darkness to the blade that goes beyond the color of its obsidian, and it worries Gwiz. He's all for destroying the blade - once he figures out how."

"Can we at least study it more to see for sure?"

"That's between you and Gwiz. Hey, if it's any consolation, he thinks one of the black chainmail shirts might fit you. He found some protections on it and the metal is very strong. Most are too small for you, but the largest one looks wide enough for you. He doesn't know if it's too short for you, you'll have to try it on. So, let's go see if it fits."

Sturm stood up, setting the journal next to the tray on the side table.

Gnumph pointed to the journal, "I didn't get a chance to look at it. What's so interesting in it?"

"Is it from that body that was hanging off the dais?"

"Yes, as is the ring."

"Well that fits. The book is the journal of the last lord Terter." Sturm recounted Haval's story, ending with, "I feel sorry for the guy. He succeeded making his way to the highlanders and arranging a trade agreement that would have saved his barony, only to die at the edge of his estate on the way back." Sturm's gaze shifted to the mountains. "Haval had a good plan."

"You want to up into the mountains and make it happen?"

"Yes, but I don't want to leave my people defenseless while I'm gone. Not only while I'm in the mountains, but also afterwards when I run caravans. I'm not so worried about the gnomes, you have shown your pluck and your slings are effective. The humans in my hamlet are another matter."

Gnumph tipped his elder's cap. "Thank you for the compliment, but you can't expect gnomes to form a shield wall to hold back an intruder."

"True, and I can't expect the humans to suddenly learn ranged weapons either. So, the answer lies in the two working together. We'll have to equip and train the humans to be your shield wall. I'll need someone to organize them and train them. You were good with that mace, could you show them how to fight like that?"

"I've had my times when I've had to use it, but I'm not a trained warrior like you. I can only show them the basics."

"That's all they need at first. I can take them further when I return." The rest of a plan fell into place in Sturm's thoughts. "Here is what we're going to do. I am going to issue a mace and a shield to every human household in the hamlet and to any gnome households that want them. I'll hold a feast at the hamlet, to issue the equipment and to lay out my vision. I'll need representatives from each gnome steading there. Hopefully after feasting together the two groups will be amendable to working together. What do you think?"

Gnumph ran the idea through his thoughts a few times, then bobbed his head. "I think it's a good plan. Where are you going to get that equipment?"

"Wood shields are easy enough to make ourselves. As for the weapons, I'll see what's available in the Vellar market. If there isn't enough there, I'll commission a blacksmith. We don't need dwarven steel for maces, blacksmith's iron will do. And, yes, I know that will take some coin, but we're flush right now with the platinum I picked up."

Gnumph interjected, "The feast would be an opportunity to hand out rewards to Gnemaley, Drel, Kjel, and Vzin — if I can get him on his feet by then."

"That's a good thought. Of course, I would reward you and Gwiz as well, it's just that I owe the two of you so much I have no idea what reward would suffice."

Gnump chuckled, "Again, thank you for the compliment. However, you have provided us with a home and safe haven. We ask for no more. In any case, Gwiz is quite happy puttering about with the tomes and samples we brought back. May I make another suggestion?"

Strum nodded.

Gnumph continued, "The hamlet has scarce extra food for a feast. The gnomes already used much of their stores for the sendoff feast at Gnemaley's. I think the estate needs to provide the food for the feast."

"You're right. In Vzin's honor we should have a boar. I'll hunt one down. The rest I can buy from the farmer's market while I'm in Vellar." Sturm considered for a moment, then continued, "I can roast the boar, but I'll need help with the rest. But who? It doesn't feel right to order people to help me with this."

"I agree. That would take away from the goodwill the feast would bring. However, you could always hire someone."

"That's what I'll do then. I'll give the people on the estate the first chance for a fair day's wage in exchange for helping with the feast. If they're not interested, I can hire people in Vellar. Alright, enough for the moment. Let's join Gwiz. He can help us make a list of what I'll have to buy."

Chapter 43: Terter Manor House, northern lawn, 25th YOC, 12th Day of Planting Month, Noon.

The feast was set up on the east side of the manor house, with a view of the mountains. A dozen tables were between the firepit and the hamlet, with three score of the estate residents filling them. Platters of boar meat, bread, and mashed tubers garnished with pecans were the meal with pitchers of cool well water or gnomish ale provided to wash it down.

Sturm stepped back from the boar, exchanging the slicing knife for a mug of ale. He took a moment to survey the tables. There was more than enough boar meat for everyone.

Boiko, a farmer new to the hamlet, stood next to Sturm with a platter in hand. Sturm slapped him on the shoulder. "We're done. Take that platter and join your family. Thanks for a job well done. Tell the other servers the same."

Sturm refilled his mug and made the rounds between the tables. At the first, he found Drel and Kjel surrounded by human teenagers and gnomes. The group was done eating and were into their ale. Drel monopolized the conversation, regaling them with stories of his heroism while occasionally patting his arm in the sling. Kjel deferentially sat back and let Drel talk. Sturm was drawn into recounting his part in the story. Eyes grew wide when Sturm got to the part of jumping on the demon's back to plunge his dagger into her neck.

Sturm disengaged from the group and moved to the next table where Gnemaley sat next to Audrie, bouncing Audrie's baby on her lap. Their dishes were set to the side, the last few morsels forgotten. Several other the women sat with them. One finished telling a joke and the others howled in laughter. Sturm didn't disturb them and moved on.

He stopped at each of the other tables. The discussions there were between farmers. The gnomes recounted how they were bringing orchards and vineyards back to production. The humans recounted how they were turning the meadow around the hamlet back into producing fields. He shared with them his visions of expanding both the gnome steadings and the human's hamlet.

Strum finished visiting with the last table. He refilled his mug. He saw people clearing away their plates and instruments appearing. It was time to make his announcements and to hand out the rewards before the music started, yet he hesitated. His godfathers were still in the manor house nursing Vzin. Sturm had hoped Vzin would rally, be able to attend and receive his reward. The twangs of a balalaika tuning to a fiddle decided Sturm. He raised his mug high and shouted, "SALUTE!"

The crowd enthusiastically toasted him back.

After a deep quaff from his mug, he continued. "Thank you all for coming! I wanted to say a few things before I lose you to the singing and dancing. I'll start with two announcements. The first is, we discovered a road into the mountains that leads to the highlanders. I plan on following it, contacting the highlanders, and develop trade with them. Everyone on the estate will profit from this. Plant extra and your excess harvest can be sold not only in Vellar but to the Highlanders. Further, I'm sure there will be some work to clear the road for wagons. Any who can take time from their crops will be paid a good day's wage for helping with that. Any of your kin who wish to join us here are welcome and can share in our prosperity."

Sturm waited a moment for the cheers and toasts to die down, then continued. "As for the second. The fight with the spiders made me realize that each household needs to be able to defend themselves. I am gifting each household with a weapon and a shield. We will hold training sessions to teach you how to defend yourselves, and how to work together in a fight. Further I will pay a day's wage for each day of training you attend."

Another cheer broke out.

Sturm waived for their attention. "There is one more thing. I wish to honor those who accompanied me into the spider valley and fought at my side. My thanks to them! I also have more than just thanks to give. There are rewards from the items we brought back. Let me start with Kjel."

Sturm stepped over to a bag near the boar roast, and as he pulled out a copper mace, addressed Kjel. "I know you love your cudgel, but I saw you eyeing a weapon we found." Sturm held the copper mace up, it gleamed in the sunlight. "Gwiz tested the metal of this mace and found it is as strong as any steel and you will never need to worry about it rusting. Kjel, you have earned this, please take it with my thanks." Sturm bowed and presented it to Kjel.

Kjel took it and swung it around with gusto to the applause of the crowd.

Sturm reached into the bag and pulled out a polished copper mirror. It had been on the wall in the demon's quarters. It was large enough to be a full-length mirror for a gnome. "Drel. You wanted this mirror for your wife. Take it with my thanks. May your family enjoy it for many generations to come." Another round of applause as Sturm set it next to Drel.

Drel grinned broadly as he ran his hand down its side. "Thank you, milord!" He tilted it to see himself in it.

When the applause died down, Sturm continued. "Gnemaley."

Gnemaley cut him off, "Please Lord Kian. I want nothing from the demon."

"I figured, but you deserve a reward for the courage you showed facing your childhood nightmare. I know what that is like, and it deserves more than merely gratitude. I also know that you want to go back and bring that forest back to life. So, your reward is my pledge to aid you with that. I will provide whatever supplies you need, and to hire whatever workers you need."

Gnemaley blinked back tears. "Thank you, milord."

After the applause for Gnemaley trailed off, Sturm continued. "Vzin also accompanied us. I am doubly indebted to him. When a spider injected me with its poison it was Vzin who got me on my feet and moving to the safety of the cave. He isn't with us. He's still under the demon's spell. I ask for you all to pray for him." The last words had trouble coming out.

Kjel tugged at Sturm's arm getting his attention, then pointed towards the manor. Cheers erupted from the crowd.

Sturm turned to look. Gnump and Gwiz flanked Vzin, aiding him to walk out of the manor house. Vzin waved in response to the cheers.

Sturm joyously grabbed his mug and raised it high, "Huzzah!"

Made in the USA
Middletown, DE
29 October 2023

41494162R00139